THE EDGE OF ALONE

A Ryan Lock Thriller

D1607491

SEAN BLACK

The Edge of Alone
Copyright © 2016 Sean Black
All rights reserved.

First published in 2016.

For Lee and Patsy

ABOUT THE BOOK

An isolated school for troubled teens. A series of mysterious deaths. A father frantically trying to rescue his daughter before it's too late.
But when the law won't listen, who can he turn to?

****

'Sean Black writes with the pace of Lee Child, and the heart of Harlan Coben.' Joseph Finder, *New York Times Bestseller* (Paranoia, Buried Secrets)

****

'This is a writer, and a hero, to watch.' *Daily Mail*

****

'Ace. There are deservedly strong Lee Child comparisons as the author is also a Brit, his novels US-based, his character appealing, and his publisher the same.' Sarah Broadhurst, *The Bookseller*

Sign up to Sean Black's VIP mailing list for a free e-book and updates about new releases

Your email will be kept confidential. You will not be spammed. You can unsubscribe at any time.
Click the link below to sign up:
seanblackauthor.com/subscribe

OTHER BOOKS BY SEAN BLACK

PART ONE

CHAPTER ONE

WHEN PEOPLE ASKED BRICE WALKER what he did for a living, he told them he was a deliveryman. It saved a long, potentially awkward conversation. And it wasn't a lie. Well, not exactly. As an answer it had the added bonus of making his occupation sound boring. Which closed down having to deal with any more questions.

In reality, Brice's profession was far from boring. Most people had no idea it even existed. Or that it was, despite what they might have believed, completely legal.

Brice, with his business partner, Mike, both of them former bail bondsmen, did collect packages, transport them across the country, and drop them off at a predesignated location. So, calling himself a deliveryman wasn't that far removed from the truth.

The aspect of the job that was hard to explain to people was that he and Mike collected, transported, and delivered human beings from one location to another. More specifically, children and teenagers, the youngest being eleven and the oldest being seventeen, boys, girls, and, increasingly, young people who described themselves as transgender. In fact, the fastest growth area for their business in the last twelve months had been transgender young people.

Personally, Brice didn't see what the big deal was if a kid was gay or transgender. But he wasn't the one paying top dollar to move them around, so he tended to keep his own views on the subject to himself. After all, he and Mike were only deliverymen, and they had just arrived at their pick-up for the day.

Sitting in the passenger seat next to him, Mike jabbed a finger at the corner of the map he was holding. "This is it," he said to Brice. "Laurel Avenue."

Brice slowed the truck, and spun the wheel. "What's the number?"

Mike peered down at the piece of paper containing the collection instructions. "Four two one eight. Should be two blocks down. The cross street is Third."

"You forget your reading glasses again?"

Mike scowled. "I don't need 'em."

"Sure you don't," Brice told him.

Mike's eyesight was a running joke between them. Brice knew he couldn't read for shit without glasses, and Mike was too damn vain to use them. It was like he was trying to deny he was getting older by ignoring the changes that came with it. Other than that, they got on pretty good. Which was just as well, because they spent a lot of time in each other's company.

A few moments later, Brice pulled the truck into a space opposite the address. It had been Mike's idea to swap out the car they'd been using for an old UPS delivery truck that he'd spotted in an online auction. He might have shitty eyesight and not want to admit it, but making collections in an actual delivery truck had been a stroke of genius. It blended in. And once they had their cargo safely stowed in back, there was way less chance of anyone seeing it. The soundproofing was better too. They'd had to make some adjustments to the rear cargo area to make it comfortable for longer journeys, but overall it made the job a lot easier.

Brice switched off the engine and killed the headlights. "What time you got?"

Mike dug his cell phone from his front pants pocket and checked the display. "Zero three fifty-three."

"Good. That means we can be on the road well before sunrise."

"If she doesn't give us a problem," said Mike.

Brice shrugged his shoulders. "What kind of problem is a fourteen-year-old girl going to give us?"

3

"You forgot about that kid in El Segundo?"

The kid Mike was talking about had pulled her boyfriend's gun from under the bed when they'd walked into her room. Thankfully the safety had been on.

"That was a one-off," said Brice. "This kid doesn't seem like the type who'll give us too many problems."

Mike eyeballed him. "If she wasn't a problem, we wouldn't be here."

"You know what I mean," said Brice, reaching back behind his seat and pulling out a bag. He unzipped it and quickly checked they had everything they might need if she *was* a problem.

Mike started to run through the equipment list. Brice found the first item in the bag and called it out. Mike put a line through it. El Segundo was also the reason they'd tightened up their procedures, including running through the checklist before every collection.

"Okay," said Mike. "Let's see here," he said, squinting at the list. "Pepper spray? Two canisters."

Brice dug around the bottom of the bag. He found the spray, took one for himself and handed off the other to Mike. Mike struck a line through it on the list and moved on.

"Handcuffs. Two pairs."

****

4

With jacket collars turned up, and baseball caps pulled low over their eyes, the two men walked quickly toward the front door. They didn't speak. They didn't have to. They both knew the drill. Plus, they wanted to make as little noise as possible on entry.

Coming out might be a different matter. Sometimes they got a screamer or someone else in the house flipped out: a brother, a sister, another family member, the dog.

If they didn't shut up when Brice asked them to, that was when the pepper spray came out. Usually the threat was enough to quieten them down. They only used it when they absolutely had to. They preferred speed and surprise, hence the early hour.

Brice turned the handle of the front door. It was unlocked. As arranged.

He stepped into the hallway, Mike a few steps behind him. Mike closed the door behind them and they started up the stairs toward the target's bedroom. It was the second door on the left-hand side. Ideally, one of them would be posted outside the house, usually beneath the target's bedroom window to prevent them escaping. Brice could have put Mike there, but ever since the gun incident they had adopted a two-man protocol.

For one thing it was safer. Two pairs of eyes. Two pairs of hands. Two pairs of cuffs. These were all better. But there were a couple of other reasons. A child or teenager was less likely to think they had a chance against two fully grown men. And, crucially, Brice having Mike there meant they could counter any allegations that might be made after the fact. It was why two-person teams were deployed in this line of work. It provided deniability against any suggestion of impropriety.

They climbed the stairs, making sure to minimize any noise. The last thing they wanted was the target waking up before they got into the room.

They reached the landing and walked toward the bedroom door. It was closed. There was a sign on it that read: "Adults: Keep Out."

Too bad it wasn't going to work, thought Brice. At least half the time there was either a sign like it on the door, or the door was locked from the inside.

He glanced at Mike. Mike nodded. Brice slowly turned the door handle as Mike's hand slipped down to his pepper spray. They started as a black cat streaked past them, heading for the stairs.

The two men walked into the bedroom. It took a second for Brice's eyes to adjust to the gloom. Looking around, he felt like he had seen this room a thousand times before. Cluttered. Clothes strewn all over the floor, even though there was a hamper for dirty laundry by the window. Posters featuring moody, long-haired indie bands or green cannabis leaves were tacked to the walls. The smell of incense hung in the air, just below the general stink of teenage funk.

In the far corner, a desk was covered with books, makeup and colored pens. Next to it was a dresser, every drawer at least partially open with clothes spilling out over the edges.

Brice navigated through the minefield of crap until he reached the bed. Their target lay in the middle, the comforter over her head. Mike had already moved to the other side of the bed, ready for Brice's signal.

They had this part perfectly choreographed. Mike pulled a single leather glove from his jacket pocket and slipped it on. Occasionally they got a biter, almost always a girl, and the glove prevented too much damage. If there was a struggle, Brice would take the legs. Control someone's upper body, then pin down their legs, and there wasn't a whole hell of a lot they could do about it. When they were assured of cooperation they could relax their grip. If the target decided to go back on their word, well, that was what the pepper spray and handcuffs were for.

CHAPTER TWO

RUTH PRICE COULDN'T BREATHE. SHE was stuck inside a water-filled quarry. She couldn't remember how she'd got there, or how long she'd been trapped, but trapped she was.

She scrambled frantically to the side, but every time she tried to get a handhold to pull herself out, she lost her grip, fell back in, and her head went back under the water. She tried to stay calm, to conserve her energy, but it was no use. She rose to the surface one more time. She opened her mouth to take a breath and tasted something solid pressing against her tongue.

She could hear voices. Men's voices. Low and soothing. But she couldn't see anyone. There was only the water all around her and the steep, jagged quarry walls.

8

Finally, her eyes snapped open. The quarry disappeared. So did the water.

Oh, thank God.

A dream. A nightmare. She was in her bedroom at home.

But the thing pressing against her mouth was still there. A man's face was staring down at her.

Her heart pounded. Fear jolted its way up her spine. Her body spasmed with terror.

She tried to get up. She kicked out her legs. They wouldn't move. They were pinned down by a heavy weight.

The man's eyes stared down at her. "Ruth," he said. Low. Soothing. It was the voice she'd heard a moment before when she had been on the edge of waking.

How did he know her name?

Was this a nightmare within a nightmare?

It had to be.

That was the only explanation.

A cruel trick of her own mind.

Wake from one horror to another.

Only this seemed real.

"Ruth," the man said again. "My name is Michael. My partner here is Brice."

Ruth followed the man's gaze down the bed, slowly realizing why she wasn't able to move her legs. They were pinned down.

Sleep fell away. This wasn't a dream. This was real. This was the here and now. Her bedroom at home. The middle of the night. With two men holding her down, and about to do what?

"We're sorry for waking you like this but, believe me, it's the safest way for everyone."

She didn't understand. They were sorry for breaking into her and her mom's house? Sorry for sneaking into her bedroom in the dead of night and waking her up with their hand over her mouth so she couldn't scream?

What was safe about any of this?

"Ruth, I'm going to take my hand away from your mouth so you can breathe a little easier. I just didn't want you hollering the place down. Okay?"

Ruth swallowed hard. The whole thing still seemed unreal. But it was real. Very real.

She nodded. Or moved her head up and down as much as the man's grip allowed her to.

"Good. That's good," he said. "We don't want to hurt you. Or for you to hurt us. Do you understand that?"

She moved her head again. She felt his grip relax a little.

"Okay, Ruth, I'm going to take my hand away now. And Brice here is going to let you get up. If you scream, or attempt to resist in any way, it'll go very badly for you. We'll have to restrain you, which we don't want to do. Unless you don't give us a choice."

He unclamped his hand from over her mouth. She struggled to breathe. Her heart was still thumping out of her chest. Thumping so hard that she could actually hear it.

Her breathing came fast and shallow. She felt like she was about to have an asthma attack. She hadn't had one of those in over a year. She didn't even know where her inhaler was. The thought that she couldn't find it made her panic even more.

The man's hand fell onto her bare shoulder where her T-shirt had fallen down. The sensation of him touching her there creeped her out. "Take it easy, okay? We're here to help you. Not to hurt you."

Not here to hurt her? Was this guy for real? They'd almost scared her to death. And they were touching her.

She could think of a thousand things to say to that. But she knew better. Not when she was still lying down, half naked, with them standing over her.

She'd play along. When she could, when she actually had some air in her lungs, she'd scream and make a break for it.

Ruth closed her eyes and tried to calm her breathing. It was hard.

"That's better," Mike said.

"Okay," Ruth finally managed to say. "I understand."

"That's good," said Mike. "Now, we want you to get up, and throw some clothes on over what you already have on. Then we're going to walk you outside."

What the hell? Walk her outside?

I'm being kidnapped.

These two guys have broken in and they're going to kidnap me.

She managed to get to her feet. "Can you at least give me some privacy to get changed?" she asked them.

"No can do. From now until we deliver you to Broken Ridge you can't leave our sight. Those are the rules."

"What the hell is Broken Ridge?" she asked.

"It'll all be explained to you on the way there."

Ruth picked up a sweatshirt from the floor and pulled it on over her head. "You won't get away with this," she said.

She saw them trade a smile, like they were in on a secret she didn't know about. "Kidnapping's a federal crime."

She wasn't sure if it was or not, but she was sure that it was. She had heard something on a TV show once about transporting a minor over state lines being a federal crime.

"Ruth, no one's kidnapping anyone. We're simply here to make sure you're safely escorted to Broken Ridge."

Again with Broken Ridge. They said it like she should know what they were talking about.

This whole thing was crazy. Two men had burst into her bedroom in the middle of the night, told her they were taking her somewhere she'd never heard of, and acting like it was the most natural thing in the world. They could threaten her all they wanted, but there was no way she'd just go along with them because they said so.

She sat down on the edge of the bed, and folded her arms. "I don't know who you are, or how you got in here, but I'm not going anywhere with you."

The man who had held down her legs, the one the other had called Brice, stepped in front of her. "That's where you're wrong. You see, you might be able to pull this crap with your mom, but it won't wash with us. Now, you can walk out of here with us or we can carry you out. Makes no difference to me. Or to Mike."

Ruth glared up at him. "Screw you. I'm going to scream and then my mom will call the cops and both your asses will be thrown in jail."

"Is that so?" said Brice, turning away, walking across to the bedroom door and opening it to reveal Ruth's mom standing just outside, tears streaming down her face.

In that split second it all came together. Everything was clear. The two men weren't kidnappers. They were here at her mother's request.

Broken Ridge? Her mom had never used that name. But Ruth knew what it was. Her mother had threatened her with it when they fought, which, since her dad had left, was a lot. She'd threatened to send her away. And now, because of a stupid misunderstanding, and because her mom was bitter and twisted from the divorce, it was happening.

"You knew about this?" Ruth said to her mother.

Her mother looked at the floor. "I'm sorry," Sandra told her daughter. "I can't cope with you on my own anymore. This is for the best. You'll see."

"What are you talking about? What do you mean you can't cope?"

Brice stepped between Ruth and her mom. She moved to go round him, but he grabbed her wrists.

"Why are you doing this?" Ruth screamed, trying to shake herself free of his grasp.

"You know why."

"To punish me for Dad leaving you. Is that why?"

"That's not true. This has nothing to do with your father. There's been all the lies. And the drugs. And your grades are . . ."

The drugs? Ruth had been caught at school with a joint that wasn't even hers. That she'd been holding for her friend. One crummy joint that she wasn't going to smoke, because she didn't even smoke cigarettes, never mind pot. And her grades had been down because of all the shit at home.

"It was a joint, Mom. And it wasn't even mine."

"That's how these things start, Ruth. That's why you need to go somewhere you can learn to follow rules."

Ruth felt Brice's grip tighten. Suddenly he let go. Before she could react there was a click. She looked down to see shiny metal handcuffs around her wrists. She'd been so consumed with rage at her mom that she hadn't even seen him put them on her. "You can't do this!"

Her mom's tears evaporated. Her crumpled features morphed into an angry expression that Ruth was more familiar with. "I think you'll find that I can."

CHAPTER THREE

RUTH SAT ON THE FLOOR in the back of the truck, and sobbed. She hadn't cried like this since she was a little girl. Not that she could remember, anyway. She couldn't even recall crying when her parents had told her they were separating. Or when they told her they were getting divorced. If anything, that news had come as a relief more than anything. At least she wouldn't have to listen to them fighting all night anymore.

She had missed her dad when he'd moved out. Missed him a lot. She had wondered why she couldn't have gone with him. But he'd explained that he only had a studio apartment in D.C., and that she would have had to change schools. Plus, he'd said, her mom would need her. It was for the best that she stayed where she was.

Although she resented not being consulted, she'd guessed that it made sense. But she still couldn't shake the feeling that her staying was her father's way of trying to placate her mother. As her mother's mood had darkened, and she began to take out her unhappiness on Ruth, finding fault with everything she did, Ruth had wondered if she was punishing her for her father's leaving.

Now, sitting in the back of the truck on the way to God knew where, with two men who could be anyone, all of it not only agreed by her mom but done at her instigation, Ruth knew the truth. Her mom couldn't hurt her ex-husband. Not directly anyway. So she'd concocted this as her way of punishing him. Ruth and her dad had always been close. Her mom had even joked about her being a "Daddy's girl." After the divorce it had become less of a joke and more of an indictment. As if Ruth should pledge unfailing allegiance to her mother rather than do her best to get on with both parents.

But if Ruth's mom was punishing her to get back at her dad, Ruth was equally sure that there was no way her dad would have let this happen. If she could just get away, find a phone, or some way of contacting him, then these two rent-a-cops, or whatever they were, would be sorry they'd ever been born. Her dad would make sure of that.

All she had to do was play along. From what they'd said, there was a long drive ahead. They'd have to stop at some point. She'd get a chance to escape. All she had to do was have the courage to take the opportunity when it presented itself.

CHAPTER FOUR

"WHO'S BEEN A BAD BOY, Jacob?"

The question sent chills through him. He knew what was coming next. He knew there was no answer that would satisfy her. Once you'd been accused, denying any wrongdoing was worse than admitting it. "I'll try to be good from now on," he said. From where he was lying, his face pressed against the concrete floor, he could see her dirty black shoes and crappy old wrinkled stockings as she paced back and forth. "I promise," he pleaded.

"Oh, my, Jacob. I know you *want* to be good. But you just can't help yourself. It's hardly even your fault."

"I can help it," he said. "I know I can."

"Words, Jacob. You mean them when you say them. But you're just not capable. That's why we figured you might need a little help in the right direction, if you catch my meaning."

He did. He knew exactly what she meant. So did his bladder. Warm urine ran down his leg as he lost control of it, his terror at what was to come all-consuming.

A lot of times he'd heard that thinking about the pain to come was worse than the pain itself. This was not one of those times.

He was about to be electrocuted. And there was nothing he could say, and nothing he could do, to stop it.

The black shoes and wrinkled stockings shuffled out of sight. He heard two sets of footsteps get closer. He was lifted off his feet and dumped onto the gurney. He thrashed and flailed but they were too strong.

The heavy leather straps closed over his chest, his waist and his legs. A cloth was shoved into his mouth. That was to stop him biting through his tongue. In the background, he could hear the low hum of the generator.

Hands grasped either side of his head. The neck strap was put in place. He felt the cool gel being slathered over his temples.

Jacob closed his eyes and wished he was anywhere else in the world than here.

"We're doing this for you, Jacob," she said. "Now you shush and be still and it'll all be over quicker than two shakes of a lamb's tail."

CHAPTER FIVE

THE TRUCK SLOWED. FROM WHERE she was sitting in back, Ruth could hear the click-clack of the turn signal.

She had planned on saying that she needed to use the restroom when they stopped, but now, after three hours on the road, it wouldn't be a lie. She had needed to pee for the past hour. The truck's suspension, or lack of it, wasn't helping matters.

She kicked out at the backpack her mom had packed for her. She wasn't even sure she was angry at her any more. What she felt went beyond that. She felt betrayed. Completely and utterly.

The only thing Ruth knew for sure was that, when she got out of this situation, she wasn't going home. It wasn't home. Not anymore. Home was somewhere you were safe.

Secure. Neither of those words applied now. Not when you could be snatched up and transported halfway across the country at any time.

It wasn't even as if her mom had given her a warning. Or asked her to do anything to change. There had been arguments over her room, and homework, a slow grind of friction between them, but no more than usual. This whole being shipped off to who knew where had come from nowhere. Or, at least, that was how it seemed to Ruth.

Brice, the taller and heavier of the two men, slid back a door leading into the back of the truck from the cab. He stuck his head round the side. "We're going to stop in a few minutes. Make a comfort stop, if you need to. Get something to eat and drink. We'll take the cuffs off you, but you have to promise not to do anything stupid, you hear me?"

Ruth gave a little nod. "I won't give you any problems."

She'd already figured that the cuffs would be coming off anyway. What were they going to do? Take her into the restroom, pull down her pants for her and stand there while she used the toilet? Official escorts or not, there would be a call to 911 if anyone saw them taking a teenage girl into a truck-stop restroom and doing that.

All she had to do now was play nice and take her chance to escape when it came. She didn't even need to get that far away, just to a phone, or borrow someone's cell, and call her father. He would take care of the rest. These two chumps wouldn't know what had hit them. Her dad had a lot of friends. Washington D.C. friends. Powerful friends.

The truck came to a stop. Brice clambered into the back with her. He removed the handcuffs and helped her to her feet. She rubbed at her wrists.

"Sorry about the cuffs," he said, sounding genuine. "If you don't give us any more problems, you can keep them off until we get there."

"So what is this Broken Ridge place, anyway?" Ruth asked him. She figured that a few questions would help get him on her side, and that if he thought she was cooperating he'd be more likely to let his guard down. She could already make an educated guess as to what kind of place she was being sent to. A school for "troubled teens." She'd watched a documentary on Netflix about one of those places. It hadn't looked nice, but it hadn't seemed awful either. It had come over like a kind of super-hardcore summer camp.

Mike appeared before Brice could answer. "Come on. Let's go get some chow."

Ruth followed Brice back into the cab. She slid across the seat and out through the passenger door. Mike put out a hand and helped her jump down.

She looked around. Behind them, trucks and cars thundered past on the highway. The landscape was flat, scrub desert that stretched off toward the horizon in every direction. There was a gas station, a couple of fast-food joints, and some kind of general store. "I need to use the restroom," she told the two men, as they walked toward the store.

"No problem," said Brice. "You do that and then we can get something to eat."

Ruth hesitated. She was hoping that there would be another woman going into the restroom at the same time. That way she could ask to borrow their phone and call her dad. He would know what she should do once she'd made the call. Looking around she'd soon realized that, even if she did get away from her two escorts, she had nowhere to go. She could try to hitch a ride with someone, but that might be even more dangerous than the situation she was in already.

"Problem?" Brice asked her.

"No problem," she said, heading for the ladies' room.

"Good. Let's keep it that way."

****

The ladies' room was empty. Ruth headed for a stall. Escape or not, she really needed to pee. As she sat there, she listened for someone coming in. No one did. But surely it was only a matter of time.

She finished up, walked out of the stall and washed up as best she could. She left the water running in the sink. If Brice or the other one was outside she wanted them to think she was still washing her hands.

How come no one else had walked in? She had seen other cars, some with female passengers or drivers, parked outside. If they had pulled off the freeway, then surely one of them must have needed to use the restroom. They couldn't all have stopped for gas or food.

Seconds passed. Then a minute. Ruth cursed herself for not trying to pick up her own cell phone before she left. Then she remembered it hadn't been on the night stand next to her bed. Her mom must have moved it. But when? During the night, before the two escorts arrived to take her.

How long had her mom been planning this? Days? Weeks? It had to have been weeks. This wasn't something you could put together in a few days. So her mom had known for all that time she was going to send Ruth away. But the past few weeks had been calm. They'd barely had an argument, never mind a full-blown row. Well, not apart from the usual stuff about Ruth picking up after herself and doing some chores around the house.

They'd shared dinners. Gone for walks on the weekend. They'd got on. Not great. They would never have the kind of relationship that some of Ruth's friends had with their moms. But things had been about as chilled out as they'd been since her dad had left. And yet her mom had gone ahead with sending her away. Of having her woken in the middle of the night by two strange men, put into a truck with no windows in back, and being driven

25

across the country to who knew where. To a school for "troubled teens."

The name itself almost made Ruth laugh. Yeah, she was troubled—what teen wasn't? If she was more troubled than most that was because of her parents' divorce, and the hole it had left in their family.

So what had made her mom do this? It had to have been the joint. Ruth had been caught with it. That was true. But no one would believe her when she'd told them it wasn't hers. That she wasn't even a stoner. She wasn't sure which was worse: being accused or not being believed when she'd never lied in her life. Well, apart from all the usual little white lies that everyone told.

A knock at the restroom door. Brice called out, "You need to finish up in there. People are waiting out here."

Ruth's heart sank. That was why no one else had walked in. No one she could speak to and ask to borrow their phone to make a quick call. Because that asshole on a power trip was standing outside making sure that no one else came in.

Play along, she told herself. Don't show you're upset. If you do, he'll figure out that you were planning something. Play it off like it's all cool.

She turned off the tap, grabbed some paper towels and dried her hands. She walked to the door, opened it and stuck her head out.

Right enough, a woman and her two daughters were standing there, looking less than pleased with Brice preventing them using the facilities.

"Sorry," Ruth said, smiling sweetly at the mom. "Would you happen to have a spare tampon?"

It made her cringe to ask, but she needed a way to stall for time, and this was the only thing she could think of. Guys, even hard-ass guys like Brice, maybe even especially hard-asses like him, tended to get super-embarrassed when you made even the faintest mention of periods or anything related. At least, that was what Ruth had always thought.

Brice stared at her stony-faced. He didn't seem embarrassed. He looked angry. Like he knew what she was doing and planned on making her pay for it.

The two girls studied the floor. The mom smiled sympathetically at Ruth. "Sure, honey." She snapped open her handbag and dug around inside. She glared at Brice. "Would you excuse us for a moment?"

She started to move round him, toward the door, toward Ruth. He put out a hand. "Ma'am, if I could have a moment of your time."

The mom really glared at him now. "Sir, I don't know what's going on here with this young lady, but perhaps I should call the highway patrol." She turned back to the two girls she had with her. "Girls, go ask your father to come here, would you?"

Brice held up a hand. "There's no need for that. Or for you to call the cops. Unless, of course, you'd like to. Let

27

me explain the situation we have here. My name is Brice Walker, and I'm currently escorting this young lady to an institutional facility. Her mother has signed her over to me, so I and my partner Mike, who's out front right now, are *in loco parentis.*"

Ruth felt her face flush as the woman's expression changed before her eyes. One minute Ruth had been a young woman who might be in trouble. The next moment, after a few words from Brice, she was the trouble. The lady's two daughters were staring at her, too, like she was some of kind of zoo exhibit. The mom's glances to them seem to be saying: *See? This is what could happen if you don't eat your greens, do your homework and keep your room tidy.*

"We're concerned that Ruth here might try to do something silly before we manage to drop her off at the school. That was why I asked you to wait for a moment. I'm very sorry to have inconvenienced you," Brice continued.

Ruth had to hand it to him. He was smooth. He made it sound like the most normal thing in the world. It definitely sounded like a speech he'd had to give more than a few times.

The woman looked at Ruth. "Is this all true?"

Part of Ruth wanted to say no. That it was all lies. Maybe the woman or her husband would call the cops. But what if she didn't? What if Brice just made her out to be hysterical or crazy? What then?

Brice would be pissed. And Brice scared her. He'd already threatened her with pepper spray. There was no knowing what he and his buddy would do to her if she really made trouble. Even if the cops were called, Brice would put her back in the truck and they'd be long gone before anyone got there.

The woman was staring expectantly at her.

"Yes, it's true," Ruth said, her chin sinking onto her chest. She'd lost this battle.

"Do you still need a tampon?" the woman asked her.

But she didn't need to lose the war. "Yes," said Ruth. "I'd appreciate that."

The woman dug one out of the box, stepped past Brice and gave it to her. Ruth thanked her and stepped back inside the bathroom. So much for borrowing a phone. She'd have to think of something else. And fast.

CHAPTER SIX

WHEN SHE'D FIRST WALKED INTO the bathroom stall, Ruth had noticed a window. It was small. Maybe four feet wide, and two high, and it was toward the top of the wall, but she thought she might be able to get through it.

With the lady outside having completely bought into what Brice had told her, right now it looked like Ruth's best chance of getting away for long enough to contact her father. She put the toilet seat down, and climbed up. She reached up to the window, found the catch and pushed it open.

That was the easy part. The next would be a whole lot harder.

She grabbed the ledge with both hands and tried to pull herself up. No dice. She fell back. It was perhaps the first and only time that she wished she'd tried harder in Phys Ed class.

Come on, she told herself. You have to do this. It's either this or going back into that stinky truck and being dropped off who knows where. Broken Ridge? Even the name creeped her out. Hadn't she heard about people getting crazy strength when they really needed it? Like women lifting cars up into the air when their child was trapped underneath. That was what she needed now.

She took a deep breath, grabbed the ledge again with both hands and hauled herself up. She gave it everything. Her elbows cleared the top. She reached up with one hand and jammed it through the open window. She caught the ledge on the other side.

Great. Now she had some purchase and her bodyweight had shifted a little. Her arms and shoulders burned with the effort but, she told herself, she'd done the hard part. She pushed her other hand through the window.

She pushed her elbows over the ledge and through the window. Behind her she was sure she heard knocking at the door. She ignored it. A second later she heard a woman's voice call out, "Honey, are you okay in there?"

She twisted her head back, and tried to calm her breathing. "Yes, fine. Thank you."

Now there really was no going back. Pulling herself up a few inches more, she shoved her head through the window. It whacked against the glass. She ignored the pain and kept wriggling until her shoulders were through.

31

The window dropped out into an alleyway at the back of the gas station. Besides a couple of garbage dumpsters, the place was empty.

Ruth had been half expecting to find Mike out there, but he was nowhere to be seen. It was about a six-feet drop to the ground, and Ruth had no way of getting into a sitting position. The ledge was too narrow for her to scoot her butt round.

The only thing she could do was twist herself round, let gravity take her, and hope that she landed on her side rather than her head. She took another deep breath and pushed through the window.

Her ankle snagged, then twisted, getting caught between the window and the metal frame. She managed to wrench it free and fell the rest of the way. Pushing out her hands, she broke her fall, and tumbled forward, no longer in control. Her hands and wrists stung from the impact and her ankle pulsed with pain.

She lay there for a moment, trying to work out if she'd broken anything. There was only one way to know for sure. Gingerly, she got to her feet. She rubbed at her wrists. Her ankle still throbbed as she put some weight on it, but she didn't think it was broken.

She looked around the alleyway. Still no one there.

She hobbled down it toward the gas station. She turned the corner, expecting to see Mike or Brice. But they were nowhere to be seen. There was only a man putting gas in his Saturn, and a couple climbing out of a large, expensive-looking silver recreational vehicle.

None of them so much as looked in her direction. She tried to figure which one might be more easily persuaded to let her make a phone call. The couple, she decided. A woman would be more likely to help a young girl who asked. If Brice hadn't gotten to them first. They were busy stretching in the morning sunshine, working the kinks out of their necks and backs.

She walked toward them, trying to seem casual. Hard to do when you'd just dropped out of a bathroom window head first, and twisted your ankle.

The man looked up first. He didn't say anything. He nudged his wife.

"Excuse me," she said, trying to sound extra polite. "I really hate to bother you, but I need to call my dad, and I've lost my phone. I know it's asking a lot, but maybe if you could lend me yours? I'd be really quick."

They seemed to shrink away. Their expressions said that this must be some kind of a scam. A strange kid approaching strangers at a gas station in the middle of nowhere. They probably thought that as soon as they handed over their phone she'd run off with it. Jump into a waiting car and take off.

Ruth didn't blame them. It did seem weird. "Please," she said again. She could already tell they weren't going to do it.

"I'm sorry . . ." the woman started to say.

Before she could finish, Ruth turned and started toward the man gassing up his Saturn. Now she probably did seem like a panhandler to the couple.

The pump clicked to a stop. The man removed the nozzle. Ruth walked over to him, making sure to keep the pump between her and the gas station so no one could see her without really looking. She repeated what she'd said to the couple. It sounded even more sketchy to her own ears the second time around.

"Sorry," Saturn man said. "Even if I wanted to, you see that sign there?"

She glanced in the direction he was pointing a stubby finger.

"You're not allowed to use a cell phone here. Sounds a bit crazy to me but that's what the sign says. Must be a reason for it."

"I could take it over there," she said.

Saturn guy wasn't looking at her anymore. His gaze had moved over her shoulder. She didn't want to look around. It was Brice. Or Mike. Or both of them.

"Maybe he can help," said Saturn guy, confirming her worst fears. She'd been found. Without being able to make the call.

There would be a price to pay for trying to escape. She was sure of it.

She had to will herself to look round.

When she did, her heart quickened, but in a good way. Neither Mike nor Brice was standing next to the gas station entrance. Or even the lady from the restroom.

It was someone with the power to save her from this nightmare.

CHAPTER SEVEN

J ACOB TOOK HIS LUNCH TRAY, shuffled across the room and sat at a table on his own. Apart from Rachel, who nudged one of her little followers, no one looked at him. No one dared. They all knew where he'd been. They all knew what had happened there. Some of them had heard his screams. The room was soundproofed, but they had still heard him scream and plead for Gretchen to stop, before he'd fallen silent.

A couple of the other kids had cleaned up the room afterwards. Chris had given them a mop, a bucket and some bleach to do the job. They hadn't talked about it. Not to each other. Not to anyone. They were level sixes. Another few months and they could be out of here. Back home with their families. Good boys and girls who had passed through the program.

Jacob had refused to follow the program. He didn't take orders. He was sullen around the fire pit. He had even laughed at Gretchen once. Right to her face. That had been a fatal error.

So, now he had paid the price. His brain was cloudy. He could barely keep his hands steady enough to spoon Jell-O into his mouth.

The others avoided him now. No one wanted to be the next Jacob. No one wanted to be led into the room and come back out like that.

But, somewhere deep inside, the old Jacob was still alive. And he would have his say. Maybe not today. Or tomorrow. But one day.

CHAPTER EIGHT

RUTH MOVED FAST TOWARD THE state trooper, who had now sauntered into the gas station and was busy filling a cup with coffee from the stand just inside the door. Any second now either Mike or Brice could appear round the corner. The couple from the RV were still staring at her. The look on their faces suggested they had been thinking about approaching the state trooper too.

Ruth pushed through the gas-station door and made straight for him. He was tall, over six feet, lean, and in his forties. He looked up as she walked toward him.

She stopped straight in front of him. Her words came out in a furious rush.

"My name's Ruth Catherine Price. I'm fourteen years old. I live in Los Angeles, California. This morning I was taken from my home by two men. They stopped here to get gas and I got away from them. I need you to help me. If they catch me . . ."

The trooper, whose name plate read "Trooper Leaf", put his coffee back on the stand. "Okay, slow down there, young lady."

"Ruth. Ruth Price." She knew she sounded dorky repeating her name like that, but she needed for him to understand how serious this was.

"Okay, Ruth. Where are these two men now?" She could already see him looking past her to the door. His hand had fallen to his service weapon. Just that little gesture made her feel safer.

"I don't know. I snuck out the restroom window." She held up her blackened, scraped palms as proof. "See?"

All that she wanted right this second was to be believed. For an adult not to look at her like she was some kind of crazy runaway. That she was telling the truth.

"Sounds like it's just as well I was here, doesn't it?" He gave her a reassuring smile. "Now, let's go sit in my patrol car. That sound good?"

It sounded better than good. There was no way anyone was going to try to pull her out of a state trooper's patrol car. No way on earth. If either of those two bullies tried it, Ruth was sure that Trooper Leaf would shoot them.

Trooper Leaf picked up his coffee and raised it toward the woman jockeying the cash register. "Back in a moment, Claudette."

She smiled and gave him a wave. Ruth followed him outside. They walked down the other side of the gas station to his car.

"Tell you what," he said. "The front's kind of messy. Why don't you sit in back?"

He opened the rear door. Ruth got in and scooted along the seat to the other side where there was some shade. The trooper closed the door. The locks clunked down. Ruth was pretty sure that was automatic. The back seat smelt of stale hamburger meat and sweat. Right now, Ruth didn't mind. She was safe.

Trooper Leaf walked round and got into the driver's seat. Sitting up, Ruth could see that he hadn't been exaggerating about the mess. The front passenger seat was covered with papers, a couple of discarded Subway wrappers and three empty Camelbacks.

"Okay, so I got your name already," said Trooper Leaf, flipping open a notepad and writing it down. "Now, if you could let me have a number for your mom, I'm going to call and let her know that you're okay."

When Ruth didn't respond, he glanced back at her. "I'm guessing she'll be worried out of her mind."

Him calling her mom wouldn't help. It had to be her dad. "She's away on business right now. It'd be easier to call my dad."

Trooper Leaf looked puzzled. "She doesn't have a cell phone?"

"She's overseas," said Ruth. "In Paris."

The trooper shifted round in his seat so he could look at her without straining his neck. "I'm pretty sure they have cell-phone coverage in France. Especially a big city like Paris."

"Yeah, but the time difference. It'll be the middle of the night there. Wouldn't it be easier to call my father? I can give you his number."

His expression said he was started to doubt her story. Ruth was pretty sure that cops were experts at telling when someone was lying to them, and she wasn't a good liar. She never had been. Her face flushed, and she avoided making eye contact with the person.

"Okay, give me that number and I'll call him. I'm guessing he can call your mom, right?"

"Sure," said Ruth, a little too eagerly. "That would be great."

She rattled off her dad's cell phone and the number at his apartment. He was pretty much the only person she knew who still had a landline instead of just a cell phone and Skype. She teased him about it.

Out of the corner of her eye, Ruth saw movement. It was Brice and Mike. They were with the man from the RV. He was pointing them toward the patrol car.

Ruth slid down in the seat. She didn't want them to see her. At least, not before the trooper had made that call to her dad. He already had his phone in his hand and had started tapping in the number.

41

Peeking out of the window, she saw that Brice and Mike were still heading straight for the patrol car. Ruth froze. They were looking straight at her. Brice had a big smirk on his face.

CHAPTER NINE

SHOULD SHE WARN TROOPER LEAF that these were the two guys? Or should she wait for him to make the call?

The call, she decided, was more important. It wasn't like they were going to do anything to a cop. Not in broad daylight. She'd speak to her dad; he'd ask the trooper to stay with her until he could get there. And her mom could go to Hell.

The trooper had finished tapping in the number. He held his cell phone to his ear. "Damn," he said. "The connection dropped." He held up the screen so that she could see there were no signal bars.

She glanced back at the two escorts strolling toward her. They couldn't be more than fifty yards away now.

"Can you try again?" Ruth asked Trooper Leaf. "Please."

"Not a whole lot of point if I don't have a signal."

Now he had noticed Brice and Mike closing in on the patrol car. His gaze didn't leave them as he asked Ruth, "Are these the two men?"

"Yes," said Ruth, her voice breaking with fear. "That's them. Can we get out of here?"

The trooper ignored her question. He opened his door and got out, his weapon drawn. Keeping the hood of the patrol car between him and the two men, he pointed his gun straight at Brice and Mike. The smirk melted away from Brice's face.

"Stand where you are," the trooper barked at them. "Place your hands slowly above your head, and lace your fingers together."

Having a gun pointed at them had what Ruth guessed was the desired effect. Trooper Leaf had their full attention. She couldn't help a little tingle of enjoyment. After all, they'd pushed her around, threatened her, and generally scared the hell out of her. Now they were getting a little taste of their own medicine. It didn't look like they were enjoying it all that much.

"Okay, now get down onto your knees. Keep your hands on top of your heads."

Brice glared at her as he struggled to lower himself. If looks could have killed, Ruth thought.

She watched as the trooper stepped out from behind the patrol car and moved behind the two men, his gun still on them. He was talking to them but, with the distance, she couldn't tell what was being said. The trooper unclipped his handcuffs from his belt.

Ruth waited for him to use them. He didn't. Now Brice was doing most of the talking. Trooper Leaf holstered his gun.

Brice kept talking. Ruth looked for a way of lowering the window. There wasn't any. She tried to get out. She couldn't do that either. Of course she couldn't. She was in the back of a patrol car. The people who usually sat back here had been arrested.

She wanted to know what lies Brice was telling. She could see him and his partner dropping their hands down. Trooper Leaf kept looking at her. Brice kept talking. The trooper put his hands on his hips. His expression was one of exasperation.

A few more minutes passed. Brice dug a piece of paper out of his pocket along with his wallet. He opened the wallet and handed it to the trooper. While Trooper Leaf looked at Brice's ID, Brice unfolded the piece of paper. They traded wallet and paper. The trooper looked over the paper, then handed it back to Brice.

Apparently satisfied that the two men weren't kidnappers, or an immediate danger, the trooper walked back to the patrol car. He came round to Ruth's side and opened the door.

"Step out of my car for a moment."

Ruth's heart sank as she got out. She leaned against the trunk.

45

"Okay, Ruth. I've spoken to Brice and Michael. They've also shown me the paperwork signed by your mother, and evidence that they are who they say they are, and that they're properly insured to transport you to this residential facility."

A lump formed in her throat. Tears welled in her eyes. She swiped them away with the back of her sleeve. She didn't want to come across as some overly emotional teenager. That would only make things worse. If they could get any worse.

"I just want to call my dad. That's all. If I can speak to him, even just for a minute, then I'll do whatever you ask me to."

Trooper Leaf bit down on his lower lip. "That's the thing. Your father, at least as far I've been told, doesn't have custody. His visitation rights are limited to one weekend a month. Is that correct?"

Where was this going? Just because she only saw her dad once a month, she couldn't call him?

"Yes, but—"

The trooper cut her off as another patrol car swung fast into the gas station and pulled up just behind them. "I can let you make a call to your mother. Perhaps she can get a message to your father."

Ruth thought she'd lose it. Start screaming. Or hit someone. Was everyone around her insane? Her mom was the one who'd arranged this in the first place. Her mom hated her dad. That was why she'd fought so hard to make sure they didn't see each other. It was her mom's payback for her father leaving.

"Don't I have the right to make a phone call to whoever I want to?"

"If you'd been arrested. You haven't been arrested."

Ruth sensed a small irritation in the trooper's voice as he said that.

"Then I'm free to go?" said Ruth.

"No, you're a minor," said the trooper. "And these two men here are fully insured escorts. Right now, they're in *in loco parentis*, at least until you all get where you're going. You know what that means? *In loco parentis?*"

Ruth had listened to enough talk from her parents and her friends about court hearings and divorce courts to know that it meant, right now, Brice and Mike *were* her parents, as far as the law was concerned. What they said went.

"But they kidnapped me! From my home."

"Your mom was there, right?"

"Yes, but . . ."

"She asked them, no, she hired them, to take you to this facility."

"But I don't want to go," Ruth protested. She sounded like a bratty teenager. She knew she did. But it was so unfair.

"I'm sorry. I don't make the law. I just enforce it. And they're not breaking any law."

"Can't I at least phone my father? Please."

The trooper sighed. She could tell that he was getting tired of the conversation. "That's not my call."

"But he's my father."

Trooper Leaf cleared his throat. "You can ask them. It's not down to me who you can or can't call. I'm sorry."

He turned and walked over to the other cop who had just arrived. Brice and Mike flanked her on either side.

"Okay," said Brice. "You've had your fun. Now we need to get going."

The lump in her throat was as hard as a rock. She wanted to burst in tears. But she didn't want to do it in front of them. She wasn't going to give them the satisfaction.

With the two escorts at either side of her, she walked all the way back to the truck. Brice opened the door and she climbed in. He unhooked the handcuffs from his belt.

"But I'm going to be riding in back. You can lock the door. I won't be able to escape," Ruth said to him.

"Maybe you should've thought about that. You think we haven't had kids try to get away before?" He smirked. With a widening smile, he snapped the cuffs around her wrists. They clicked into place. He led her into the back of the truck and helped her sit down. "Want to know something funny?"

She didn't. She had a feeling he was going to tell her anyway.

"We were going to let you keep the cuffs off, ride up front with us. All comfortable and everything."

Ruth stared up at him. "Let me call my dad, please."

"No can do," said Brice. He clambered back into the front of the truck. The engine sputtered into life.

Now the tears came. Her sobs drowned by the engine, Ruth Price closed her eyes and lay down on her side.

CHAPTER TEN

THE DELIVERY TRUCK RUMBLED TO a halt. The jolt woke Ruth. She sat up as best she could. It wasn't an easy thing when you were lying on your side with your hands cuffed. Finally, after a struggle, she managed it. She sat with her back against the side panel. The engine was switched off. She could hear Mike and Brice get out and slam their doors.

They weren't going to leave her in the back on her own, were they? It had been getting warmer over the past few hours. Now it was hot enough that she could feel a trickle of sweat running down her back and into the crack of her butt. Her mouth was dry, her lips cracked.

The back door of the truck was flung open. Blinded by the blazing sunlight that poured in, Ruth raised her cuffed hands to shield her eyes. She blinked, the light still hurting.

"Wake up, Sleeping Beauty," said Mike, hopping into the back of the truck, and pulling her to her feet. Brice joined him and together the two men helped her down out of the truck.

Apart from a scraggly line of barbed-wire fence, there was nothing to see. Flat Western desert landscape stretched off in every direction, only interrupted by cactus and juniper trees. It looked like the kind of place that someone in a movie about the Mafia would visit to bury a body. The thought flitted through her mind.

"Can I have some water?" she croaked.

"Sure thing," said Brice, disappearing back to the front of the truck and reappearing a few moments later with a bottle. He unscrewed the cap and held it up to her mouth. She took a sip, running her tongue over her lips to moisten them. She titled her head back a fraction and took another drink. Then another.

"Better?" Brice asked.

Ruth nodded. "Yes, thanks."

Since the incident with the cop back at the gas station, she had decided not to give them any more trouble. To do what they asked. Kiss their ass if she had to. She would get another chance to escape, she was sure of it. Until then it was best just to go along with what they wanted until someone let their guard down enough that she could make a run for it. This time she wouldn't make the mistake of trusting anyone. With the way she felt right now, she wasn't sure she'd ever trust anyone again.

51

"Where are we?" she asked the two escorts.

"This is it," said Brice. "Broken Ridge Academy."

Maybe this was their idea of a joke. She looked around, but all she could see was the same barren desert dotted with juniper, cactus and tumbleweed.

"Here," he said, taking her elbow and guiding her to the front of the truck.

It was there in front of them. A series of long, single-story buildings that looked like military barracks were set one behind another. Off to one side was what looked like a ranch house. In the far distance she could see some other buildings. Maybe barns, or something.

The first thing that stood out to Ruth was how orderly everything seemed. The surroundings might have been wilderness but everything Ruth was looking at was spick, span and freshly painted.

"I'll go get your bag," said Mike, opening the passenger door of the trunk, appearing a few seconds later with the backpack her mom had filled. He dumped it on the ground at Ruth's feet.

"You want to go get the Wicked Witch of the West, or should I?" Mike asked his partner.

Ruth noticed Brice shoot him a knock-it-off look. "No need," said Brice. "Here she comes now."

Ruth followed his gaze to the front porch of the ranch house where a frumpy woman in her fifties, wearing the kind of white and red polka-dot dress you usually saw on little girls at church, started down the front steps toward them. Her hair was a limp, mousy brown, cut into a bob. Not a modern bob, but something you might have seen on a housewife from the 1950s.

"Good afternoon, Miss Applewhite," said Brice. "This is Ruth Price."

Gretchen Applewhite smoothed down the front of her dress as she walked toward them. She was smiling sweetly. "Gentlemen, could you please remove those handcuffs from Ruth? You know how I feel about the use of restraints on our young people."

Mike jumped to it, scrabbling for his key and unlocking the cuffs. "Sorry, Miss Applewhite, she tried to escape when we stopped for gas."

Gretchen stood directly in front of Ruth. Ruth rubbed at her wrists, grateful that she was now free of the cuffs. "Thank you," she said to Gretchen.

"You're quite welcome, my dear. Now, I'll have someone come out in a moment and collect your bag, so you can leave it there for now. Gentlemen, I assume you'll want me to sign the transfer papers. You can come into the house and we can do it there."

Brice shifted his weight from one foot to the other and back again. "Actually, we're in kind of a hurry. We have a pick-up in Scottsdale this evening. Overnight transport to a facility in Montana."

Ruth assumed that this meant another kid like her was about to be taken from their home in Scottsdale and driven in the back of the truck all the way to Montana. She didn't know who it was, or what their crime was, but she already felt sorry for them.

"As you wish," said Gretchen.

Brice dug into his pocket and pulled out a sheet of paper. "If you can initial here and here, and sign at the bottom," he said, handing off the paper to her along with a pen.

Gretchen took the paper, initialed and signed it and handed it back to him. He folded it, jammed it back into his pocket and started toward the truck. Mike was already climbing into the cab. It was like they couldn't get out of there fast enough. Standing next to Ruth, Gretchen watched them start the engine and turn the truck around with the same smile on her face and a slightly misty look in her eyes.

The truck disappeared in a cloud of dust. The speed with which they'd taken off had set Ruth on edge.

She waited for Gretchen to move, or to say something. But she just stood there with that same creepy look on her face.

"So, how long do I have to stay here for?" Ruth asked her.

Gretchen turned her head. Her expression didn't change. "That all depends on you, my dear."

In other words, if she behaved and and followed orders, she'd get to go home. At least, that was what Ruth thought she'd meant.

"So, what?" asked Ruth. "A couple of months?"

"You're how old?" Gretchen said.

"Fourteen," said Ruth. "Fifteen in December."

"Well, you'll stay until you're eighteen, or until we decide you can be a normal functioning young woman who doesn't try to constantly test boundaries."

"Eighteen?" Ruth blurted out. "You're kidding me, right?"

The smile had begun to melt from Gretchen's face. "Perhaps at your old school the students were allowed to speak to adults like that." The smile was gone. "This isn't your old school, young lady. We demand respect."

"I just asked a question."

Gretchen reached out, grabbed Ruth's hand and quickly bent it back at the wrist. Pain surged up her arm. It was so sudden, and so violent, that she froze with shock. For someone who looked so frail, Gretchen Applewhite was surprisingly strong. "We've had hundreds of young women like you at Broken Ridge over the years. Smart mouths. Grubby habits. Dirty little secrets. Thought they knew better than everyone else. No respect for their elders." Gretchen's face was so close to Ruth's that she could smell her breath.

"They all come in here thinking they'll be able to twist us round their little finger. Just like they do at home. Or flout the rules. Just like they do at school. Well, allow me to tell you something for nothing, they are quickly disabused of either of those notions."

55

She was still bending back Ruth's wrist, almost to breaking point. Ruth wanted to lash out with her free hand. But she didn't. Something told her that fighting back would bring something far worse.

"I'm sorry. I really am," Ruth pleaded.

Gretchen let go of her hand and took a step back. "Oh, you will be sorry, young lady. I promise you that."

CHAPTER ELEVEN

AS THEY TURNED BACK ONTO the highway, Brice eased off the gas pedal. He'd been driving like a bat out of hell since they'd left Broken Ridge.

In the passenger seat, Mike looked at him. "I thought that the Scottsdale collection wasn't until tomorrow."

"It is. But that place weirds me out Quicker we could get out of there, the better."

Mike laughed. "Yeah. Me, too. I almost feel sorry dropping kids off at that dump. That Gretchen lady. Something ain't right there."

"You should have met her old man, dude."

"Weird?"

"Weird doesn't even begin to cover it."

Brice rolled his head, trying to relax his neck from all the hours behind the wheel. "Hey, if you don't want to do the time, then don't do the crime."

CHAPTER TWELVE

THE BUILDINGS THAT RUTH HAD thought looked like army barracks when she'd arrived were the dormitories where the students of Broken Ridge slept. As instructed, she left her bag outside to be collected and followed Gretchen up the steps of the ranch house.

Ruth nodded, scared to speak in case whatever she said upset Gretchen. On the front porch, Gretchen told Ruth to wait. She disappeared inside the ranch house, closing the door behind her.

Ruth was alone. There was no one else to be seen.

For a second, she thought about making a break for it. She could head back down the track that the truck had driven up. Maybe she could make it to a road and hitch a lift.

The problem was that she was hungry and exhausted. Not just physically, but mentally as well. She still hadn't even begun to process what had happened. One second she'd been in her bed at home and now she was in the middle of the desert at a place run by some crazy woman. She didn't even know for sure which state she was in, never mind what town they were near. She had no money. No phone. And, right this second, no hope.

All she could think about was that she might have to stay here for over three years. That thought alone made her feel sick. It couldn't be true, could it? You couldn't be kept somewhere against your wishes for years?

Her dad wouldn't let that happen anyway. Even if she couldn't contact him, he'd realize something was up when she wasn't home at their next visit. That was a few weeks away, but right now a few weeks felt a lot more manageable than more than three years.

If she had to, she could deal with this place for a few weeks until her dad came and got her out. Keep out of Gretchen's way. Maybe try to make some friends with the other kids. She wasn't the most popular girl at school, but she had friends. She could get by. She could make this work. You could make pretty much anything work for a few weeks.

The door of the ranch house opened. A man stepped out. He was about six feet tall with the build of a football player. He had short blond hair and blue eyes. Ruth guessed he was in his early thirties, or maybe a little older.

He was dressed in khakis and a blue polo shirt with "Broken Ridge Academy" in small gold lettering on the front.

He didn't look at her. He strode straight past and down the stairs. At the bottom, he stopped and turned. "Come with me, Price."

She scrambled to follow him as he kept the same fast pace toward the dormitories. As he walked, he didn't look back.

One of the dormitory doors opened. A dumpy brunette woman appeared, wearing the same uniform as the guy showing Ruth around. She was followed by a long line of teenage girls. They all wore puffy white blouses, and flip-flops. They were spaced out, with a few feet between each of them. They stared straight ahead. Didn't talk. They looked like robots.

The man Ruth was following stopped and watched them pass. When they were gone, he started talking.

"All of our students live together as families. Males and females are segregated. You may not speak to a male student unless explicitly granted permission. If you do so without having permission, you *will* suffer a penalty and lose your current level. Levels, penalties and what we expect of you will be explained in more detail later on. But, in language that your typical slacker teenager can understand, it's a little like a video game. You start at level one, the lowest of the low. No privileges. If you do what you're told, when you're told to do it, don't give us any

61

attitude, and don't breach the rules, you can gain points. Gain sufficient points and you move up a level."

He turned to look at her as the final student in the line turned a corner and disappeared. "Life here at Broken Ridge is as hard or as easy as a student chooses to make it."

Ruth's head was spinning as he set off again, heading for the building the line of students had just left. They reached a door. He pulled out a bunch of keys, sorted through them, found the one he was looking for, and unlocked it.

"Turn around," he said.

It took a second for Ruth to react. Her head was spinning from all the talk of levels and families and penalties.

"I said, turn around, Price."

She did as she'd been told, turning around so that her back was to the door and she couldn't see the code that was being punched in. She heard four or five beeps, then the sound of a bolt sliding back.

"You remember what I said about doing what we say *when* we say it?"

She wasn't sure whether she should answer him or not.

"Price?" he prompted.

"By not following my instruction to turn around immediately you have earned one penalty point. You are now at minus one. Not a great start. You obey staff at all times, not just when you feel like it." He gave the word *feel* a sulky teenager/Valley girl pronunciation.

62

Her reflex was to object. She had just arrived. She had turned around, just not right that very second. It wasn't like she had disobeyed. But she already knew better than to argue. He'd only give her another penalty point.

"Yes, sir," she said, a hint of sarcasm creeping into her voice without her even thinking about it.

He let out a theatrical sigh. "That's one more penalty for using that tone of voice with me. Good job. You are now at minus two points."

What? This was bullshit. How could you punish someone for how they said something? It wasn't even as if she'd tried to sound like a smart-ass.

"Turn around, Price," he said. He sounded pissed off, but she guessed that was okay. After all, he was staff. This was just like school, or dealing with her mom.

"Got any more to say?" he asked.

She looked down at the ground. "No, sir," she said, trying to remove any intonation from her voice.

"Better," he said, opening the door. "Follow me. Stay three steps behind me. If you aren't able to accurately judge a three-step distance, then there are distance markings on the walls. Those are the arrows. They also indicate the one-way system that is employed in all our family houses. Walk against the flow at any time and you'll also incur a penalty. Understand me?"

"Yes, sir," she said. She hadn't realized until now how much effort it took to sound neutral. She and her friends all spoke in a way that sounded like they were making fun of each other, or that they thought the other person was an idiot. They didn't mean anything by it—well, not most of the time anyway. It wasn't even conscious.

The hallway stretched out ahead of them. It was freshly painted in white. Apart from some framed posters of sunsets with motivational quotes—*Be the person you're capable of being; Obedience is strength not weakness; Change yourself. Change others. Then change the world*—the walls were spotlessly clean, apart from the arrows. They were black, pointed in the same direction, and were spaced four feet apart.

The doors they passed had been painted blue. They all had the same electronic keypads as the outside door but they didn't have a separate lock that needed a key. At least, not so far as Ruth could see.

She was still in shock. But she also knew that if she wanted to get out of here she needed to pay attention to her surroundings. Without the staff noticing what she was doing. She didn't plan on sticking around any longer than she had to.

They stopped at a door. Ruth had to skid to a halt to avoid breaking the three-step rule. The staff member turned his head toward her, his index finger hovering over the key pad. Keeping her face expressionless, she looked down at the immaculately clean concrete floor and turned around.

"Good. You're getting it, Price. Fast learners always do much better here than students who try to fight the system."

She heard the beep as he punched in the digits. She listened hard. Maybe different digits made a different sound. If they did, she couldn't tell.

She heard the bolt open. She turned around, half expecting another penalty because she hadn't waited to be told she was allowed to. The staff member pushed the blue door open.

"This, Price, is going to be your new home while you're here."

He walked into the room. She held back, hovering in the doorway.

"You can come in. The three-step doesn't apply in here." He turned to face her and smiled. "Not enough space to keep three steps from each other at all times."

He wasn't kidding. The room itself was tiny. At least for the number of occupants.

There were three windows spaced equally alongside the far wall. They looked out onto a paved central courtyard. Within the room, there were three rows of thin mattresses laid out on the floor. Each row was made up of six mattresses. Each mattress had a single, equally thin foam pillow, two sheets and a rough wool blanket. Along one wall was a series of open lockers. The contents of each locker looked to be identical. Toothbrush, toothpaste, a hairbrush, clothes, a wash cloth, and a towel.

The walls were white. No arrows, but the same range of motivational posters. On the wall opposite the lockers there was a chart. Ruth couldn't read it from where she was standing, and she didn't want to walk over to it without permission. She stood where she was and tried not to break down in tears. That was what she wanted to do.

Apart from when she found out that her parents were divorcing, she couldn't remember ever feeling so low before. This was her new home? Maybe for years. A week here would be bad enough.

Her mind flitted back to her room at home. To her posters, her clothes, all the things that made it home. She thought of the cat that her mom had bought her (no doubt to make up for the divorce). How she always came back from school to find Merlin curled up in the middle of her bed. He wasn't a replacement for her dad being there, but he had been a comfort, something that made home feel a little less empty. She thought about all of that, looked around the bare room she had to share with strangers—a room that offered no privacy—and now she really had to fight back the tears.

There was a knock at the door. An older girl was standing there. She was dressed in staff uniform, although Ruth didn't think she could have been old enough to be an actual staff member. She looked like one of the girls Ruth had seen earlier, walking in line.

"Rachel, this is Ruth Price. She just arrived. I was showing her the dorm," said the male staff member, who still hadn't told Ruth his name.

Rachel swept a hand through a mane of long, glossy chestnut hair. She was tan, with a perfect smile and long legs. She might have stepped out of a swimsuit advertisement in a teen girl magazine. "I can take care of that for you," she said.

She might have been smiling but the look in her eyes was far from friendly. Ruth recognized it from the popular girls in her classes at high school back home.

"That'd be great if you would. I'm supposed to have a meeting in a few minutes."

"Leave it with me, Father," said Rachel.

Father? The guy didn't look old enough to have a daughter Rachel's age. Not just that, they didn't look related. Then there was the way she had said it. It had come off creepy.

Rachel glanced back at Ruth. "Mr Fontaine is our house father. We call him Father. Staff may address us by our family name or our first name."

"We're like one big family. Isn't that right, Rachel?"

"It is. One big happy family," said Rachel.

Fontaine left them. Ruth could hear him whistling to himself as he walked back down the corridor. She stood awkwardly in the middle of the room. Rachel walked over to her, circling her slowly, looking her up and down.

"What are you here for?" she asked Ruth. "Dope? Booze? Whoring around?"

Ruth shook her head. She hadn't done any of that. She wasn't sure a few puffs of a single joint made you a doper. "I don't know," she said.

"No reason?" Rachel sounded incredulous.

"No," said Ruth.

"There has to be a reason."

"I guess there does," said Ruth. "But I don't know what it is."

"Oh, wow, that's really sad." Rachel tilted her head back and laughed. It was a real mean-girl laugh. "Hey, maybe your parents just don't like you."

CHAPTER THIRTEEN

DONALD PRICE PACED UP AND down outside the entrance to the Four Seasons Hotel on Pennsylvania Avenue in Washington, D.C. In one hand, he held his cell phone, pressed hard to his ear. In his other he had a lit cigarette. Along with weight gain, and a stomach ulcer, smoking had been another unforeseen consequence of separation. He'd gone from being a former smoker of fifteen years' standing (he'd stopped when Ruth was born) to a pack-a-day habit in a little under six months.

He brushed a stray cone of ash from the lapel of his sports coat and took a breath. "I'd like to speak to Ruth. I haven't spoken to her since the weekend, and I don't want her thinking I've disappeared off the radar."

On the other end of the line his soon-to-be ex-wife, Sandra, offered to take a message.

"She's not there?" he asked.

"Not right now, no. Or haven't you been listening?"

"You just said she couldn't come to the phone. I thought that maybe she was doing homework or something."

"I'll tell her you called—"

"No," he said, cutting her off. "Not good enough. I want to speak to her."

From other friends of his, guys who were either separated or divorced, he knew he had to make a concerted effort to maintain a relationship with his daughter. If he didn't, it would slip away. Leaving messages, which would suit Sandra down to the ground, was the start of it.

He'd already had to spend tens of thousands of dollars in attorney's fees just to be able to see Ruth one weekend a month and have two weeks with her over the summer vacation and a week at Christmas. It was money he'd hoped to use toward her college education, but the system was so hopelessly weighted against fathers that he'd had no choice but to use it to pay his attorney's kids' college tuition.

It could have all been avoided if his ex had been reasonable. But she hadn't been, and it didn't look like she was about to start now. If anything, over the past few months, she'd gotten worse.

Their relationship was now one of mutual contempt that was no longer even thinly disguised. Thinly disguised contempt had been about three months back. Now "openly hostile" would have been the more accurate description. And, despite Donald's best efforts, maybe Sandra's too, their daughter was in the middle. The one thing his ex knew she could use to hurt him, like he had hurt her. It was messed up, but hardly new when it came to couples splitting up. Children as the battleground for their parents' failed relationship.

"She's not here," Sandra said finally.

"Where is she?" Donald demanded. Wouldn't it have been easier for her to tell him where she was? Rather than making every single thing an uphill battle.

"Don't speak to me like that."

"Like what?"

"Like that."

It was as if they were reading from a script they'd run through so often that the pages must have been dog-eared from use and covered with coffee stains. "I tried her cell but it was switched off, or out of service," said Donald.

"She's at a friend's. She probably turned off her phone and forgot to turn it back on again. You know how forgetful she can be sometimes."

"Do you have a number for this friend?"

Sandra hesitated.

Something was off. He sensed it. You lived with someone as long as he and Sandra had been together, and you knew when they were lying. Or holding something back, not telling you the whole truth.

"No."

"You let her go to a friend's but you don't have a number for them?"

"I do but, listen, I'm really busy right now, okay? I wasn't expecting you to call."

"Sandra, stop. What are you not telling me here?"

"I have no idea what you're talking about."

"Yes, you do."

"This is harassment, Donald. Am I going to have to go talk to my attorney again, see if he can ask the judge to take another look at your visitation rights?"

Donald looked up. He had stopped in front of the hotel's valet parking stand. A well dressed D.C. couple were staring at him. He didn't blame them. He must have looked like a maniac, standing there, almost screaming into a cell phone while in his other hand the Marlboro burned down to the filter.

He hit the end-call button. He'd only say something that would make an already bad conversation even worse. He could call back later, speak to his daughter then.

He looked across at the couple, and shrugged an apology. "Sorry. Soon to be ex-wife," Donald Price said to them, with a nod to his phone.

The man shot him an understanding smile. His female companion caught it and glared. The smile evaporated.

Donald walked past them and back into the hotel's lobby. He had a meeting in five minutes about a deployment of security personnel to the Turkish-Syrian border and he still hadn't finished writing the brief.

CHAPTER FOURTEEN

S O, CHRIS ALREADY TOLD YOU about the levels?" Rachel asked Ruth.

So that was his name. Chris Fontaine. Although he expected to be called "Dad" or "Father". There was no way Ruth was going to call him that. She already had a dad. She didn't need some creepy replacement.

"Yeah. You start at one and go up to six. When you hit level six Ms Applewhite will start preparing your exit plan."

"You mean that's when you get to go home?"

"If you want to, once the exit plan has been agreed, then yeah."

If you wanted to? This girl was cracked.

"So you'll be leaving soon?"

Rachel shrugged. "I guess so. I turned eighteen a few months ago, so I could have gone then if I'd really wanted to."

The conversation was getting more and more bizarre. Who in their right mind would choose to stay here? A place out in the middle of nowhere, where you had to sleep in a room full of other kids, on a mattress.

Rachel seemed to sense Ruth's incredulity. "If you leave without an exit plan, you get a one-way ticket and fifty bucks in your pocket. If your parents don't want to take you back then you're better off staying here."

That made a little more sense. Even a mattress on a floor probably beat living on the streets.

Rachel twirled a finger through her hair. "Anyway, you're like a million miles away from all that. It usually takes kids at least a year or two to move up to level six."

Ruth's heart, not for the first time in the past twenty-four hours, sank again. She wasn't sure how she'd handle a month here. Never mind a year. She reminded herself that she wouldn't have to. Not when her dad found out what had happened. What her mom had done.

But, right now, it would be better if she just played the game, went along with the program. No matter how crazy it seemed.

"The best thing you can do is to take one day at a time," Rachel continued. "Do what you're told, when you're told to do it, and everything will be fine."

Those were almost the exact same words Chris had come out with. Rachel had delivered them in exactly the same robotic way he had.

"That's what you've done?" Ruth asked.

"Yeah, I guess," said Rachel.

Ruth tried not to stare at her. She already had the idea that if Rachel wanted to, she could make her life even more miserable than it was now. Who in their right mind could like a place like this?

CHAPTER FIFTEEN

AN HOUR LATER THE OTHER girls who lived in the room began to filter back. Although *filter* might not have been the right word. They appeared in a marching column that only broke up when they stepped into the room. As best as Ruth could tell, they ranged in age from about thirteen to seventeen. They all wore the same uniform that Ruth had been ordered to change into.

The uniform was white and consisted of a long skirt and the hideous, puffy blouse she'd noticed earlier. Instead of shoes or sneakers, each girl wore red or yellow flip-flops. That seemed to be the only color variation that Ruth had seen. No one wore make-up and, apart from girls with short hair, they all had their hair tied back in a ponytail.

A couple began to chat as they came into the room. A few nodded at Ruth or said hello. When Rachel appeared behind them, they clammed up. They all seemed wary around her. She wanted to ask what was up with the red and yellow flip-flops, but didn't dare.

In the corner, Ruth noticed a girl who seemed to be around her age sneaking glances at her. The girl had red hair cut into a short bob, and was overweight. She also looked, thought Ruth, completely miserable—even by teen girls' standards. Her shoulders slumped and, other than darting glances at Ruth, she stared at the floor, not making eye contact with anyone else in the room.

If no one else was going to introduce themselves, Ruth figured that she would have to make the first move. Even if she didn't plan on sticking around, it might be useful to make a few friends while she was here. If nothing else, she might be able to get some information that would help her escape.

Ruth walked across to the girl with red hair. "Hey," she said.

The girl glanced up at her. She looked like she might be about to burst into tears. It seemed a strange reaction to someone saying *hey*.

"I'm Ruth."

"Mary," said the girl, her eyes returning to the bare concrete floor as she spoke.

Ruth glanced around the room. Rachel had disappeared. Some of the girls had gone back to chatting, although they kept their voices down to a low whisper, speaking just loudly enough so the person they were talking to could hear them.

"So what you in for?" Ruth asked.

Mary blinked her eyes. "In for?" she asked.

Now that Ruth was closer to her, she could see that the desert sun had brought out a mass of freckles on Mary's face. "Yeah, why did you get sent here? What'd you do?"

Still no answer. It was as if Ruth was speaking French or something.

"I'm here because my mom's a crazy bitch who thinks she can punish my dad by sending me here. At least, that's all I can figure."

Mary stopped blinking. Her eyes widened. She stared at Ruth.

"So? What about you?"

Mary cleared her throat. "I'm here because I lack self-discipline. Especially when it comes to looking after my body. Broken Ridge is helping me. A lot!"

Ruth was suddenly aware of someone standing behind her. She turned to see Rachel. Her arms were folded across her chest, and her right foot was tapping out a beat on the floor.

"I was just telling Ruth how good this place has been for me, Rachel," Mary blurted, her words coming in one big rush.

It didn't take a genius to work out that all the other girls were intimidated by Rachel's presence. Ruth didn't blame them.

"Right," said Rachel, who was staring at Ruth. "You two had better get changed. Phys Ed starts in five minutes, and you don't want to be late again, do you, Mary?"

"No," said Mary, her eyes cast down to the floor.

Rachel turned toward Ruth. "Mary really needs to get as much exercise as she can. Chris says that being fat is the outward manifestation of being weak."

God, what a judgmental bitch.

Rachel looked Ruth up and down. "You could probably do with losing a few pounds yourself."

All the girls in the room had started getting changed into T-shirts and shorts. Without answering Rachel, Ruth went over to her open locker, grabbed what she needed, went back to her bed area and started to get changed.

The clothes that she'd had with her had already been taken away. She doubted she'd see them again. She was left with what she'd been given shortly after she'd arrived. She guessed that everyone wearing the same clothing was another way of making people conform, of converting them from individuals to little robots who didn't challenge anything and always gave the right answers.

A few minutes later she followed the others out of the room. They spaced themselves out and, led by Rachel, walked down the corridor and outside.

It was late afternoon but the air still bubbled and shimmered with heat. Rachel led them to an area of open ground away from the residential blocks. They stood in a single line and waited. No one looked at anyone else. No one spoke. They just waited, silently, in the baking heat.

A few minutes later, just as Ruth was starting to think she might pass out, Chris Fontaine appeared. He stood directly in front of them. "Good afternoon, ladies."

"Good afternoon, Father," they all said in unison. Only Ruth didn't join in.

Chris looked at her. "I said, good afternoon, Price."

Ruth hesitated. She knew she had to say it. There would be a problem if she didn't. But calling this guy who was a complete stranger her dad, when she already had a dad, creeped her out. Maybe she could compromise.

"Good afternoon," she said, remembering to keep her voice as neutral as possible.

She could almost hear the collective intake of breath from the other girls.

Chris Fontaine glared at her. "Good afternoon what?"

She wasn't going to call him *Father*. No way. He could deduct a hundred points if he wanted. They could create a whole new level just for her. It wouldn't matter. She wasn't staying around here. Even if she couldn't run away, as soon as her real dad found out where she was he would get her out.

"Good afternoon, sir."

Further down the line she heard Rachel mutter. "Just say it, bitch."

Chris ignored *that* interruption. Obviously the rules were different for different people. "Okay, Price, have it your way. Everyone drop and give me ten."

Slowly, all the girls got down onto the bare desert ground. Ruth followed them.

"Not you, Price. You stay right where you are. Take it easy."

Ruth watched as the other girls began to count off ten push-ups. Rachel breezed through hers while the others struggled. At the end of the line, Mary was finding it hard after the first. Her face was even redder and sweat poured from her forehead into her eyes. She swiped it away with the back of her hand.

"Come on, ladies," Chris barked. "Everyone does ten. No exceptions." He started to walk down the line toward Mary. "That includes you, Tubby."

Mary, giving it everything she had, managed to squeeze out a couple more push-ups. Finally, her arms gave out and she collapsed face down on the ground.

Chris crouched down next to her. "Come on. That's pathetic. Three push-ups? You're fifteen years of age. Heck, my grandma can do more than that."

Mary levered herself back up onto her hands. She managed another push-up. "That's better." He glanced back to Ruth. "Now, Price, what are you going to say to me?"

82

Ruth didn't want to give in. To call him *Father*. At the same time, she didn't want to see everyone else being punished for what she'd done. She didn't care if they hated her for it. She just didn't want to see someone like Mary having to suffer because this guy was on some weird power trip.

Ruth lowered herself onto the ground. Chris gave up on Mary and marched over to Ruth. He grabbed her under the arms, and yanked her back onto her feet.

"I said stay where you are, Price. Okay, that's ten more push-ups for everyone."

The girls who had done their first set, and got back to their feet, started to get back onto the ground.

Ruth glared at Chris.

He smirked. "What is it, Price? You think you're special? You think you're different? I've seen this kind of bullshit a hundred and one different times. And I got news for you. It doesn't fly here."

He walked back over to Mary at the end of the line. "You useless sack of crap. Everyone else has done their ten. What makes you so special?"

"I'm sorry."

"Yeah, you are. You're a sorry excuse for a human being. Now I want to see two more from you."

Mary lowered herself, her elbows flaring out. She pushed herself back up as Chris kept screaming at her.

There was nothing else for Ruth to do. After all, they were only words. They didn't have to mean anything. She took a deep breath. "Good afternoon, Father," she said, staring straight ahead.

Chris stopped screaming at Mary. "What was that, Price? What did you say?"

"Good afternoon, Father," repeated Ruth.

"Get up," Chris said to Mary. Slowly, Mary stumbled back onto her feet as the others finished up their second set of push-ups.

Chris walked back to the middle of the line. "See, wasn't so hard, was it?"

"No," said Ruth.

"No what?"

Ruth bit down hard on her lower lip. "No, Dad." She felt as if a little bit of who she was had just been taken from her. She guessed that was the idea behind this place. Then and there, she promised herself she wasn't going to let that happen. She'd say what she had to say, do what she had to do, but on the inside, where it counted, she was going to stay the same Ruth. Except she knew that wasn't going to be possible. After what her mom had done to her, how could it be?

"Okay," said Chris, clapping his hands together. "Let's run, ladies. Down to the corral and back. Three circuits. Two miles."

"Yes, Father," they shouted back in unison.

This time, Ruth joined in.

CHAPTER SIXTEEN

W HAT DO YOU MEAN YOU can't tell me?"

Donald Price tapped the bottom of his pack of smokes, dug out a fresh cigarette, and lit up. He leaned over and pushed open the window. The last thing he needed right now was to set off the smoke alarm.

"I'm very sorry, Mr. Price," said the secretary of Ruth's school.

Donald Price took a deep drag, and slowly exhaled, careful to push the smoke out through the crack in the window. "All I need to know is whether my daughter was at school the past few days."

"I can't release that information to anyone who isn't a named person."

Donald closed his eyes and tried to count down slowly from ten. He made it to five. "Listen to me. I'm her father. Surely I'm entitled to know if my daughter has been at school or not."

"I understand your frustration, I really do, but I can only release information about one of our students, including their attendance, to a named person."

They were going round in circles. He could feel himself on the verge of losing his temper. And that wasn't going to help him find out what the hell was going on.

After he'd spoken to his ex-wife, he'd messaged Ruth on Facebook. She hadn't replied. That really worried him. She hadn't posted anything on any of her social-media accounts for the past eighteen hours either. It might not have seemed like a long time, unless you were a teenage girl, or the father of one. In which case you realized that eighteen hours was an eternity.

He had worked his way through her Facebook, Instagram and Snapchat accounts, figured out who she interacted with most, and messaged a couple of them. They hadn't heard from her either, and one of them, who was in a couple of Ruth's classes at high school, had told him she hadn't been in school either.

Calling her cell phone just led him to voicemail. He'd left a couple of messages, which had started out casual and become more urgent. The last time he had called her cell, an hour ago, it had been switched off—or out of power. Now he really was worried.

He'd planned on calling his ex-wife back, but first he'd thought he'd try the school. If she were in class, he couldn't have much to concern him.

"Listen, thanks anyway," he told the school secretary, before ending the call.

He took another deep drag and pulled the smoke down into his lungs. He'd finish this cigarette, then call Sandra and go one more round. This time she'd give him some answers or he'd cancel her next alimony payment. That was the one guaranteed way of getting her attention. It would probably land him back in front of a judge, but he needed to know that Ruth was okay, and right now he had a bad feeling.

CHAPTER SEVENTEEN

THEY TRUDGED BACK DOWN THE corridor toward their room. There was no problem keeping three steps between each person. The problem was making sure it wasn't more than three steps.

Ruth had never been a fan of running, and she hadn't changed her mind. She was covered in sweat and she stank. She hadn't finished last, but that was only because that honor had gone to Mary.

The only person who didn't seem to be tired was Rachel, who had finished the run first, barely out of breath. Another reason for Ruth to dislike her. Why was it that the bitchiest girls always had the easiest time of it? It was something she'd wondered about before. She'd have thought that breezing through life looking pretty, with good genetics, would make you more pleasant, not less.

In their room, the girls grabbed towels and headed back down the corridor to the bathroom. Beyond the stalls there was a separate room with a dozen shower heads that blasted out lukewarm water. Ruth was too exhausted to care that it wasn't hot. She showered, dried off, changed back into the regular academy clothes, and followed them out of the block. It was time for dinner, and she was starving.

The dining room was big enough for everyone to eat at once. Like everything else, male and female students were separated. You had to sit with your family group. In this case, the eleven other girls that she shared a room with.

The other rule was that there was no talking. You came in, you got a tray, you stood in line for your meal, you took it to your table. You ate, in silence. Then you had to wait for everyone to finish before you could take your tray back up, and stack it.

As she sneaked glances around the dining room, she was met with a strange sight. All those teenagers sitting there without talking. The cafeteria at her school was a zoo, one of the loudest places on campus. This was like a monastery. Or, in the case of her table, a nunnery. Though she did notice a couple of girls' eyes darting to the table opposite, which was occupied by teenage boys.

For her part, Ruth found her attention drawn to one boy in particular. It wasn't that he was cute. That wasn't why she found herself glancing at him, and hoping that Rachel didn't notice. It was that he seemed like some kind of a zombie. She had seen him stand in line for food and shuffle back to his table, like there was something wrong with him. It was his eyes. They were completely dead. Even the way he moved was strange. His flip-flops scuffed along the floor, like he didn't have the strength to lift his feet.

The other boys seemed to keep out of his way. They wouldn't even sit next to him. There was a spare seat either side of him, like he had some kind of infectious disease. She planned on asking someone about him later. Maybe Mary, or one of the other girls, would know what his deal was.

Once they had all finished dinner, Ruth fell into line behind the other girls. Rather than heading back to their room, they walked outside.

A few hundred yards away a bunch of fire pits had been dug into the ground. A group of boys were busy stacking wood into them. When they had finished, members of staff, Chris among them, moved around the pits, starting fires. Each group moved to their pit and sat around it in a circle. It seemed kind of cheesy, but after the day Ruth had had, she didn't mind a little cheesiness.

When they had all settled down, Chris was first to speak. "So, today our little family got a new member. I'd like everyone to welcome Ruth Price."

"Welcome, Price," they all sing-songed.

"So would one of you like to explain to Price why we sit around the fire pit every evening and how it's helped you become a better person?"

Almost every girl's hand shot into the air. It reminded Ruth of being back in grade school, when most of the kids still wanted to please their teacher.

Chris pointed to a girl with lanky blonde hair and elfin features, who was sitting almost directly opposite Ruth. "Amanda."

Amanda beamed at having been chosen. "The fire pit allows us to confront the truth of who we really are, and tells us how we can leave behind all the old habits that have been holding us back. It helps us be the best possible version of ourselves."

"Very good, Amanda," said Chris.

Amanda smiled at the praise. Rachel glared at her. Chris seemed not to notice.

"And how has it helped you?" Chris asked.

Amanda glanced down into the flames. "Well, it made me realize that my eating disorder was my way of trying to hurt my parents. The fire pit helped me understand that I needed to stop being so stupid and selfish, and such a . . ." She hesitated.

"Go on," Chris prompted. "You can say it. You can say anything here. That's one of the other rules of the fire pit."

"It helped me understand that I needed to stop being such a selfish little . . . bitch."

91

There was an almost audible intake of breath. Ruth assumed that cursing was a fairly major infringement. This time, though, Chris seemed to let it go. "That's very good, Amanda." She beamed like it was Christmas morning, and Santa Claus had brought her everything she'd asked for.

"Anyone else?" Chris asked. Another forest of hands shot into the air. "Yes," he said, nodding toward a girl who was sitting two people down from Ruth. Ruth had noticed her during their run. She had been at the front of the pack. She was tall, and athletic, with long, light brown hair. She looked like the kind of girl who would have been on the lacrosse team at Ruth's high school.

"Broken Ridge has helped me realize my own worth."

"Go on," Chris prompted her.

"Well, before it was all about boys and dating. If a boy liked me I felt good. If he dumped me I felt that somehow I wasn't worth anything."

"Boy?" said Rachel. "There was a lot more than one, Abby."

"Yeah," said a girl who was sitting on the other side of Chris. "I can think of like a dozen you've told us about."

"Yeah. At least," someone else chimed in.

Abby, a fidgety girl with large brown eyes and oily skin, was staring at the flames. Ruth could see that tears had started to form in her eyes. Her shoulders were hunched and her arms folded while her knees were pulled up into her chest.

"You're making excuses for your behavior, aren't you?" said Chris.

"No, I just said 'a boy' as an example," said Abby.

"There you go again," said Rachel. "You said that because you were hoping we'd forget what you'd told us about all the others. You're minimizing."

"Yeah, you're minimizing," said another girl, who hadn't spoken yet.

"Okay, there were a lot," said Abby, trying to stave off the attack.

"I saw her looking at Mike when we were having dinner last night," someone said.

Apart from Abby, Ruth noticed that everyone sitting around the fire pit seemed to perk up as soon as this was said. A few of the girls even smiled.

"Yeah, I saw that," said someone else. "And I caught her masturbating last night. During the night when she thought we were all asleep. It was totally gross."

"Is that true?" Chris asked. "You know that we don't tolerate self-abuse at Broken Ridge."

"I did not," Abby said.

"There you go again," said Rachel. "Why do you always have to deny? Why can't you face up to things, and take responsibility for your behavior?"

"Yeah, why?"

Now it seemed like everyone wanted to have their say. The criticism and denunciations came thick and fast.

"You've never been honest."

"You haven't really changed. You pretend like you have, but you still behave the same."

"Touching yourself in a room where we all have to sleep is totally gross. You should go down to level one for that."

At some point in all of this, Ruth wasn't sure exactly when, Abby burst into tears. Her sobs seemed to spur the other girls on. A few even made fun of the fact she was crying. Chris let the comments keep coming, only intervening to say, "This is good. Everyone should let Abby know exactly what they think of her promiscuity and how it's damaged everyone else. Like it damaged her family back home."

On and on it went. Abby sobbed. The others piled on. It was almost as if they were trying to outdo each other. As if they could somehow gain points by being mean and hurtful.

Ruth knew what girls could be like. Especially when they were in a group and had turned on someone. But she had never seen anything like this. It was like a feeding frenzy. They were the sharks and Abby was the injured fish that Chris had just thrown over the side of the boat.

Eventually the wave of vitriol and character assassination subsided. When it had run its course Chris changed direction.

"I just want you to know, Abby, if any of that seemed harsh it's only because everyone here cares about you. We don't want you to slip back into your old ways. We want

94

you to keep growing, and become the best version of yourself that you can be."

Ruth very much doubted that was the reason they'd all piled on. Some of them, like Rachel, seemed to take sadistic pleasure in the whole thing. For the others, Ruth got the sense that they joined in because if the group was picking on Abby, it couldn't be picking on them.

Chris dug into his pants pocket and pulled out a pack of tissues. He peeled one off and handed it to Rachel. They passed on the tissue until it reached Abby. She took it, and wiped away the tears. "That's better," said Chris, his tone now one of paternal concern. "Now, Abby, I'd like you to thank the group for their concern."

Ruth couldn't take much more of this. Was this guy for real? He'd just turned the others on Abby, watched as they'd torn her limb from limb, and now he wanted her to thank them for the privilege.

"Thank you," said Abby, her voice hoarse and cracked from all the crying.

Ruth kept quiet, but she couldn't help rolling her eyes.

Now Chris was staring at her. "You have something to add, Price?"

Damn. Why had she rolled her eyes just now?

"No, I don't think so," she said, quickly adding, "Thank you."

"There's no hiding here, Price. If you have something to say, then we encourage you to come right out and say it.

The truth will set you free. It's the way we all make progress."

Ruth couldn't help feeling she was being pulled into a trap. There was no way, from what she had already seen, that the truth would set her free. If she told Chris what she really thought, it would only be bad for her. At the same time, she hated them all for what they had just done. It was like watching someone pull the wings off a fly.

"I only just got here," she said. "I guess I'm still finding my feet."

"And?" said Chris.

Ruth shrugged. "Nothing. That's all."

"You don't strike me as someone who's afraid to share their opinion."

"She doesn't think she should be here!" someone blurted out.

Ruth looked over to see Abby, still dabbing at her eyes, staring at her. "She was telling everyone earlier that she got sent here because her mom's crazy and she's doing it to punish her dad for getting a divorce."

"She called her mom a bitch," said Mary.

Ruth felt like she'd been punched hard in the stomach. She couldn't believe that the two girls who'd been picked on the most had just turned on her for nothing. Thrown her to the wolves.

"Is that true?" said Chris.

Taking a deep breath, Ruth decided she wasn't going to go down without a fight. "Is it true that I said it or true that my mom's a crazy bitch who sent me here to get back at my father?"

A smile played at the corner of Chris's mouth. In the flickering light from the fire it made him look even more sinister. He gave a little nod.

"They're both true," said Ruth. "I said it, and I believe it, because it's true."

She returned his smirk. If she was going to be the new villain, then she planned on playing the role properly. They could say what they wanted about her. None of them knew her. She would let whatever they said wash over her. Even they didn't believe half the things they said. They only said them because it was what was expected, or because it would save them from being bullied. And that's what this was. Bullying. Not therapy. Not trying to help people confront their behavior.

One of the others tried to jump in. Chris held up his hand to silence them. "I have a feeling there's nothing I could say now to persuade you that your mom did this for your own good. Is that fair?"

Chris's response wrong-footed her. She'd thought he'd attack her. It was another trap. It had to be.

"Yes, that's fair," Ruth said. She could feel everyone's eyes on her.

"So, we can be fair sometimes," Chris said, with a smile.

Rachel shot him a look that suggested she didn't like him going easy on Ruth. Maybe she thought he was giving

97

Ruth special treatment. Special treatment that was usually reserved for her.

Ruth didn't say anything.

Chris stood up. "That was productive. Let's leave it there for tonight."

The girls exchanged glances. Some looked crestfallen. Ruth had stood up to Chris and he'd let her. There hadn't been any punishment. He'd let it go.

"Back to your dorm," he said.

"Yes, Father," the girls chorused.

Ruth didn't join in. Chris ignored that too. He walked away from the group.

Rachel stood up. She was giving Ruth daggers. "You heard him."

They formed up into a line. As Rachel walked past Ruth, she whispered, "I know what you were doing there. Don't think you're going to get away with it."

CHAPTER EIGHTEEN

THEY WALKED BACK TO THEIR dorm room in silence. Once they got inside, the atmosphere was muted. One of the girls went over to Abby and gave her a hug. Rachel shot them a filthy look.

A few of the girls began to chat among themselves. Again they kept their voices low so Ruth couldn't hear what they were saying. They didn't look at her. They didn't speak.

Ruth got changed into the pajamas that had been provided. A few of the others were doing the same. It was only then that she remembered she didn't have any toothpaste. She walked over to where Mary was lying on her bed, staring up at the ceiling, eyes open. "Hey, do you have any toothpaste I could use? I'll give you it back when I get my own."

Mary didn't look at her, just kept staring.

"Hey," said Ruth.

Mary rolled over onto her side so that her back was to Ruth. Ruth took the hint. She guessed that talking back to Chris like that hadn't made her very popular. Or maybe Mary just didn't want to be associated with someone who was a troublemaker. That was understandable, especially if you were already vulnerable, like Mary was.

She walked into the bathroom. One of the other girls, whose name she didn't know, had just finished brushing her teeth. She still had her tube of toothpaste in her hand.

"Can I have a squeeze of your toothpaste?"

The girl looked at her, grabbed her tube and walked away.

Whatever. Ruth brushed as best she could with just water. She rinsed her mouth, washed her face and headed to her mattress. She lay down on her back. She could get toothpaste from someone tomorrow. No doubt tomorrow would bring a different drama. Someone else would be in the spotlight. Things would move on.

Around her the other girls were getting into bed. A few minutes later the lights went out. A full moon bathed the room in a soft white glow. The bed wasn't as uncomfortable as it looked. Plus, she was tired. She fell asleep quickly.

****

Ruth woke to water splashing across her face. Her eyes opened. It took her a moment to orientate herself. Even with her face and hair soaking wet, she was still trapped somewhere in the zone between being completely asleep and awake.

A hand slapping her face bridged the gap. She looked up to see Rachel standing over her. Ruth tried to get up but she couldn't move her legs. She glanced down as best she could to see two girls sitting at the bottom of the bed, holding them down.

She tried to sit up. Hands pushed down on her chest, forcing her back onto the bed. Someone on either side grabbed her wrists so that she couldn't raise her arms. No matter how hard she struggled, she couldn't move. There were just too many of them.

Looming over her was Rachel. Ruth caught a flash of metal in Rachel's right hand. A pair of scissors.

"You even think about screaming and it'll be more than your hair getting cut, Price."

"Why? Why are you doing this?"

"You're a troublemaker, Price. Everyone here can see it. You have been since you arrived."

The scissors disappeared from Ruth's sight. There was a snipping sound and Rachel held up a lock of hair.

Ruth thrashed her head from side to side. More hands emerged from the darkness. They pressed against her neck and skull, holding her head in place.

Rachel kept cutting. Ruth closed her eyes, fighting back tears of rage and humiliation. It was no use. The tears came. She couldn't stop them.

When Rachel had finished, they relaxed their grip. The others melted back to their beds. Rachel stood over her, the scissors still in her hand. She stared at Ruth, assessing her handiwork.

"Huh, I didn't think it was possible for you to look even more dykey, Price, but it really is."

Ruth's fists clenched with rage. She had never wanted to hurt someone as badly as she wanted to hurt Rachel. But now wasn't the time. Not when Rachel still had a pair of scissors in her hand, and wouldn't hesitate to use them.

"If anyone asks, this was your idea. You even think about telling any of the staff what happened and I promise you'll regret it. This was just a little taste of what happens to people at Broken Ridge who don't get with the program. You understand me?"

Ruth stared at her. When she'd arrived, Ruth had assumed that this was just like high school, but on steroids. Rachel was the mean girl with the band of followers, all of them desperate to curry favor so that they didn't become a victim.

Ruth had been wrong. Looking into Rachel's eyes, she now saw something else. It was something a lot more frightening, and dangerous. Rachel wasn't just mean, or a bully, it went beyond that. Rachel was broken. Whatever quality that made someone a human had been lost in her.

"I get you," Ruth told her.

PART TWO

CHAPTER NINETEEN

Ten days later

T HE MOTEL CLERK LOOKED UP as the black Ford Explorer pulled into a space directly in front of his office. Two men got out. One was white, the other African-American. Both over six feet tall, they were casually but neatly dressed, and clean-shaven. They both wore sunglasses.

The way they walked toward the motel office door made the clerk think they were either military or law enforcement. There was an air-force base about a forty-minute drive from the motel. Maybe they were headed there. From time to time, outside contractors working at the base stayed here.

The white guy was first through the door. He removed his Ray-Ban sunglasses, and smiled at the clerk. "Good afternoon."

The black guy kept on his sunglasses, heavily tinted Oakleys. He didn't smile. He hung back by the door, keeping an eye on their vehicle, and the street outside.

If it hadn't been for their smart appearance, the clerk might have put this down as a robbery. "Good afternoon," he said. "May I help you, gentlemen?"

"We require two rooms. Adjoining, if possible."

Not a robbery. The clerk relaxed a little. He made a show of checking availability on the computer in front of him, even though, out of a total of forty units, only half were currently occupied, and most of those were taken by longer-term residents who paid on a weekly basis.

A few taps on the keyboard later, the clerk looked up. "You're in luck. I have two adjoining rooms that came available yesterday. How long will you be staying with us?"

"Five nights, give or take. We'll pay cash up front if that's agreeable to you. If we're staying longer, we'll let you know."

At the mention of possibly staying longer, the massive black guy pulled his sunglasses down to the tip of his nose and glared at his companion, who just laughed.

"Certainly, sir, cash is fine. I will have to see some form of identification, though."

"Sure," said the white guy.

107

Both men dug out wallets. Each presented a California driver's license. The black guy handed his to the white guy, who slid them both over the desk toward the clerk. He jotted down their details as the white guy counted out the cash in crisp twenty-dollar bills. The clerk took the cash, and handed back the two California driving licenses, then walked into the back office and returned with two room keys. Each was attached to a heavy wooden fob. He pushed them over the counter. "Would you like me to show you to your rooms, gentlemen?"

"Thank you, but that won't be necessary."

The clerk gave a little nod. Customers who paid cash up-front were always welcome. And these didn't look like two men who were going to be throwing any wild parties. But it was still a little weird, and he was a naturally curious type. "So, are you here on business?" he asked.

Both men stared at him. They didn't reply, just stood there, looking at him. There was something about them that frightened him. Having been robbed a half-dozen times, he didn't think he scared easily. But the way they were looking at him was unsettling.

The clerk swallowed, hard. "No matter," he said quickly. "Enjoy your stay. If you need anything at all, you just let me know."

"Appreciate that," said the black guy.

"One other thing," the other added, as they both headed for the door. "We won't require maid service, and we'd prefer not to disturbed unless absolutely necessary."

"Of course," said the clerk. It wasn't a request he would have agreed to usually. People who didn't want their room cleaned were usually taking drugs, smuggling hookers, or something similarly seedy.

Right now he wasn't going to argue. Not with these two. All he wanted was to get them out of his office. If he didn't see them again until they checked out, that was all the better.

CHAPTER TWENTY

THE TWO MEN GOT BACK into the Ford Explorer. The driver started the engine, pulled out of the space, and drove the two hundred yards to where their rooms were located at the end of the motel. He pulled the Explorer into a small parking lot that was shielded from the road by the motel building. He reached up to the visor and pressed a switch. It activated two motion-sensor cameras, one mounted inside and one on the dash that covered the front of the vehicle.

Cameras activated, the two men got out. The tailgate lifted with the click of a button on the key fob. They each grabbed two black canvas bags from the back. They walked, in silence, back to the front of the motel and entered their rooms.

Once inside, each man performed the same basic surveillance sweep. Not that they expected to find anything. For one thing, apart from one individual in Washington D.C., no one knew who they were or why they were there. For another, the names and credentials they had given the motel clerk were fake.

Checks finished, each man unpacked. Shirts were hung up. Pants neatly folded. Everything put away in proper order, including each man's SIG Sauer P229 handgun. The weapons were purely a precaution, to be used only in the most extreme of circumstances. Neither of them expected anything extreme to occur but, as they had both learned the hard way, it was always better to be prepared for the unexpected.

The connecting door opened. The white guy walked into his companion's room. He took in the less than palatial surroundings. "Ready for your interview?"

Across the room, Ty Johnson looked up at his business partner. "This whole thing is bullshit. You do realize that, right?"

Ryan Lock smiled. If Ty was right, and he most likely was, he was never going to hear the end of it. But Donald Price was a man at his wit's end, someone Lock knew and trusted, not an individual given to spending thousands of dollars on a neurotic whim. Price was worried about his daughter, Ruth. And if Lock and Ty could offer him reassurance that she was in good health that had to be a good thing. "Whether it's bullshit or not remains to be seen."

Ty shook his head. His expression suggested that the world had gone crazy. "Checking up on some spoilt middle-class kid who's been sent to brat camp. Come on, man, it's a complete waste of everyone's time. Dude's pissed at his ex, I get that. But this is a long way to come to prove she's wrong."

"Then if that's all true, this'll be easy money."

Ty turned away, clearly not convinced. And when Lock had gotten the panicked phone call from Donald Price, he had shared Ty's skepticism.

Then he'd sat down and begun his research on Broken Ridge. He hadn't shared any of it with Ty.

Lock wanted his partner to go in fresh, without any preconceived notions. Maybe the ex-employees who alleged dangerous practices were disgruntled because they'd been let go. Perhaps the former students who claimed they'd been abused were resentful. There were usually three sides to a story: one side, the other side, and the truth. Between them, he and Ty would work out which was which.

Lock checked this watch. They had only two hours. "Let's go find someplace to eat."

CHAPTER TWENTY-ONE

GRETCHEN APPLEWHITE HAD A BAD feeling. She couldn't quite put her finger on it, but it was there. It hung over the ranch like a great, dark cloud, ready to burst at any moment.

She sat in her office in the main ranch house, and stared up at her father Albert's portrait. Broken Ridge had been his baby, a place where parents could send their children when they had nowhere else to turn. A place of discipline and security that was insulated from the ravages of modern society.

From the early 1960s on, Gretchen's father had known that sooner or later the country's experiment with permissiveness would fail. And that when it did, people would need someone, and somewhere, to turn to. A place especially for their children.

It had taken time, but he had been proven right. From humble beginnings, when there was only the ranch house and the land that had come with it, the academy had blossomed. Then had come the first of the storm clouds. Accidents, kids who had gotten out of control. Journalists asking questions. And law enforcement. Her father had been forced to sell out to a large company that had taken his model and used it to make millions. They'd allowed him and then Gretchen to stay there, but they put constant pressure on them to deliver the numbers. They were all about the bottom line.

And now, to make things worse, there were fresh storm clouds on the horizon. She could see them far off in the distance.

There had been accusations and allegations, lies and mistruths. Against the staff. Against the way they did things. Against Gretchen herself. The people who owned the place now were growing restless.

But Gretchen had to go on. She had to see through what her father had begun. Sure, Broken Ridge wasn't the answer for every child sent to them, Gretchen had always accepted that. Some were beyond help, or simply too stubborn. But most, with a little encouragement and some tough love, came round. They learned to love the routine, and the peace of mind that came with it.

But, still, she couldn't shake the feeling that forces were massing against them. Somewhere out there on the horizon.

There was a knock at the door. Three quick taps in rapid succession, a signature knock. "Come in, Chris," said Gretchen.

He walked in, a broad smile on his face.

What would she have done without Chris? How would she have coped? He had been a true blessing. Not only did he understand their mission, he never deviated from it. The students were lucky to have him, even if they didn't always show their appreciation.

"Mr. Cross is here," said Chris.

Oh, yes. Gretchen had almost forgotten. They had someone coming to interview for a counselor role. Chris had been pretty excited about it ever since Gretchen had shown him the application.

The candidate was a former US Marine from California. He had responded to an online ad seeking staff. Because of their remote location it was hard to get good people. Those they did hire often didn't last past the first month. Often they were as undisciplined as one of the more troubled children, or they had their own ideas as to how things should be done, and questioned Gretchen's methods, which was one quick way to get fired.

The Broken Ridge system could work only if the staff were united. The children, especially the more resistant ones, could sense hesitation in a staff member and would quickly exploit it. A chink in the armor, or a disagreement between staff, even if it was only a look, and the children sensed it. Gretchen's father had taught her that the single

115

greatest asset they had was their unity. Once that was breached, the whole thing would disintegrate. Discipline was everything, and that extended to the adults.

"Well, then, Chris, show him in."

Chris about-turned and raced back out the door. Gretchen had rarely seen him quite so excited about a potential staff member. She suspected it was because the man had been a Marine and, according to his letter, had seen combat. That was the sort of thing that impressed a man like Chris. A man who had never had the opportunity to fight for his country.

Gretchen would take more convincing. Especially with all the vultures that had been circling recently, ready to damage the reputation of everything her father and she had built over the years.

CHAPTER TWENTY-TWO

TY JOHNSON HAD ARRIVED AT Broken Ridge ten minutes before he was scheduled to have his job interview. He'd been dropped off at the bottom of the long track leading up to the academy by a bus he'd picked up in town. His clothes were thrift-store smart. Cheap, slightly tired, washed and frayed, but neatly pressed and starched. The kind of clothes worn by a proud former Marine a little down on his luck, who needed a job and wasn't all that particular about what it might involve. But someone who also wanted to make a good impression.

He'd measured out the length of the rutted road in a series of long strides. In the event that he wasn't offered the advertised position at Broken Ridge, this visit could serve as reconnaissance. A tiny video camera clipped into his shirt transmitted a live feed to an app on his cell phone, ready for the footage to be dumped onto a laptop at a later date. Cell and data coverage out here was poor to non-existent, which prevented him being able to send Lock a live feed. Not that it mattered. Ty was fairly sure he could handle whatever lay ahead.

Up ahead lay a ranch house that stood next to a series of long, barrack-style buildings. Beyond that, open land was dotted with a couple of semi-derelict barns and outbuildings. Hundreds of acres without another house or person in sight. If he hadn't known better, he would have assumed it was a dude ranch. One that had seen better days.

The email he'd received a few days before had told him to come to the main ranch house. Ty had decided to ignore that instruction, and take a little unscheduled tour. If he was challenged, he'd play dumb and cite the fact he was early. Tell them he wanted to get a feel for the place. Which would be true. He did.

Turning left at the ranch house, he sauntered across to the first dormitory building. Instead of going inside, he skirted around the perimeter of the building. There were single windows at regular intervals. Some had blinds drawn down. None appeared to have locks. They were simply plates of glass dropped into a frame. Good for keeping people in, or out, but really bad news if there was a fire, or other emergency.

Ty kept walking. At the far end was an emergency exit door. It was chained and padlocked. He took another left and walked back along the front of the building, taking his time, stopping at the windows that weren't covered with blinds. All the while, the body cam did its work.

Glimpses of pin-neat dorm rooms crammed with mattresses and lockers were broken up by equally Spartan classrooms arranged with desks and chairs that all faced the wall. Each set was separated by a partition so the student wouldn't be able to see the person either side of them.

Apart from the motivational posters there were no personal effects in the dorm rooms. There was no student work pinned up on the classroom walls. No charts. No certificates naming a student of the week. No gold stars or merit badges on display. And, Ty asked himself, so what? Kids should come to school to learn, not to spend eight hours being told how they were all special little snowflakes. Sure, by American standards, the set-up seemed basic, but he imagined that most kids in Africa or India sitting in schools just like this were happy for the opportunity.

"Can I help you?"

The question came from a lanky white guy in shorts and a blue polo shirt. Ty recognized him from the school website as Chris Fontaine, the academy's deputy director. Lock had already background-checked the dude. What had come back wasn't good, and he had used it to challenge Ty's reluctance to take the gig. As a negotiation strategy, Lock presenting him with his findings about Fontaine and some of the other staff had proven effective.

Ty stopped, squaring his shoulders, and looked at Fontaine. "I'm here for a job interview."

Fontaine's hand shot out and he grinned. "Of course. Mr. Cross, right?"

"Correct."

"Chris Fontaine. Deputy director. It's a real pleasure to meet you."

Ty looked at him, his expression blank, although Ty's blank expression could be read by most people as one that ranged from low-grade threat to utterly terrifying. Not that he could help it. He just had one of those faces.

He and Lock had decided that if Ty was to assume a fake identity, he might as well do a little character work to go with it. They'd figured their best chance of gaining information about Broken Ridge was for him to play someone who would carry out orders without question, was smart enough to do what was asked of him, but no more than that.

Ty slowly extended his hand. "Nice to meet you, Mr. Fontaine. And thank you for giving me the opportunity."

They shook, Fontaine repeating, "Great. Great," over and over.

"So, as you'll see, our little school is on the basic side, but that's what we feel provides the most benefit to the young people who are sent to us. It allows them to focus on themselves. Set themselves straight without all the distractions they have at home."

Ty went back to looking blank. Seconds passed.

"Well, great," said Fontaine. "Let me take you on down to the ranch house and you can meet Ms Applewhite. And don't worry, the interview process here is really informal so there's nothing to be on edge about. Just be yourself. All we're trying to work out is whether you'll be a good fit. There aren't any right or wrong answers."

CHAPTER TWENTY-THREE

TY STARED ACROSS THE DEEP wooden desk at Gretchen Applewhite. He was directly opposite her, on a hard-backed dining chair. To his right, Chris Fontaine sat with his hands on his knees, one toe tapping on the floor, a ball of barely contained energy. Gretchen was peering through pink-rimmed reading glasses at Ty's, or rather, Mark Cross's, job application.

It was only six pages long, but she must have been leafing through it for at least five minutes. She turned a page. She scanned. She flipped back. She flipped forward. Ty's nerves were gone. Now he was just plain irritated.

He sat there quietly, and reminded himself that while Ty didn't do interviews, the fictional Mr. Cross needed this gig. Another minute passed. Gretchen let out a sigh.

Ty leaned forward in his chair. It creaked. "Everything okay with my application?" he asked. "Anything you'd like me to clarify for you?"

She looked at him over the top of her reading glasses. "No, thank you."

Ty shot her a shit-eating smile. "Well, if there is, you only need to ask."

Gretchen smiled back and returned to flipping back and forth through the pages. Ty had the feeling this was a power play. She was the boss, which meant everyone else could wait. That worked for him.

Finally, she took off her glasses, placed them in front of her and propped her elbows on the desk so that her chin was resting on doughy knuckles. "Well, Mr. Cross, I must say I'm very impressed."

"Thank you," Ty replied. He'd also been impressed when Lock had handed him the completed application to sign, complete with a detailed bio, social security number, and bankcard, all with the name of someone who didn't actually exist. The whole package had cost them, or rather their client, Donald Price, around five Gs to put together.

Price's contact, who specialized in what he euphemistically termed as 'surrogate identity formation', was apparently one of the most accomplished forgers in the country. He'd done time in the joint for any number of scams and cons, until the United States government, in the form of the State Department, had made him an offer he would have been crazy to refuse. That was how Donald

Price had known about him. This was an off-the-books job that would cost his career, if it came to light. Having someone fake identities for the United States government was one thing, doing it for your own purposes was frowned upon. Lock and Ty had promised to make sure it stayed on the down low.

"Have you worked with young people before?" Gretchen asked.

"Not quite as young as those you have here, but with young recruits, yes," said Ty. "The young men and women who enlist often come from challenging backgrounds."

Chris almost bounced out of his chair. "Exactly what we do here. Forge character."

Gretchen cut him off with a single withering look. Chris cleared his throat and went back to lounging in his chair, and tapping his foot.

"You'll find some of the behavior you may encounter here is particularly difficult. Even for a man such as yourself. Often by the time young people reach us they've been all but ruined by a lack of boundaries. Drugs, alcohol, under-age sexual activity, you name it, we have to deal with it. And the way we do that is by applying a strict policy of discipline. Where there is chaos in their life, we see it as our mission to bring order. Which isn't to say it's all negative or about punishment. They have the chance to complete their education via directed independent study, they learn to appreciate and value their bodies through physical exercise, and they are encouraged to examine the bad choices that placed them here."

She stopped, looking pleased with herself. Ty had the feeling she was hoping for a round of applause. He also had the distinct impression that this was a well-rehearsed speech that she'd given to worried parents hundreds of times. He had to admit, it didn't sound too bad. If you had a teenager who'd gone off the rails those were the words you'd want to hear. It made Broken Ridge sound like a one-stop solution. Roll 'em in wrecked, and pick 'em up all shiny new and fixed.

"It sounds like an excellent program," he said.

"Something you feel you can get on board with?" Gretchen asked him.

Ty reminded himself that Cross needed this job if he wanted to eat that week. He tried to interject just the right amount of enthusiasm to reflect that fact. "I'm positive that I can."

"And you have no problem with it being a live-in position? Obviously you'll have certain periods free, but we do expect dorm fathers to be here overnight on a regular basis."

"No, ma'am, that's fine," Ty said. There wasn't much an older white woman on a power trip liked more than being called *ma'am* by someone like him.

Gretchen stood up. She tidied the papers in front of her and set them to one side. "In that case, welcome aboard. Mr. Cross." Then she flattened down that weird-ass 1950s plaid dress she was wearing, patted at her hair, and stuck out her hand.

Ty shook it as, next to him, Chris beamed like someone whose mom finally approved of one of his friends. "Thank you for offering me this opportunity to see what this wonderful program is really all about," said Ty, without a single hint of irony.

CHAPTER TWENTY-FOUR

Y OU ARE GOING TO LOVE it here, Mark. You mind if I call you Mark?"

"Not at all, Chris," Ty said.

They were walking toward one of the dormitories. According to Chris, this block housed a dozen or so young men who ranged in age from thirteen to almost eighteen. Ty was going to fill the role of housefather. No one had mentioned why the last person in the role had left, and Ty had known better than to ask. Mark Cross wanted the job too much to ask a lot of questions. He wanted to be a team player. And Ty Johnson wanted to be inside, seeing what was really going down. Right now, they had both achieved their objectives.

A group of teenage girls marched past them in single file. Ty scanned their faces for Ruth Price. He didn't see

127

her. One of the girls did look at him, though, one of the older ones, holding his gaze before he looked away.

Chris must have caught something of it. "You're lucky, getting assigned one of the boys' dorms. The girls are the ones you really have to watch out for. Manipulative as hell, especially if you're a dude, if you catch my drift . . . Plus they really band together."

Ty could feel his skin start to crawl, but he tamped it down. "I hear you."

"And they're all in sync, if you catch my meaning," Chris went on. "So, like, for four or five days of every month all hell breaks loose. It's like my old man used to tell me, 'Never trust anything that bleeds once a month and doesn't die.'"

Ty had never heard any man, old or otherwise, say something like that. At least, not one who wasn't a complete asshole. With young Chris there must be some weird genetic component to his personality, as well as whatever he had picked up along the way, in his lack of respect for females.

Lock teased Ty about being a ladies' man, who dated women like he was trying to set some kind of record. Up to a point, it was true. Ty had dated a lot of different women. He enjoyed female company, and not only for the sexual part. He enjoyed the whole enchilada. A couple of women he'd dated said it might have come from him having been raised by a single mom. He didn't know if that was true. He just knew he enjoyed female company.

Enjoyed women too much to be disrespectful toward them.

But Ty was always clear going in with someone that he wasn't looking to settle down. He was married to the job, like Lock was. But he sure as hell didn't see women, or anyone else for that matter, as some kind of sub-species. He had no respect for men who did. He didn't even think of it as sexism. It was just plain old insecurity that manifested itself as bar talk.

Don't trust anything that bleeds once a month and doesn't die, Ty repeated to himself. He glanced at Chris. *I'd only need one shot to make you bleed.*

Ty pushed down his distaste and they moved on with the official tour of Broken Ridge Academy. Chris talked more about the ethos of the program. About how it was a way to provide structure and discipline to teenagers who had suffered a complete absence of both at home and school.

"What you have to understand," said Chris, as they stepped into an empty classroom, "these aren't always bad kids. Most of them are good kids, or bad kids with a good kid wanting to get out, and break away from all that bad peer pressure. They've just never heard the word 'no'—at least, not from someone who actually meant it, and wasn't going to turn it into a 'yes' because that made their own life easier. It probably sounds crazy to someone who was in the Marines, but half our kids had never even made their own bed before they came here."

That part didn't sound crazy at all. While he'd still been serving he'd not only met FOB (fresh off the boat) recruits who couldn't make their bed, but they didn't know how to read or write beyond maybe second-grade level, and some didn't know how to brush their teeth or shower properly.

Neither did anything else Chris had said about boundaries or discipline sound crazy to Ty. It sounded just the opposite. Leaving aside Chris's eagerness to impress someone he obviously thought was a bad ass, some of what he was saying made a lot of sense. Kids, these days, did lack basic consistency because adults didn't provide it. It wasn't exactly the adults' fault, because maybe the pendulum had swung too far the other way: away from the rights of parents and schools to set the rules and toward the rights of teenagers who weren't yet developed enough to make good choices, or weren't yet able to know what a good choice was.

As they stood in the middle of the empty classroom, with its single-student corrals, Ty noticed that not one desk looked out. They were all either facing a wall, or where there was a window, a board had been tacked up to obscure the view of the outside.

"We don't like the students having any possible distractions," Chris told him, seeming to anticipate Ty's or, rather, Mark's next question.

"So if they're staring at the wall, how do they look at the teacher?" In fact, he didn't see any kind of board or teacher's desk for that matter either.

Ty hadn't exactly been an academic star. Hell, back in the day where he grew up in Long Beach, graduating high school was pretty much like getting yourself into an Ivy League college. But he did know that students usually faced the teacher rather than a wall or a piece of wood.

Chris walked over to a tall metal cabinet. He opened it to reveal a series of metal shelves. He pulled a workbook from the middle one. "Study is self-directed. Each student comes in, takes a workbook, goes through their exercises, and a member of staff spot-checks that the work has been completed," he said.

That sounded like a whole bunch of horseshit to Ty. Perhaps because, in the military, you were shown how to do something, and someone took you through it until they were satisfied. It was labor-intensive, but it was pretty much the only way. Handing a grunt an M16 a rifle and a booklet on how to use it would have been all kinds of bad news. But, thought Ty, maybe algebra was different. It seemed like a half-assed system to him, but maybe it was too early to judge.

"So what happens if they're not getting something?" he asked Chris.

Chris spread his arms wide. "Then all they need to do is come ask. If the member of staff monitoring them doesn't know, or doesn't know how to explain it, they'll find someone who does."

Ty quickly reminded himself that he didn't want to come off too critical. That didn't fit with the role he was playing. He nodded. "That's a relief. Because I'm not sure how much algebra I'd remember from high school."

Chris grinned and punched his shoulder. "Don't worry. I have you covered on that one. Hey, talking about everyone helping out, I know you haven't officially started, but I have to take one of the girls' Phys Ed classes. You mind giving me some help with it?"

Ty smiled right back. "Absolutely not. Tell you the truth," he said to Chris, leaning in a little, a small sign that they were already buddies, "I'd be happy to get started."

"See, that attitude right there. That's what I told Gretchen having a Marine here would give us. Some positive vibes."

The guy would have lasted about ten seconds in the Corps, Ty thought. His idea of a Marine was all about the external, of how you came across. Ty knew different. Being a warrior was all about the internal. It was a state of mind: a way of being.

Not that any of that mattered right now. If Ty having served kept Chris happy, and his suspicions at bay, all the better for finding out what kind of place this really was, and whether Donald Price really did have cause to be concerned about his daughter.

CHAPTER TWENTY-FIVE

I T WAS THE MIDDLE OF the afternoon, and it was
baking hot. Not the optimal time of the day to be
getting teenage girls to run outside. But right now,
Ty, or Mark, was the FNG (the f—ing new guy) and, as
such, he wasn't about to point out to Chris that running in
these conditions was just plain dumb. Maybe if you were a
fighter on the last stretch of cutting weight before a bout it
made sense. Other than that, it was just plain stupid,
bordering on dangerous. The human body could cope with
a lot, but dehydration could get you into trouble real fast.

The group of teenage girls from Chris's dorm was
already lined up as Chris and Ty rounded the corner. Ty
scanned the faces.

Bingo.

In the middle of the line of girls was Ruth Price. He was ninety-nine percent certain it was her. Her hair was cut short, but he'd studied the photographs her father had provided long enough to make the positive identification. Unsurprisingly, it turned out that divorced fathers like Donald Price had no shortage of pictures. Lock had also managed to cull some very recent ones from a couple of social-media accounts.

So, at least the first part of Ty's mission was already completed, and he hadn't even officially started working at Broken Ridge. He had established that Ruth Price was here. His tiny body cam would provide official confirmation. He angled his feet so that the lens would capture her face.

On the walk outside, Ty had excused himself to go use the bathroom. Inside, he had switched out the data card on his cell phone that he was using to archive the body-cam footage. He'd also checked that it had been recording. So far, so good.

On the way out, he'd also put on his shades. He was glad that he had. Not only did they shield his eyes from the sun's brutal glare, they also allowed him to do a quick assessment of Ruth, without it appearing too obvious.

Compared to the slightly pale, puffy Goth teen last glimpsed on social media, she looked in good shape. Her skin was tanned to a light brown, she had lost ten to fifteen pounds, and her posture was much improved.

Overall, her skin looked clear, and she seemed to be in better physical health.

On a purely visual assessment he'd be able to tell Lock and their client that Ruth Price seemed to be in good shape. Not just holding up, and uninjured, but better than she had been before.

But that was on a first pass. Watching her stand, hands behind her back, feet spread shoulder wide, there was something else about her appearance that was impossible to miss if you actually looked properly. It lay in her eyes.

In the social-media pictures taken just before she'd left for Broken Ridge, she was out of shape and had bad skin and posture. That was all true. But she had seemed happy as she mugged for the camera and goofed around with her high-school friends.

Now, she was tan and trimmed down, but her eyes seemed dead. Like she'd checked out of human life. The look didn't even qualify as sullen. Or bored. It was an absence of anything, more than a presence of something.

It was a look Ty had seen before. It was a deadness that he associated with some kind of trauma. It gave him immediate cause for concern.

Chris tapped his shoulder. "You want to lead the run?"

Ty half turned toward his new colleague. "Sure, I can do that. What's the usual route?"

Chris pointed out toward the eastern horizon. "There's a dried-up riverbed about a half-mile or so that way. I usually run them down and back. Y'know, just as a warm-up."

Given the group in front of him, it didn't sound to Ty like a warm-up. He reminded himself that he was there to gather intel. And by leading the group he'd get to set the pace, maybe ensure that everyone made it back warmed up rather than passed out.

Ty walked to the center, ten paces back so everyone could see him. He clapped his shovel-sized hands together. "Okay, ladies, we're going to run down toward the dried creek and back. I will lead. Do not get out in front of me. Understood?"

"Yes, sir," they all said in unison.

"Okay, let's move out,' he added, feeling slightly ridiculous to be talking to a bunch of teenage girls like that.

But, he'd figured, Chris wanted to see a performance, and they'd hired him because of his military background, so if their expectation was a drill sergeant straight out of Central Casting then that was what they would get.

He turned and set a slow jogging pace. The girls fell in behind. Ty didn't look back, just kept moving. The pace would probably seem slow until the heat set in.

The jog down didn't take too long. By the time they reached the dried-up creek, Ty was sweating from the heat. Run, jog, sprint or just stand, this kind of heat would make you break a sweat. That was why no one but gringos would be crazy enough to go running at this time of day, unless someone was chasing them.

Chris caught up with him. "Maybe we could pick it up a little on the way back. They're barely out of breath."

"Sure thing," said Ty. "I heard you say 'warm-up', was all." He locked eyes with Chris as he said it.

Chris held up open palms. "Totally get that. I should have been clearer."

This was the male dance. Each of them working out who was the alpha relative to the other. Not that it was ever going to be close. But Ty didn't want to push it too far. "Hey, I'm the new guy here. Why don't you lead, show me the pace you like, and I'll pick up any stragglers from the rear?" he offered.

"I can do that."

Chris took off with no further instructions. An older brunette girl with a long ponytail, who looked almost college age, was first to take off after him. She practically raced off and, rather than falling in behind, ran beside him. Ty was fairly sure she was the same girl who had checked him out earlier. The other teenagers fell in behind.

If Ty's pace had been a little on the slow side, Chris Fontaine's wasn't. He set off like he'd just heard the bell ring for chow. The guy was a foot taller than most of the girls, with the stride to go with it. There was no way they were keeping up.

As promised, Ty brought up the rear. He noticed that Ruth was holding her own. She was near the back, but not last or second last. That honor went to a short, overweight girl with brown hair cut into a bob.

Among the pack of runners, Ty had noted her, too. She had stood out. Not just because she had the same dead expression in her eyes as Ruth Price and a few of the others. But because of the thin red scars, some small, but deep, and others long and thin that ran up and down her arms and legs: a tapestry of mental anguish turned inside out.

Ty had to slow so that he was next to her. Her face was flushed from running, and she was sweating heavily. As he jogged alongside her, she stared straight ahead.

"You're doing good," he said to her.

She snuck a glance at him. "Thank you, sir."

His immediate reaction was to ask her to not call him *sir*. He already felt old.

She was really struggling now. She looked like she might be about to throw up. But she kept going, albeit with more stumbling than actual running involved. Finally, she slipped, her left knee giving way under her. Ty caught her just in time, grabbing under her arm, and hauling her back to her feet. "You okay?"

"Yes, sir. I'm sorry, sir. I'll try harder."

She broke back into a jog, but she was limping. She must have pulled something when she'd slipped. Or maybe she'd twisted her ankle. The ground was hard and uneven. It was hardly a proper running track that absorbed some of the impact.

"Okay, stop," Ty told her. She did so, looking even more terrified than she had a moment ago. At least he knew there was still something there, beyond the abyss. "What's your name?"

"Harper," she told him.

"That's your first name?" Ty asked.

"No, sir, my first name is Mary."

"Okay, Mary, if you've hurt your leg, let's not make it any worse, okay?"

"But if I stop running . . ."

Her eyes were fixed on the rest of the group who were almost back to their starting point by now.

"I ordered you to stop and I'm a member of staff. You'd be in more trouble if you disobeyed a member of staff, correct?"

"I guess so."

"Okay, then you stopping is on me. Now, what hurts?" It seemed a strange question given all the scar tissue.

"I think it's my ankle."

Ty bent down. "Okay, let me take a look. Take your weight off."

He took her injured foot and got her to rotate it as best she could. From the way she reacted he was fairly sure it was a minor sprain. Nothing that a little rest and maybe an ice pack couldn't cure.

"Okay, Mary, you lean on me, and we'll finish this up. Keep as much weight off that foot as you can. If you need me to carry you, you just holler."

Something approaching a smile flitted across her face. It was a little lop-sided, like she'd somehow forgotten to use that expression.

With her arm around Ty's waist, they walked back toward the others. Chris stood next to the girl with the long ponytail. Neither looked happy, which, as far as Ty was concerned, was too bad. Chris wore a pained expression while Ponytail Girl looked seriously pissed. Ruth was studying the ground, moving around a stone with the toe of her sneaker.

"Mary here twisted her ankle," Ty said. "We're gonna go find her some ice before it starts to swell up."

Chris walked over to them. "Mark, can I speak with you for a moment in private?"

"Sure."

The two men stepped away from the group of girls. "You recall what I said to you before about how manipulative the girls here can get?" Chris asked.

Ty already knew where this was going, but he'd play along. It wasn't every day he had someone call him out as being naïve. It was kind of entertaining. Ty had grown up in the ghetto. You didn't do that, survive and thrive, by being easily taken in. "Sure, I remember," he said.

"Great," said Chris, giving Ty an Atta-boy pat on the shoulder that, under different circumstances, might have garnered a different reaction. "So Mary here is, how do I say this? She's kind of an attention-seeker. She doesn't like to do the Phys Ed stuff, so she fakes being injured to get out of it."

Now the question was just how far Ty would let this go. He'd seen her trip and pull up. He knew she hadn't been faking. And as for being an attention-seeker, that was kind of an interesting way of phrasing it. There was the usual teenage girl attention-seeking behavior that revolved around clothes, makeup and taking selfies, and then there was carving up your limbs with a razor blade so you could feel something. Ty wasn't a psychiatrist. But he was fairly confident that the latter was a little more serious than attention-seeking, and should be treated as such.

Lock had talked to Ty a lot over the years about "offering the victory." What it came down to was allowing, when it suited your agenda, an asshole to be an asshole. Allow them to think they had the advantage over you.

If Ty argued the point it could quickly go south. And, to figure out what was going on here, he needed to have Chris on his side. Chris was a talker, unlike the boss lady, Gretchen. He could learn a lot about what was really going on at Broken Ridge from him.

"I get it," said Ty. "Guess I have some learning still to do. I'm kind of used to people being straight up."

"Which is great," said Chris, giving Ty another pat on the shoulder. "But here it can be a weakness." He took a step back from Ty. "So are we good?"

"Yeah. Thanks for the advice."

141

"Terrific." Chris marched back toward the group of girls. Ruth was standing next to Mary, who was doubled over, rubbing her twisted ankle.

"Okay, Harper, you can go run it again," Chris shouted at Mary. He turned toward Ruth. "Price, you can go with her, seeing as how you're so concerned."

Ruth started to object, but quickly shut up. Chris and Ponytail Girl glared at her. The others did their best to fade into the background.

Out of instinct, more than anything, Ty started to move forward. He checked himself. If he intervened now he was pretty sure it would end with his employment, which had barely started, being terminated. You didn't cut across your manager. Not on the first day.

Ty stood, arms folded, and watched as Mary and Ruth set back out toward the dried-up creek a half-mile away. Chris walked behind them. Mary could barely move past a jog. She half walked, and half limped.

At one point, Ruth went to help her. Chris barked for her to mind her own business. She stepped away.

Behind his sunglasses, Ty took everything in. On his chest, the body cam recorded the scene.

There was discipline. There was holding kids to account. There was building character through asking people to face adversity.

What Ty was watching unfold in front of his very eyes was none of these. Not least because he could tell that Chris was getting off on the power trip. Ty could imagine

142

someone with good intentions doing this. It wasn't that either. This was a grown man proving what a tough guy he was by humiliating a couple of teenage girls.

****

By the time the two girls had made it back, Ty could see the pain of every step etched onto Mary's face. Ruth Price was back to being checked out. She had shown compassion for another girl and paid the price.

There followed a series of exercises. Crunches, push-ups, planks. The group worked through them, Chris screaming at the slower ones or those who struggled. Ty moved among them, correcting bad form and trying to encourage them on. All the while thinking it was a bunch of horseshit. If you wanted to make sure that a person grew up to hate physical exercise, and completely avoid it as an adult, this was the best way to do that.

Chris, meanwhile, seemed happy to be proving his point. "See what you can do when you put your mind to it, Harper," he said to Mary, her face now streaked with tears.

Finally, mercifully, it was over.

"Okay, ladies, go get showered and dressed for dinner. And don't be late."

As they headed back to their dorm, Chris glanced at Ty. "It's tough love. It ain't pretty. But it works."

Ty kept his own counsel.

"You should stay for dinner, Mark," Chris added.

143

"I'd like that," lied Ty, "but I have some things to do if I'm going to be moving my gear in here tomorrow."

CHAPTER TWENTY-SIX

THE BUS RIDE BACK INTO town gave Ty a chance to cool down a little about what he'd just seen. Taking out the last part, where Chris had punished an injured kid for the crime of twisting her ankle, it hadn't been all bad.

But what if he'd been right about her faking it? Ty hadn't known for sure that she was injured. Yes, she'd slipped and seemed to have hurt herself. But if that was her way of getting out of running, she could easily have faked a slip.

As for the rest of it, it was hardcore. No talking, boys and girls separated, regular physical exercise that was mandatory. But it was hardcore compared to any regular school in the US. Some of which were, if people were being honest, like a zoo.

Compared to many other parts of the world, Broken Ridge wasn't all that hardcore. Having traveled the world, Ty knew that in many places school discipline was extremely strict. Go to places in Asia or Africa and the kids were literally terrified of their teachers.

What else?

The kids he'd seen had appeared to be in good physical shape. Hell, Ruth Price had looked a ways healthier than she had back at home with her mom. She was eating right, getting her vitamin D from being outside, and moving around; all the stuff that used to come as the standard package for a kid of Ty's generation and before.

There were no TVs, video games or cell phones that Ty had seen. Even the staff didn't appear to be carrying phones. Maybe that was down to lack of coverage in the area or maybe it was policy. He could ask Chris tomorrow. But those were all plus points in Ty's book. Half the time people wandered around like zombies, their eyes glued to some screen or another.

The teaching seemed kind of basic. Or non-existent. But then again, these kids had been sent to Broken Ridge to get their heads on straight. If they'd been using drugs or booze or doing whatever else, then presumably the priority was to fix that first. If they needed to, they could catch up on the academic part when they got home.

The bus rolled to a stop. The door hissed open. An old lady got on with a shopping bag, the kind on rollers. The driver stood up to help her. Ty watched all this, impressed.

He couldn't imagine seeing something like that in LA. People on the coasts could rag on the 'fly-over' states all they liked, but out here there were good people with solid values.

The bus pulled away. A County Sheriff's patrol car rolled past it. The cop in front glanced at Ty for a second, then he was gone.

Okay, Ty thought, so Broken Ridge was basic, but hardly a brutal regime. So why did he still have a nagging sensation in the pit of his stomach? It came back to Mary, the girl with the scars. But presumably that was why she was there. They hadn't looked fresh. He would ask Chris about her history tomorrow, see what he could find out. It might allow him to ask about Ruth, too, seeing as how she'd got in trouble for helping out Mary. He'd run it past Lock first, but that could be a good way in. If he'd gone in asking questions about Ruth straight away, they'd have smelled a rat.

The bus was moving through the edge of town. Although the place was so small that there wasn't much distance between the edge and the center. It was early evening. The place wasn't so much quiet as dead. There was no one out on the streets, likely because of the heat. Most people were probably cooling off in a local bar or at home having dinner with their family.

The only place that looked busy, judging by the parking lot, was the place where Ty and Lock had eaten lunch. The food hadn't been at all bad, which would explain the number of cars parked outside.

The elderly lady began to get up. The bus was still moving, and she was a little unsteady on her feet. Ty got up from his seat to see if she needed assistance.

"May I help you, ma'am?" he said, putting out a hand to steady her, as he had done earlier with Mary.

She smiled, and extended her arm to him, but didn't say anything. Not at first anyway. He took her bag and, rolling it behind them, walked with her down to the steps of the bus.

The driver pulled over at the end of a small street of neatly kept houses with white picket fencing and American flags on display. Ty took the woman's bag down the steps, then turned back to help her down.

"Thank you, young man," she said to him.

It sounded a lot better to his ears than being called *sir*. That was for sure.

"Say," she said casually, "are you working at the school? Broken Ridge?"

Ty didn't think too much of her asking. She was probably trying to figure out what he was doing on the bus if she hadn't seen him before. He couldn't imagine there would be many other things that would bring someone like him here. At least, not as far as a local would be concerned.

"Yes, ma'am. Just started there today."

Her expression shifted. The smile dropped away. "Well, shame on you," she said, turning her back on him and walking away, wheeling her shopping bag behind her.

CHAPTER TWENTY-SEVEN

A TEN-SECOND CHECK TOLD Ty that no one had been in his motel room since he'd left. He wanted to take a shower, but that would have to wait. Lock would be impatient to see the footage and get a situation report.

He walked to the connecting door and gave three quick taps. "Honey, I'm home."

He heard Lock get up and move to the door. It opened. Lock handed him a cold beer.

"Man, you are going to make someone a great wife one of these days," said Ty, taking it.

"Hilarious," said Lock. "How'd it go?"

Ty stepped into Lock's room. Lock had his laptop open on the small dresser that was doubling as a desk. He had the windows open, and a notepad next to the laptop.

Papers were spread out over the bed. Since they'd taken the call from Donald Price, Lock had been deep into his research about not just Broken Ridge but the entire industry it was a part of.

He had become a little obsessive about the whole thing. Not to mention opinionated. That was why Ty had decided to attempt to be as objective as he could. He felt like their investigation needed some kind of counterweight.

"Well, I guess if private security doesn't work out for me, I can always go work as a camp counselor."

"You got the job?"

Ty shrugged and hefted the beer can in a mock toast of self-congratulation.

"Guess they really are having trouble finding staff, then," said Lock.

"Funny," Ty replied.

"Just getting you back for the wife wisecrack."

Ty shrugged. That was fair. "So they want me to start officially tomorrow. But it's pretty much a live-in kind of a deal, like we thought."

Ty dug out the two memory cards with the video footage he shot and palmed them to Lock. Lock took them to the laptop and placed the first card into the card reader that was hooked up to the laptop with a USB cable. He set the laptop to transferring the date, then turned back to Ty.

"This beer tastes awesome," said Ty, tilting back the can and finishing the final third. "I kind of want a shower, so how about I give you the bullet points, and save the details for when we go eat?"

"Sounds good."

"So, the set-up is pretty much as we thought it would be. Just like all the other schools in the organization," he said.

Lock's research had thrown up that a few years back Broken Ridge, which had been set up by Gretchen's German-born father Albert, had been bought out by a large private investment company. Albert had originally set up Broken Ridge as a school for 'wayward' teenagers. When the state had withdrawn funding after an abuse scandal, Broken Ridge had gone private, just in time to catch the first major wave of interest in schools for troubled teens from parents with money who wanted the best for their kids.

The ethos was one built upon strict discipline, psychotherapy that tended toward the confrontational, and a system of rewards and punishments that aimed to modify behavior. When it worked, it worked well. The big question, though, wasn't the immediate effectiveness, but what happened afterwards: the long-term outcomes.

"Okay, so the good news is Ruth Price is definitely there."

"The bad news?" Lock prompted.

"Not sure there is any. Not yet anyway, or none that I could confirm today. She's in good health. Her hair's shorter and she's dropped a few pounds. She seems well fed and looks like she's getting enough sleep."

"So if it's all good, why am I sensing a 'but' here?"

"Psychologically, I don't know. She had a look about her. In her eyes. But that could just be because she's still pissed at what her mom did, or because she's having to follow the rules there. She's a teenager, so who the hell knows, right?"

"Okay, go get that shower. I'm going to call Don Price in D.C. At least we can set his mind at ease a little. That his daughter's there and she's in good health. I'll save the other stuff until we know more," said Lock.

"Cool," said Ty, tossing the empty beer can across the room and into the wastebasket without it touching the sides.

"Hey, Ty?"

Ty turned back from the connecting door.

"Good work," said Lock.

"Place ain't that bad, Ryan. It's not Disneyland, but it was never meant to be."

Lock nodded and turned back to his laptop while Ty closed the connecting door behind him, and headed for that long-anticipated shower.

CHAPTER TWENTY-EIGHT

MORE THAN ANY OTHER TIME of the day or night, Ruth had grown to loathe and fear her time around the fire pit with the other girls from her dorm. Everything else she could just about handle. She had actually come to enjoy the exercise more than she'd thought she would. She was so far ahead on her schoolwork that she was able to help some of the others when they got stuck — if Rachel or one of the other girls who were bad for snitching weren't around. And she had found a friend, despite a rocky start at their first fire pit.

It was her friendship that was about to put her in a world of torment around that evening's fire pit. She was sure of it. Nothing got under Chris's skin more than one of the girls sticking up for another. It drove him crazy. Ruth was fairly sure he saw it as a challenge to his authority. Not that it took much. She had also quickly learned that, for a grown man, Chris was one of the most insecure people she had ever met. No doubt that also explained him sleeping with Rachel, which was all but an open secret at Broken Ridge.

At dinner, Ruth sat apart from Mary, who kept looking at her. Every time she did, Ruth turned away. She had tried to help Mary today and it had only landed her in more trouble. It was the new guy who had thrown her off. At first he'd terrified her. But then she saw something else: humanity. But he was new. They'd soon have him playing by the rules, or he'd be gone.

She still felt sorry for Mary. You had to be inhuman not to. Mary had no place being somewhere like this. But being her friend, showing compassion, had only made Ruth's situation worse. That pretty much summed up the place, as far as she was concerned. Compassion was seen as a weakness. Pretty much any display of emotion was used against you: anger; anxiety; love. They were all deemed, despite what the staff said, weaknesses. Acting a good little robot was the way to go. If you wanted to stay sane.

Right now, and pretty much since she'd got there, staying sane had been Ruth's priority. Now even more so than before. Her last hope, her father, had failed her. At the end of the first week, she had been allowed to write two letters. She already knew from Mary that Gretchen, or another staff member, would read them before they were

155

mailed. Mary also knew that the school primed parents ahead of time, warning them that students often made false accusations against staff and the institution in general. They even gave parents a list of things that their child might claim had occurred. Of course, the switch was that these things did occur. But the parents were already set up to discount them out of hand.

Armed with that information, Ruth spent hours in her little cubicle crafting two letters. One was to her mother, the other to her dad. Both letters were very different from what she would have written if she had known they would be delivered unread by anyone at Broken Ridge.

Writing the one to her mom was the hardest. She thanked her mom for "intervening." To make it sound plausible Ruth wrote that at first she had resented her mom's decision to send her to Broken Ridge. But as the days had passed, and the initial shock had worn off, she had come not only to understand it but also to appreciate it. She knew how difficult it must have been, and the financial sacrifice it involved. She wound up by telling her mom how much she loved her, and how she was going to do her very best.

In reality, Ruth knew that her dad would be picking up the bill for this, one way or another. She also knew that she would never forgive her mother for doing it. She didn't plan on cutting her out of her life, but their relationship would never be what it had been once upon a time. Beyond her anger, that was the saddest part of all of

THE EDGE OF ALONE

this. That she and her mom would never be the same. That the damage had been done as soon as Ruth had been woken by two men standing over her bed, put into a truck, and driven here against her will.

The letter to her dad was easier. She kept it as neutral as possible. She borrowed some of the material she had used in the letter to her mom. But in between the lines her dad would know that she hadn't agreed to any of this. She didn't have to say that she needed his help. He would know.

She handed over the two letters. Her mom sent a letter in reply. Ruth got it five days after she had sent her own. She heard nothing from her dad. At first she thought they must not have mailed it. Surely that had to be it. But then Mary told her that she had been in the ranch house and had seen both of Ruth's letters being placed in the mail sack that was driven into town.

Ruth's heart had broken. How could her dad not have replied? Even if he had and they had kept his letter from her, why hadn't he shown up? Why hadn't he sent help? Or come to see her himself? Why hadn't he made the trip and demanded that he could see she was okay?

She had no idea. All she knew was that none of those things had happened. There had been no letter, no call, no visit, no attorney turning up to demand that her father be allowed access or to ensure she was safe.

He had abandoned her. She was on her own now. The only person she could rely on was herself. That was the real lesson of Broken Ridge. Today had been proof of it. She had to protect herself because, when it came down to it, no one else would.

CHAPTER TWENTY-NINE

LOCK AND TY TOOK A corner booth at the far end of the diner. They ordered coffee and talked about general stuff for just long enough to shake off anyone casually listening in.

"You speak to Carmen today?" Ty asked him, taking a sip of his coffee.

Carmen was an LA-based criminal defense attorney whom Lock had been dating for a couple of months. Part of the reason he had taken this gig was that he had promised her he would keep a check on the high-risk assignments. Compared to their usual work, which had ranged from protecting an adult movie star from a violent stalker to going undercover inside a maximum-security prison, this was about as low risk as life got.

"Yeah, she just caught a double homicide out of Newton."

"Lucky gal," said Ty.

"She thinks so."

The waitress came and took their order. They had left her a good tip at lunchtime so she was glad to see them back.

The diner had emptied out a little since Ty had passed it on the bus. There was no one in the adjoining booth and behind them was a wall. Unless someone had their booth tapped, they were free to talk.

"You speak to Don Price?"

"Yeah, I brought him up to speed."

"How was he?"

"Glad to take the call. I think he felt better knowing that we've seen her and that she's okay." Lock drank some coffee. "He had a lot of questions about the place."

"Such as?" Ty asked.

"The stuff you'd expect. How are the kids treated? What are the staff like?"

"And?"

Lock grimaced slightly. "Security protocols. Access. Perimeter. Cameras. Proximity to local law enforcement. All the questions you'd expect a guy like Donald Price to ask about a place that has his daughter."

"What you tell him?"

Lock glanced out of the window as a local PD cruiser pulled into the diner's parking lot. "I answered his questions to the best of my ability. Then I reminded him that we weren't about to assist in abducting his daughter from a facility where she has been legally placed."

Ty had also noticed the patrol car. The two cops had gotten out and were heading inside the diner. They were both male, white, late forties and carrying about a hundred excess pounds between them. "How he take that?" Ty asked his friend.

"Same as he took it the last time we had that conversation."

Ty gave him a look, as if to ask, "Which was how?"

"Politely."

"But you don't believe him," said Ty.

Lock tapped two fingers on the tabletop to indicate that the two cops were now within earshot. "I tell you, I'm really lucky to have met Carmen when I did."

Ty caught on. "No kidding. Lady like that doesn't stay on the market too long."

"Tell me about it," said Lock, watching the two local cops walk up to the counter.

They weren't looking at him and Ty, which was good. Lock planned on talking to local law-enforcement. Just not yet. He wanted a handle on who was who in the local community first.

Finally, the two cops got their food to go, and headed back to their patrol car. In the meantime, Lock and Ty's dinner arrived. It sure as hell wasn't LA or New York food, but it looked pretty damn good, and was just as tasty and filling.

Heads down, they resumed their conversation where they had left off.

"If he thinks his daughter's at risk, he's going to ask us to get her out of there," said Lock, before he took another bite of cheeseburger.

"But we're not gonna?"

"Nope."

"I thought you were all high on how bad some of these schools are."

Lock stared at Ty over the top edge of what remained of his burger. "I am. But I'm not about to catch prison time over it. If there are problems there, and it looks like his daughter is in danger, he can seek legal remedy. He has the connections and the resources to do that."

"I hear ya. By the way, we seen any money come in beyond the retainer?"

Lock smiled. Ty had an eye for the bottom line right now that had a lot to do with a lease he'd just taken out on a brand new Mercedes. Lock had done his best to talk him out of it. As with Ty's choice of female companionship, it had proven to be a losing battle.

"Paid in full. In fact, he's a little ahead."

"Now that's the kind of client I can get behind." Ty waved a finger, remembering something, the lady from the bus. He'd been so focused on giving Lock his bullet points that he'd forgotten to mention her when he'd gotten back to the motel. "I had an old lady on the bus back ask me if I worked at Broken Ridge."

"And?"

"And when I said that I did she said, 'Shame on you.' Kind of came out of left field too. I was helping her with her groceries when she said it so she must have been carrying some strong opinions."

Lock mulled that one over. Broken Ridge having a bad reputation locally could work to their advantage. "Wonder why she said it?" He was thinking out loud.

"And I thought you were supposed to be the smart one."

"I mean, did she work there one time? Is it local gossip? Did something happen? And, if so, when? What's the angle? If there's a grievance, it comes from somewhere, smartass," said Lock.

The waitress headed over with the coffee pot. "How are you boys doing over here? Enjoying everything?"

They both answered in the affirmative. She gave them a refill and left them to resume their conversation.

"So where d'you say this woman got off the bus?" Lock asked.

Ty described the street where the driver had stopped to let her off. Lock figured she should be easy enough to find in a town so small. "Well, the less popular the place is, the easier that makes my job. But you just be careful out there tomorrow. Remember your cover and stick to it."

Ty smirked at him across the table. "What they gonna do? Put me in detention?"

"Ty," said Lock, suddenly serious. "The digging I was doing today . . . People have died at Broken Ridge, two kids and one member of staff since it first opened. All three happened a while back, and the place was pretty much cleared of any wrongdoing, but this is not a zero-risk environment, so don't go getting complacent. Okay?"

Chapter Thirty

THE FLAMES FROM THE FIRE pits flickered in the darkness. The day's heat had given way to a chilling desert cold. Ruth sat, knees pulled up, her arms stretched out so that she could warm her hands by the flames.

When they had gathered at the pit, Mary had sat next to her. Ruth had got up and switched places with Abby. Abby seemed to be happy about having a seat closer to where the action was likely to be.

Chris hadn't begun with what had happened with Mary and, by extension, with Ruth. He'd held off. Instead, he'd started out by lecturing them on the importance of keeping the dorm, especially their main bathroom, clean. He had even picked out Rachel as someone who wasn't doing enough cleaning detail.

Ruth had watched Rachel bristle at the comments. She was not used to being criticized at all. Certainly not to her face, and certainly not by Chris.

Ruth wondered if there had been a lovers' tiff, or whether maybe Rachel had just stopped putting out. Rachel and Chris were hardly the most discreet people when it came to their being involved. Rachel pretty much dined out on it, not just with the other girls but with some of the staff too. Though she never said it straight out, Rachel made it pretty clear that she expected to be treated differently because Chris was second only to Gretchen in the pecking order.

But Rachel hadn't climbed the levels as quickly, or become Queen Bee, without knowing how to play the blame game. She listened earnestly to Chris's criticism of her as "being lazy sometimes". She also took a few jabs from some of the others. Abby made sure to get in a little payback: "We all have to contribute, Rachel." Mary was silent, even when she was asked to comment.

When it came to Ruth's turn, she had already decided to take advantage of the opportunity that had presented itself. Her dad, half joking, had told her that the key to success in D.C. was directly related to a person's ability to kiss ass. That was why he'd been stuck at the same level for so many years.

"Ruth, what do you have to say about keeping the dorm and the bathroom clean?" Chris said.

Ruth looked straight at Rachel. From the way the other girl's eyes narrowed, Ruth was sure she was anticipating a little more payback, just like she'd got from Abby and some of the others. Instead, Ruth said, "I think it's a little unfair of any of us to criticize Rachel when she already does so much for everyone in our dorm. We all need to take responsibility. But that also means picking up the slack when people are really busy, like Rachel is."

Rachel smiled, then turned toward Chris with a glare. "Thank you, Ruth. I'm glad someone else understands that I can't do *everything* in the dorm."

Chris, perhaps sensing that if he pushed Rachel much harder, he'd never get into her pants again, started to backtrack. "I think we all appreciate you, Rachel," he said.

That drew a snicker from Abby and a few of the others. Now it was Chris's turn to glare. Ruth was waiting for him to start handing out punishments, but he let it go.

"Now that we have allowed everyone to have their say then I expect the cleanliness of the common areas will no longer be an issue," Chris said. "It's a matter of everyone taking responsibility and pulling their weight."

Now he was staring straight at Mary who was sitting there, head down, rubbing at her ankle. Even though Chris was staring at her, she kept her head down, her eyes on the ground.

Finally, it was Rachel who said, "Mary! Chris would like to address you. Can you at least look at him?"

Slowly, Mary lifted her head. "Yes, Daddy?"

167

The way she said it totally creeped Ruth out. A couple of the other girls exchanged looks.

"You don't have to call me that, Mary," Chris told her.

"It's a little over-familiar," said Rachel, chipping in.

"Yeah, only Rachel gets to call him that," Abby whispered, loud enough for Ruth to hear.

Chris must have been really regretting his criticism of Rachel, thought Ruth. It had completely changed the dynamic of the group.

"Mary, we need to talk about what happened today on the run. You pretended to be injured to garner sympathy," said Chris.

"Yeah, Mary," said one of the other girls. "Why do you always pull stuff like that? Like you think we're dumb enough to believe you. We all know it's because you're a fat tub who doesn't want to exercise."

Now they were back on familiar ground, thought Ruth. Naked, personal attacks designed to humiliate and belittle. Or, as Chris liked to put it, 'You have to break something down before you can build it back up."

"I was injured," said Mary. "I twisted my ankle."

"You were faking it," Chris said sternly.

"I wasn't," Mary shot back, a steeliness creeping into her voice that Ruth hadn't heard much of before. It had always been there, a kind of repressed anger, but Mary rarely allowed it to surface. When she did, she didn't direct it outwards. She got a blade of some kind and directed it at herself.

"If you're to move forward and progress, you have to confront your behavior. Not deny it."

"I'm not," said Mary, not prepared to give up and play the game.

"Okay, I'll ask the group," said Chris. "Raise your hand if you believed that Mary was genuinely injured."

No one raised their hand. Mary took them in with a sweep. She stopped at Ruth.

Ruth tilted her head back and they locked eyes. She could see the pleading in Mary's.

Ruth already knew what would happen if she raised her hand. It would make her life even more difficult than it was already about to be for helping Mary earlier. There was no way of winning. Chris had made sure of that.

If Ruth raised her hand, she would be the lone dissenter. Not a good thing to be around the fire pit. The pressure would be off Mary and on Ruth.

If she kept her hand down? She would be safe, but she would have sacrificed not just her friend but the person in the dorm who was most troubled and least able to defend herself from what would follow. Ruth would still take some lumps, but she wouldn't be the focus of tonight's fire pit.

"Price?" said Chris. "Don't you want to raise your hand? I mean, you helped out Mary here."

Ruth looked at Chris. She could still feel Mary's heavy stare, and sense her desperation, her need.

169

Moments like this were what made her dread the fire pit. Ruth already knew that she would never forget what was happening now as long as she lived. She was torn. The last thing she wanted to do was to abandon Mary to the pack. Betrayal. That was what it would be if she didn't raise her hand.

But hadn't she been betrayed? By her mother, who had sent her here. By her dad, who had ignored her cry for help. And hadn't Mary thrown her under the bus that first night? Wouldn't Mary do the same tonight if the tables were turned?

Ruth had to survive. There was only one way to do that.

"No," said Ruth. "I don't want to raise my hand."

Now she'd said it, she might as well be all in. "I think Mary was faking. I'm sorry I got sucked in."

She still couldn't look at Mary. Chris must have sensed as much.

"Okay, Price. Now, you know I'll have to punish you for your part in what happened today."

Ruth stuck out her chin. "Yes, I accept that."

"Even though you were trying to do a good thing."

"Yes."

"All because Mary lied to us about being hurt," said Chris.

"Yes," said Ruth.

Now that she'd kept her hand down she wasn't sure it would have felt worse to have stood up for Mary. This was awful. She hated herself for what she had just done. But she had done it now. Going back would be worse.

"Okay, Price, I want you to look at Mary and tell her how her deceit has hurt you," said Chris.

Rachel, who loved nothing more than the smell of blood in the water, jumped in. "Yes, Price. We all know she's your friend, and then she does that. You need to share your truth with her. Make her realize how lame that whole deal today was."

"Look at her!" yelled Abby, whose body was almost vibrating with the excitement of this latest twist in the dorm's drama.

Ruth scooted round so she was staring at Mary's tear-filled eyes. She couldn't do it. She knew what she had to say: she could form the words in her mind. *Mary, you need to stop pulling other people into your dramas. You need to take responsibility for yourself. Stop being so weak.* She just couldn't say them. She had come this far. But she couldn't do it. It was the eagerness of the others for her to say them. It made her feel sick. Sicker than she already felt for having done what she already had.

Slowly, Ruth raised her arm into the air. "I just lied," said Ruth. "She did hurt her ankle. Everyone here knows it. This whole thing isn't about facing who we are, and being honest. It's bullshit."

Abby started laughing. A nervous giggle. A couple of the others joined in.

171

Mary looked confused. Her eyes were still full of tears. Ruth wasn't even sure that she had heard what she'd just said.

"You didn't lie!" Rachel almost screamed. "Tell her! Tell her she's a faker! Tell her she's a liar!"

"Price?" said Chris.

"Yes, Chris?" said Ruth, not even attempting to conceal the sarcasm in her voice. She was already about to face a world of pain. There was nothing they would do to her now that hadn't already been going to happen.

Chris tried to play it off. "Okay," he said. "That's all fine."

He began to get to his feet. Now there was silence. This didn't happen. The fire pit didn't finish early like this. Not unless something major happened. Ruth guessed that this was major.

"Price, Harper. Follow me."

A ripple passed through the girls around the fire pit. Groups around other fire pits were looking at them as Chris stood up and Ruth and Mary followed.

Ruth already knew where they were headed. With every step, she cursed her own stupidity. If she had stood up for Mary from the get-go, it would have been bad, but not this bad. If she had kept her hand down, and spoken the words in her head, she would have been home free.

Instead she had managed to capture the worst of both worlds. Now she would pay a very heavy price. So would

Mary. By first her cowardice, and then her bravery, Ruth had doomed them both.

CHAPTER THIRTY-ONE

RUTH STOOD WITH MARY OFF to one side. They watched as, one by one, pails of water were thrown over the dying embers in the fire pits. Almost everyone was already back in their dormitories. They were the only students left outside.

Chris and two other staff members stood guard over them. No one spoke. They were waiting for Gretchen to arrive.

As they stood there, Mary struggling to stay upright on her twisted ankle, Ruth reflected that she had learned some things from her short time at Broken Ridge. The power in making someone wait was one of them. The staff at Broken Ridge were experts at it. They waited until you confessed your sins. They waited while you almost cooked to death in the baking sun. They made you wait to eat, to

174

drink, to use the bathroom. But perhaps the most effective wait of all was this one: the wait to decide your punishment.

While you stood there, you couldn't help but wonder, dread, what you were about to face. Gretchen was the most feared member of staff for a reason. Her punishments were rarely deployed, at least directly, by her. But they were legendary for their cruelty.

Figuring that the damage was already done to her own chances of an early release, or a move up a level, Ruth turned toward Chris. "Can't you at least let Mary sit down?"

Chris actually smiled. It was more frightening to Ruth than him shouting. "Sure," he said. "Mary, you can sit down if you really need to." He placed a sarcastic emphasis on *really need to.*

Mary didn't so much sit as collapse on the ground. Immediately, she began to massage her ankle again, rubbing at it in small circles, kneading it with her fingers. Ruth wasn't sure why anyone would think she was faking now. You could see the pain etched in her features. Her shoulders were hunched, her elbows tucked in tight, her chin on her chest.

No one said anything else. They just stood round, guarding Mary and Ruth. Though where they were going to go was anyone's guess. Mary couldn't walk, never mind run.

175

Ruth had worked out that escape from Broken Ridge was possible. It wasn't a Supermax prison. But the chances of being caught were high. And what would happen to you when you were brought back didn't bear thinking about. Although, ironically, that level of punishment was what she was likely about to face. More stupidity she could have cursed herself for. If you were going be busted, then trying to get out of here once for all had to be a better crime for it than this.

Ten minutes later, Gretchen arrived. They heard her coming through the darkness before they saw her. Her slippers scraped over the rough ground toward them. She was wearing a robe, and under it some kind of long nightdress. To Ruth's eyes she looked like a crazy homeless lady rather than the person who was in charge of all these people.

Chris walked over to meet her before she got to them. He talked in low whispers to her. She didn't say much in response, not that Ruth could hear anyway.

The other staff members seemed uncomfortable and on edge. It was well known that Gretchen did not like hearing about problems. That was why so much went on behind the scenes. No one wanted to be the one to go tell Gretchen that there was an issue with something.

Staff turnover at Broken Ridge, according to the kids who'd been there awhile, was high. Partly because a lot of new staff didn't agree with the way the place was run but also because Gretchen often took an irrational dislike to them. Chris was one of the longest serving, and because he'd always been so loyal, he was allowed to get away with a lot, including his affair with Rachel, who was a barely legal student and had probably been under-age when he'd first crossed that line.

The discussion between Chris and Gretchen broke up. Gretchen shuffled over to them in her slippers. She was breathing hard through her nose, almost like a toddler at the end of a tantrum, trying to compose itself.

"Ruth Price and Mary Harper, please come with me," Gretchen said to them, turning on a flashlight.

Mary struggled to her feet somehow, and half walking, half limping, followed Ruth, who was following Gretchen. Chris and the other two staff members flanked them.

They weren't on the way back to the dormitory. They were about to experience some of Broken Ridge's alternative accommodation.

It was in back. Way in back. Completely separate from all the other buildings.

When they got there, Gretchen stood back as Chris pulled the key to a padlock off the chain hanging from his belt. He unlocked the padlock and wrenched open the door.

Ruth heard something inside the barn, maybe more than one thing, scuttle for cover. The barn was big and open. There was moldy hay on the dirt floor. In one corner there were three dirty old mattresses. In the opposite corner there was a sink with a cold tap. There were two buckets to use as a toilet. That was it.

This was solitary confinement, Broken Ridge-style. Not quite the most feared place there: that honor went to what the kids called "the naughty room", which was where Gretchen was known to administer electro-shock therapy. But the barn came a close second.

Mary stumbled over to a mattress and sat down. Ruth stood, turning so that she was facing Gretchen, Chris and the two other staff members.

"One week," said Gretchen.

Mary started to sob. Ruth was going to argue, but there was no point. Arguing would only get their stay extended further, especially when Gretchen was in this kind of a rage.

Gretchen withdrew along with Chris and the other two staff. Ruth stood in the middle of the barn. No change of clothes, not so much as a toothbrush. Just the mattresses, the sink and the buckets. Plus, whatever else was living there.

The door was locked. The padlock put back on. It clicked shut.

Ruth walked over and sat down next to Mary. She put her arm around her.

"I'm sorry. I'm so sorry, Ruth. This is all my stupid fault," Mary spluttered, between sobs.

"It's nobody's fault."

"No, it is. It's my fault. If I'd looked where I was going. If I hadn't been so slow . . ."

"Listen," said Ruth, firmly. "It's this place. It's evil. Pure evil."

CHAPTER THIRTY-TWO

THE FULL MOON GAVE THEM some light through the barn's only window. Without it, they would have been in darkness. That was something to think about before tomorrow night. They hadn't been left with so much as a torch.

Part of Ruth was relieved at being put in here. Sharing your every waking and sleeping moment with at least a dozen other people was tiring in a way she could never have imagined. There was simply no let-up. Even when you went to the toilet, someone was often posted outside the cubicle if you hadn't reached the necessary level of the program.

Ruth also knew that the enjoyment of being away from barked orders, and constant teenage-girl bitchiness, would fade. And probably quickly. To be replaced by what, she didn't know. Whatever it was, she would handle it. She had handled everything so far, hadn't she?

Mary, though. That was something else entirely. Mary needed help, from someone who knew what they were doing, a professional person—and fast. Ruth would do her best, but she wasn't at all sure her best was going to be enough.

She was assuming they'd be brought food of some kind. They weren't just going to leave them here to starve for a week. Ruth made a mental note that they had better make sure to eat everything they were given or, if not, they should ask for it to be taken away. Even crumbs would attract more critters into the barn, and by the skittering sounds she was hearing, it didn't need any more.

"Okay, so here's what we're going to do," Ruth said softly to Mary. "We're going to try to get some sleep. I'll be here right next to you, okay? Things are always better in the morning."

"This is all my fault," Mary repeated.

"You need to stop telling yourself that. It's not true."

Ruth lay down next to Mary. She closed her eyes. She was beyond exhausted, but she knew getting to sleep would take some time, if it came at all. If she didn't sleep, she could try at least to get some rest. Worrying about whether you would sleep or not was a surefire way to stay awake.

She lay there, trying to calm her mind. She listened to Mary's breathing. It was cold and getting colder. She put an arm around Mary. Mary cuddled into her, like a little kid. After a while, maybe it was an hour, maybe it was two hours, Ruth finally fell asleep.

CHAPTER THIRTY-THREE

WITH LOCK'S WORDS OF CAUTION from the previous evening still at the front of his mind, Ty climbed onto the bus to take him back to Broken Ridge. Today would be his first day on the job. He had kept on the motel room, but he would be living at the academy. At least for the next three days and nights.

He'd taken a last-minute decision to pack his gun. He doubted he'd need it but it was always better to be fully prepared. In any case, no one had told him he couldn't have a gun with him. If someone saw it, and he was asked, he was sure he'd be able to explain it. This was not a part of the nation where having a handgun was seen as out of the ordinary. It wasn't like he planned on sticking it on his hip and strutting around the academy with it there.

Because cell-phone coverage in the area was best described as patchy, he'd agreed to check in with Lock when he could. Meanwhile, Lock would be in town, asking questions, and getting more of a feel for how the locals saw Broken Ridge. He was also scheduled to meet with at least one former employee who'd been shut down from speaking publicly about the place by an NDA (non-disclosure agreement), but who seemed to harbor serious concerns. Needless to say, Broken Ridge had described her as a disgruntled former employee with an axe to grind.

On the bus, Ty kept an eye out for the little old lady. He didn't see her. Apart from a couple of sleepy-eyed farm laborers, he and the driver were the only people on the bus. The driver, the same one as the previous day, had given him a look when he'd seen Ty's bag, but hadn't said anything.

Ty decided to sit up front. Maybe the driver could use a little help to start talking. Once they'd pulled away, he leaned in a little.

"I'm kind of nervous. Starting a new job today."

The driver glanced back at him for a split second. "Congratulations."

"First real job since I came out the military. Tough economy, I guess. Been looking for a while."

"Tell me about it," said the driver.

"You serve?"

"Never got the chance."

184

Ty had heard that one a lot. It always came from people who wouldn't have taken the chance if it had come along. Which was fine. The military wasn't for everyone.

"So, the people at this place seemed like good folks. I'd heard some mixed stuff. Y'know, like they'd had some problems."

The driver's eyes flicked in the mirror toward Ty and beyond him to the two dozing farm laborers. "Yeah," said the driver. "I really wouldn't know too much about it. The people there pretty much keep themselves to themselves."

"Guess they don't use your bus, then." Ty laughed. The driver seemed cagey and Ty figured it was best to back up and keep it light.

"No, sometimes they do. I've had the odd runaway."

Ty's ears pricked up. "Oh, yeah? What do you do?"

"Drop 'em off in town, and call the Sheriff's Department. They usually come, pick 'em up and bring 'em back pretty damn quick."

"Pretty damn quick, huh?" said Ty, pushing his luck a little.

He needn't have worried. The driver was warming to the topic. "Oh, yeah, anything out there and the sheriff is real responsive."

"How come?"

The driver laughed. "Boy, you are new around here, ain't you? Well, maybe I can save you putting your foot in it. The lady that's in charge, Gretchen, the sheriff's her brother-in-law. Plus, and this is between us, with the kind of money that place makes, I'm guessing the school kicks in some bucks. Tax base is kinda narrow out here to keep things running. Hey, you know what they charge at that place?"

Ty did. In fact, when Lock had told him, he'd made him repeat it and then write it down because he'd refused to be believe it. Tuition at an Ivy League college was probably cheaper. "No, what?"

The driver repeated the number that Lock had given him. Ty let out a low whistle. "No kidding."

"Yeah, crazy, ain't it?" said the driver. "I guess, though, if you have that kind of cash and you're worried about your kid, it makes sense. Better than them ending up dead in a ditch somewhere, pregnant at sixteen, or jacked up on drugs."

"Yeah," said Ty. "Better than any of those things."

CHAPTER THIRTY-FOUR

As TY STEPPED OFF THE bus, he checked his cell phone for a signal. There was a single bar out of a possible five. He decided to give it a shot. He pulled up Lock's number on the display and tapped the call icon.

No luck. It wouldn't connect.

He kept walking along the road toward Broken Ridge, his bag slung over his shoulder. As he went he started to tap out a text message for Lock that he could send as soon as he got a signal. He was sure there was some kind of cell-phone coverage in the area, it was just patchy.

Gretchen being related to the local sheriff was hardly surprising. In small, isolated communities those kinds of connections were far from unusual. By and large, people in this type of place tended to stick together. That went

187

double when you factored in the money that a school like Broken Ridge brought into the local community.

As Ty finished up his brief text message to let Lock know about the local sheriff's connection to the school, all kinds of things were suddenly clicking into place. Such as why a school where three people had either died suddenly or been killed had been allowed to remain open.

That particular death had been explained, but knowing the connection between the school and local law enforcement, maybe the explanation didn't quite hold up. The staff member who had been killed was a young woman in her early twenties, by the name of Kelsey Reese.

Kelsey had taken a job at Broken Ridge immediately after graduating from college in California. Six months into her time at the school, she had been walking alone near it. In fact, she'd been on the dirt track Ty was walking on now when she had been shot once at close range. She'd bled out before anyone found her.

A local man, Willard Lowsen, had been arrested. He had confessed to killing Kelsey. It was a confession he later retracted, but by then it was too late. He was already serving the first year of a life sentence without possibility of parole. Willard had been talking about making an appeal against his conviction when two members of a notoriously violent prison gang had stabbed him to death in his cell.

Before the murder, Willard Lowsen had already had a stack of convictions, and had only just been released from prison for a sexual assault. From what Lock had told Ty, no one was going to miss him. And certainly not enough to ask any questions. He'd had motive, and he'd had opportunity. DNA on the murder weapon, and on the body of Kelsey Reese, matched to him. It was pretty much a slam-dunk, even without the confession he later claimed had been beaten out of him by the local sheriff.

A couple of bars showing a signal finally appeared on Ty's cell phone. He was about to hit the send button on the text to Lock when he heard the rumble of an engine closing in fast from behind. He stepped off to the side of the track as a pick-up truck ground to a sudden halt. The rear tires threw up a plume of dust. Ty had to cover his mouth with his hand to avoid catching a lungful.

The driver leaned over to the passenger side of the cab, his face obscured by a ball cap pulled down low over his eyes. Ty turned slightly so that he was side on to him. The driver took off the cap, and Chris Fontaine grinned like an idiot at him.

"Sorry, man, I went to see if I could give you a ride from town, but the motel manager told me he'd seen you getting on the bus," he said.

That was weird, thought Ty. Chris hadn't mentioned anything about picking him up. Neither was he sure that he'd mentioned where he was staying to the man. Although, to be fair, when it came to places to stay in the nearby town, it was a pretty narrow field. Ty wondered what else Chris had asked the motel manager.

Chris popped open the passenger door. "Hop in."

"Thanks."

He had already decided that the less he said, the less chance there was he would slip up on his cover story. At the same time, he realized that it would only get harder to maintain his new identity as time went on. He would start to relax, and that was when he was most likely to make a mistake.

There was still something he felt he needed to say to Chris. It would be in keeping with the person he was pretending to be. Someone who really needed this job right now. What was it that actors always talked about? The character's motivation.

"Listen, Chris, about yesterday, I kind of feel like I owe you an apology."

Chris glanced across at him, puzzled. "For what?"

"Well," Ty began, "I know you were really rooting for me to get this gig."

"I was. Believe me. Positive male role models are really hard to come by for these kids."

Yeah, no kidding, thought Ty.

"It's easy enough for us to find women to work here, but guys are another story," Chris continued.

"Anyway," Ty cut in, "I really appreciate all your help. I just didn't want you thinking I was trying to step on your toes yesterday. Y'know, with that kid who was pretending she'd hurt herself."

Chris took one hand off the truck's steering-wheel and waved away the apology. "No problem. Don't give it another thought. I've been suckered by some of these kids dozens of times. It's easily done. And, you have to remember, some of them have had literally years of practice, pulling the wool over their parents' eyes before they finally got called out on their bullshit and were sent here for us to straighten them out."

"Cool. I didn't want you thinking . . . well, I don't know what I was worried about you thinking. I just wanted you to know that I really appreciate the opportunity."

Chris gave a broad grin that allayed any of Ty's niggling worries. "Man, we're lucky to have you. That's what I told Gretchen. And don't worry about those two girls either. We had more trouble with them last night at the fire pit, and we had to put them in the time-out room."

Some questions immediately sprang to Ty's mind, but he held off asking them.

"Believe me, it's been coming with those two," said Chris.

Before he got on to what time out involved, Ty figured he'd ask some more general questions. He knew that Chris would get off on playing mentor to the new guy.

"So, when a kid comes in, can you tell how resistant they'll be?" Ty knew from reading the staff manual that *resistance* was one of the buzzwords at Broken Ridge. It was revealing: it suggested the need to break down, to counter with an opposing force. It was a word that Ty was familiar with in a military context. It often cropped up when talking not just about an enemy force but interrogation. In fact, Lock had discovered that many of the psychological techniques used at private institutions, like **Broken Ridge**, were pretty much straight out of the CIA manual on enhanced interrogation techniques. They also had more than a passing resemblance to the techniques employed by cults. Techniques that were often highly effective, but that, according to psychologists, often came with a hefty price that was paid down the road by the person who had been exposed to them.

"Sometimes," said Chris. "But it can go the opposite way too. Like that kid Mary, for instance. She's not openly hostile, like some of the students are, but her behavior can be a lot more difficult to deal with."

Ty decided to keep playing the eager student. "How do you mean?"

Chris slowed the truck to a crawl. They were getting close to the ranch house, and Ty could sense him warming to the subject, keen to give the new guy the benefit of his experience.

"It's not confrontational," said Chris. "She's not going to cuss, or be deliberately disobedient. It's more that she works the angles. Like yesterday, for instance, trying to get you to feel sorry for her."

"I see what you're saying," said Ty, even though he really didn't. Or, rather, he did, but he didn't agree. The kid had hurt her ankle. She hadn't been faking. Maybe Ty had never done this job, but he knew the difference

192

between those two things. "And what about the other young lady? What was her name?"

"Ruth Price?"

Ty nodded. "Yeah. You think she just got drawn in by it?"

Chris laughed at that question. "No, she's just straight-up trouble. Has been since day one. Doesn't think she should be here."

Ty didn't think it was wise to say anything to that. He stayed quiet.

"She's still in complete denial. That's why we put her in time out with Harper. See if we can't start to break her down," said Chris, as he pulled up in back of the ranch house so that Ty could drop off his gear. "Course, then we build 'em back up again. Better than they were before. Like the military in that regard."

It was the military way to some degree. Ty could see that. But there was also one important difference. At least in America, the people who served their country in the military volunteered to do so. Here, they were all conscripts.

Ty grabbed his bag and fell in behind Chris. They were headed for the dorm that Ty would be in charge of. He allowed Chris to go on ahead, and dug his cell phone out of his pocket. He still hadn't sent Lock the text he'd drafted.

Now, looking down at the screen, he could see there was no signal again. Chris, who'd been rambling on, suddenly turned back toward him. Putting the phone away quickly would only look suspicious. In any case, Chris couldn't see the screen and who Ty was texting.

"You're out of luck," Chris said to him, with a nod in the direction of Ty's cell phone.

"No signal?" asked Ty, looking skywards.

"That, and we use a jammer. Kids were smuggling in phones. Only way we could really stop them making calls was by installing one. If you need to make a call you can use the landline in the ranch house. Or you can walk back down to the road. It's a complete pain in the ass at times, but it's also kinda nice being off the grid."

Ty smiled politely, and followed Chris inside.

CHAPTER THIRTY-FIVE

ARY WAS STILL ASLEEP WHEN Ruth woke. She managed to untangle herself from the other girl without waking her up. If they were going to be stuck in here all day, there didn't seem much point in waking her.

Ruth crossed quietly to the sink, and tried to turn on the tap. It took three attempts before she finally managed it. It coughed and spluttered before a trickle of sludgy brown water appeared. She waited until it ran clear, gathered some in her cupped hands and splashed her face a few times. The water was freezing cold, but it felt good against her skin.

The night might have been cold, but she could already begin to feel the heat outside beginning to build. She wasn't sure how hot the barn would get during the day.

195

She guessed they would find out soon enough. At least they would be shielded from the direct sunlight.

With Mary still fast asleep, Ruth took a few minutes to look around. There was a ladder that led up into a hayloft. Gingerly, she climbed it. She was halfway up when she heard someone outside and came down quickly as she heard someone removing the padlock.

The barn door opened. Ruth's heart sank a little as she saw who it was.

Rachel. No doubt come to gloat.

In her right hand, Rachel was carrying a brown canvas shopping bag. She stopped when she saw Ruth standing at the bottom of the ladder. Ruth put her finger to her lips and pointed at Mary, still asleep on the dirty mattress in the corner.

She was half expecting Rachel to fetch some cold water from the sink and use it to wake Mary. She didn't. Instead, she walked across to Ruth and handed her the bag. "Breakfast. I asked to be the one who brought it to you. I got you some extra stuff too from your lockers. Clean underwear. Toothbrushes. Toothpaste. A fresh bar of soap. That kind of junk," said Rachel, keeping her voice down to a whisper so as not to wake Mary.

Ruth took the bag from her, uncertain what to say to this new version of Rachel.

"This whole thing is such bullshit," Rachel hissed. "Chris is such an asshole."

"Okay, who are you and what have you done with Rachel?" asked Ruth.

Rachel smiled, although it might have been a smirk. Ruth was still a little too disorientated to tell.

"Very funny," said Rachel. She turned to the corner. "How's Mary doing?"

"I mean it," said Ruth. "What have you done with Rachel?"

Rachel took a step back. She crossed her arms, the body language of the Rachel that Ruth had come to know and hate. "I play the game, Ruth. That's all. Hate the game, don't hate the player. Now, do you want this stuff or not?"

Ruth may not have trusted Rachel, but she wasn't going to turn down breakfast and clean underwear. She took the bag as Rachel held it out. "Thanks."

"You're welcome," said Rachel, sounding half bitchy and half sincere.

"So if you're just playing the game, how come you're still here? You could walk out any time you want to."

"I could, but where would I go? My parents still don't want anything to do with me. If I leave here I get fifty bucks and a bus ticket home. How long do you think that would last?"

Ruth saw Rachel's point. "But you'll have to leave some time?"

"I guess," said Rachel. "I'm working on a few things. Making some plans."

Ruth peered into the bag. Rachel hadn't lied. It was crammed full of stuff. Ruth even glimpsed a pack of cookies that she knew were Mary's favorites.

"Look, I know I'm a bitch," Rachel said. "And that's not me acting. Not all the time anyway. This place has been hard on me too. It's set up so that we're against each other, but I'm not making any excuses for how I've been." She turned back toward the barn door. Before she stepped back outside, she stopped. "I'll be back at lunchtime, if they let me. Make sure you hide any of the stuff I shouldn't have given you."

CHAPTER THIRTY-SIX

C HRIS HAD ALL THE BOYS in Ty's new dorm line up against the far wall. He reeled off their names as each boy took his turn to step forward. They ranged in age from around thirteen all the way up to seventeen. Apart from one African-American and one Asian, they were white.

Like the other kids Ty had seen at Broken Ridge the previous day, they all looked to be in good physical health. Again, Ty figured that a lack of junk food, and regular exercise, coupled with sunshine and fresh air, would take care of most things.

"Gentlemen, this is Mr. Cross. He's going to be your dorm father, starting today." Chris picked out the oldest-looking kid from the line. "Lewis, can you help Mr. Cross with any questions he might have?"

"Yes, sir," said Lewis.

"Lewis here is at level six," Chris explained to Ty, then turned back to the boys. "Mr. Cross here served our country in the Marine Corps, so he's going to be firm but fair."

Ty had suspected that Chris would work in that detail. It was kind of embarrassing. Some guys he knew went out of their way to mention their service. Ty wasn't one of them. If someone asked, or it came up in conversation, that was one thing.

Chris tapped Ty's elbow. "Okay, I'll leave you to it. If you need me, just holler."

"Thanks."

Ty already had the schedule for the day. Apart from Sunday, when the students had to attend church and write letters home, it was the same schedule every day. The idea was to get the students into a routine. Whatever else might have been wrong with the place, giving young people a routine wasn't the worst idea. The right routine created good habits.

The problem was that, in Ty's experience, good habits that stuck were usually self-generated. When they were imposed on a person they tended to fall away when the imposition stopped. In other words, there was every chance the kids who'd been playing video games and eating Cheetos would go right back to that when they left.

Once Chris had gone, Ty led the boys from his dorm outside. They automatically fell into line, three steps apart, without him having to remind them. He saw them sneaking anxious glances at him when they thought he wasn't looking. There was no question that he intimidated them. That was hardly a surprise. Most people he met who didn't know him, and quite a few people who did know him, were scared of him. Never mind his specialist skills, his Long Beach background, or his status as a retired Marine, a six-foot-five-inch black man with muscles would usually have that effect.

Outside, he took the boys through a series of light stretches and warm-up exercises. As he did so, he explained the thinking behind each exercise and told them which area of the body or muscle group it was working. The warm-up finished, he led his dorm on a run. He kept the pace light. He also made a point of encouraging any stragglers rather than simply barking at them to go faster. He would save the barking for when it was needed. That way it might actually have some impact when he needed to deploy it.

On the way back, he changed up the gears for a hundred yards, making them alternately sprint, jog, then walk. The walking section allowed anyone who had fallen behind in the sprint the opportunity to catch up. He offered more encouraging words to those students he could see were struggling but making the effort.

"Good work," Ty told them, as they stopped outside the dorm building.

He asked them to partner up and took them through a series of push-ups, burpees, sit-ups and planks. Each student took turns to do the exercise while the job of their partner was to count off the repetitions and encourage them along.

Where a student was struggling, Ty reduced the number of their reps. That drew some surprised looks. For some of the older boys, he increased the numbers so that they matched that person's abilities.

Because there was an odd number of boys in his dorm, Ty partnered up with Lewis, the oldest and highest level of the students. If Broken Ridge had a model student, Ty figured that Lewis would be it. A husky, athletic kid, he was polite and deferential without coming across as an ass-kisser.

It was a reminder to Ty that whatever had gone wrong here, and he suspected that he and Lock had only skimmed the surface, a program like this one needn't be all bad. It could get results, given the right material to begin with.

They finished up, and Ty let them go hit the showers, which was the next item on the schedule. He held Lewis back for a moment. "Lewis, is that your first name or your family name?"

"Family name, sir."

"Your first name?"

"Aidan, sir."

"How long you been here?"

"Three years, sir."

"Mr. Fontaine mentioned something to me earlier. The time-out room. What's that?"

Aidan Lewis looked uncertain, like he wasn't sure if he should answer or not.

"I asked you a question, Lewis."

"It's not really a room, sir. It's an old barn. You get put there if you really mess up."

"Ever been there yourself?"

"Yes, sir," said Lewis. "In my first month here. I was pretty out of control. Broken Ridge really saved me."

"So what's the deal with this barn? You get put in there and then what?"

"Nothing, sir."

"So why is it a punishment?"

"It's not the nicest place, I guess. Not very clean. And there's nothing to do. I was only in there a couple of days, but it gets to you pretty quick," said Aidan.

It sounded to Ty like Broken Ridge's version of solitary confinement. "Okay. Well, let's hope I don't have to send any of the guys from the dorm there," he said.

"I don't think you will, sir. They're a pretty good group."

"That's encouraging to hear. Okay, go shower."

Ty watched Aidan leave. He took out his cell phone, and stared at the empty signal indicator on the screen.

CHAPTER THIRTY-SEVEN

LOCK PARKED THE FORD ON a narrow side-street a block away from the Sheriff's Department. He checked his cell phone. No update from Ty. Not even a brief text informing him that everything was running smoothly. Or that it wasn't.

He had one message from Donald Price. He'd left it while Lock had been driving. He'd call him back after this meeting. As of right now, he didn't have any fresh news, and he had a lot of ground to cover today, including a trip out to see the parents of a student who had died while attending Broken Ridge a few years back. Lock wanted to tally their story with the media reports surrounding the death.

He climbed the steps to the front entrance of the Sheriff's Department. According to their website, they had

204

a sheriff and four deputies, plus a support staff of another half-dozen civilians, to cover an area of approximately a thousand square miles. It seemed like a lot of ground to cover with so few people, but the population was sparse. In fact, the staff and students at Broken Ridge probably accounted for about ten per cent of the total number of people residing in the area. Apart from the town itself, and the school, most people were scattered, living in small family groups on vast ranches, or more modest small farms.

Pushing through the main door, Lock walked into a small, fairly informal waiting area. A row of plastic seats was lined up against a wall. They faced a long desk. Doors behind led to the offices.

Lock immediately noted two things that told him a lot about crime in the area—or, rather, the relative lack of it. The plastic seats weren't bolted down. And there was no security screen or other barrier between the waiting area and the main desk where visitors were greeted.

A bored-looking deputy was busy tapping at a slightly dated personal computer. He glanced up as Lock came in. "Man, I wish I'd taken one of those touch-typing classes when I was in high school."

"What stopped you?" Lock asked.

The deputy stared off into the middle distance. From the look of him, high school couldn't have been all that long ago. But he seemed to be having trouble recalling the reason. "Guess I was worried about the other guys teasing me. Girls took that stuff."

"It's never too late," Lock told him.

"Guess that's true. Hey, so how can I help you?"

So far, so congenial, thought Lock. "I'm here to see Sheriff Dwyer."

"You have an appointment?"

"No, I don't," said Lock. "If he's not around, maybe I can arrange to speak with him later." He hadn't wanted to telegraph his visit. He was hoping that if he arrived unannounced, the sheriff's answers to his questions might be a little less guarded. If the sheriff wasn't here, he'd see what he could get from the deputy sitting in front of him. He already had a hunch that this guy didn't have all that much of a filter.

As a rule, the higher up the chain of command you went in any organization, the more circumspect people were about sharing information. Not only because they actually had it, but also because people who were guarded with the outside world tended to rise to a higher rank. At the top, the world was populated with politicians, whether they had that title or not.

"Oh, no, he's around," said the deputy, getting up from his computer.

He took the name Lock gave him, and wandered into the back offices while Lock waited. He took a seat, dug out his cell phone, and dropped Donald Price a quick text to let him know he would call him later with an update, but as of now he had nothing to worry about.

The deputy reappeared. He smiled. "The sheriff will be right with you." He sat down at his computer and went back to pecking at the keyboard.

Two minutes passed before the sheriff himself appeared. It took Lock a moment to recognize him. The picture that was on the department's website must have been taken at least fifteen years and a hundred fifty pounds ago.

"Come on through," the sheriff told him.

Lock was a little surprised that he hadn't yet been asked what he wanted to speak with the sheriff about. He followed the man through to the largest of four offices. The sheriff waved at the chair opposite as he lowered himself into a seat behind his desk. From the mess on it, they might not have had much actual crime in this area but they still appeared to generate a lot of paper. Now came the question.

"What can I do for you?"

Lock had his answer prepared. He was a private investigator from California. He had a wealthy client, who would remain nameless, who was considering sending his wayward son to a number of residential programs. He had been tasked with conducting some informal background checks on each one. More to get a feel for them than anything specific. One of those programs was operating at Broken Ridge.

Across from him, the sheriff shifted buttocks. "Shouldn't you be asking the folks out there at Broken Ridge?"

Lock smiled. "Oh, I will be, but obviously they want the business."

"I hear you," the sheriff said. "Tell you the truth, I only have good things to say about the place. Not that I know everything that goes on, but the kids come into town to do voluntary work from time to time. They're real nice. Good manners. Look like they're well cared for. I'm afraid there's not much to tell. That's the plain truth."

"But not the whole truth," said Lock, shifting up a gear. "There have been some problems with the place."

"Problems?"

Surely no one was this dumb, thought Lock. The three deaths were well documented. Broken Ridge had worked hard to push them down the main internet search engines if you used broad search terms, but they could be found with only a small amount of persistence and savvy. He didn't say anything: he'd let the sheriff fill the silence. Or not. Either way, it would give him an additional measure of the type of man he was dealing with.

The sheriff spoke first. "Oh, you mean . . . the kid who died. Tragic, completely tragic. I really felt for the parents. Can't imagine anything worse than that happening to someone. Y'know, I've had to go inform people of deaths in this job. Doesn't get any easier."

He sounded sincere to Lock, but he was also quickly shifting the discussion from the specific to the general. No doubt he was hoping that Lock would drop it. He was about to be disappointed.

"Are you talking about the death of Jennifer Oates?"

"Oh, yeah, Jennifer Oates," said the sheriff. "That's a name from the past."

Lock was starting to get a little more suspicious. The sheriff was playing this down a little too much for Lock's comfort. He would ramp things up, see where it got him.

"Seven years ago. It isn't that distant."

The sheriff didn't take the bait. At least, not that it showed on his face. "I guess not. But to answer your question, there wasn't anything suspicious. And, believe me, we looked."

"You were sheriff back then?" Lock asked.

"Just elected. Learning the job."

"So you may have missed something?"

That got a reaction. The sheriff shifted buttocks again. The chair he was sitting in creaked at the adjustment. "Are you sure you're here asking questions for someone who's looking to send their kid to Broken Ridge?" he asked Lock, elbows suddenly propped on the desk.

"A young girl dies, that's going to be a cause for concern. Two die plus one staff member is murdered and that's a major red flag. Wouldn't you agree, Sheriff?"

It was the sheriff's turn to try to stare Lock down. Lock let him have his moment.

"I'm just trying to ensure that the deaths weren't suspicious and that it's a safe environment for my client's son," said Lock. "That's all. I apologize if it comes over any different than that."

The sheriff appeared to be studying him from across the desk. "No," he told Lock. "They weren't suspicious. They were both accidents. Well, a suicide in one case. But what you or anyone else has to understand is that, the kids who get sent to Broken Ridge, they already have all kinds of problems. Otherwise they wouldn't be sent there by their parents in the first place."

It struck Lock as a slightly circular argument. But it was one that was well rehearsed by anyone connected to an institution like Broken Ridge that had run into a problem. It was simply an extension, as Lock saw it, of telling parents to expect horror stories from the letters home they received.

"Well, in that case, your word is good enough for me. Like I said, I'm sorry if I came off pushy, but this is a good client of mine, and he wants to make absolutely sure that he finds the right place for his son."

The sheriff switched buttocks a third time, and nodded sagely. Lock rose from his own chair and reached out to shake the man's hand.

"My client's one of those guys that, as much as he doesn't like his son's behavior, if anything happened to him at one of these places . . . Well, let's just say it would get real ugly, real fast," said Lock, turning and heading for the door. "And he has the money to do it."

"Hold on," the sheriff called after him.

Lock turned back.

"Close that door for me, would you? Then come sit back down for a minute."

Lock did just that, easing into the chair. He'd hoped that the suggestion of a scorched-earth reaction to any problems would get this kind of response.

"There was nothing suspicious about any of what happened. But, and this is completely off the record, and stays between us . . ."

Lock stretched his arms out. "Absolutely. It goes no further. All my client wants is a recommendation from me. He's not big into the fine details unless he has to be." Truth be told, Lock was starting to like the sound of his fictitious client. He thought he'd be a lot lower maintenance than the people who actually hired him.

"Here's the thing. The lady who runs Broken Ridge, well, she inherited the place from her father. And he had some quite old-fashioned views about how kids should behave. He was real old-school."

Given that this was all off the record, Lock wished the sheriff would get to the point. "I get it. Old-school."

"And perhaps the place hasn't quite moved on. Not that some of the kids they get don't need discipline. They do. Otherwise they wouldn't end up there. But Gretchen

Applewhite can get a little heavy-handed. At times. Mostly she's very pleasant."

"What are you saying?" Lock pressed. "She has a temper?"

"Yeah, that would be it," said the sheriff. "A temper. Sometimes."

Lock didn't want to push too much more than he already had. He could already sense the sheriff's unease at talking about this. The unease was perhaps more revealing than what he was actually saying. "So perhaps Broken Ridge may not be the best fit?"

"Not what I said. Not my words. And that's not for me to say, really."

Lock rose and shook his hand again. "Thanks for taking the time. I appreciate it."

He walked out past the deputy, who was still pecking away at the keyboard with two fingers. His cell phone rang. Ty's name flashed up on the screen. Finally.

CHAPTER THIRTY-EIGHT

TY STOOD AT THE EDGE of the blacktop, cell phone in hand. He was still sweating from having run all the way down there. He'd told Chris he'd promised to call his girlfriend today. Chris had offered the landline in the ranch house. Ty had politely declined.

Lock took a little time to answer.

"Where are you?" Ty asked him.

"Local Sheriff's Department."

Ty heart sank a little. "Shit."

"What's the problem?"

"I've been trying to get in touch with you to let you know that the local sheriff and Gretchen are tight. Like related tight. Broken Ridge kicks money into the department."

"That would make sense," Lock said.

"They give you a hard time?"

"Not really. But he was kind of reticent about saying anything negative. Listen, I used a cover. Said I was a PI working out of California who was looking at various school options for a wealthy client. Made out that it was a standard background check."

"He bought it?" Ty asked.

"Seemed to. Listen, you have to remember, this isn't LA."

Ty grimaced at that. "No, it's worse. It's easier to ping on these folks' radar."

"Ty, relax. It'll be fine. They're not going to make a connection between you working there, and my showing up to ask a few questions."

"I hope you're right," said Ty. "You know, not much happens round here. Two people they don't know show up at the same time?"

"Okay, look, if you think they're getting suspicious just get out of there."

The suggestion that he run away didn't sit well with Ty. He had never run away from anything in his life and didn't plan on starting now. Plus, it wasn't exactly what he considered a high-risk environment. "Forget it. I'll be fine. And don't worry if you don't hear from me. They have a signal blocker up at the school to stop the kids using cell phones."

"Huh," said Lock. "That sounds kind of over the top."

"Well, they may not be dangerous, but that doesn't mean they're not a little bit out there."

"So how's Ruth? You seen her today?"

"Not exactly, no."

Ty filled Lock in on Ruth and her friend's punishment. Lock was silent until he'd finished.

"Okay, well, keep an eye on the situation as best you can."

"Don't worry," said Ty. "I'm on it."

CHAPTER THIRTY-NINE

LOCK FINISHED THE CALL WITH Ty. He opened the driver's door of the Ford Explorer and got in. Even though he'd parked it in the shade, the interior was boiling hot. He turned on the engine and cranked up the air-conditioning.

For the first time since they'd taken on Donald Price as a client, and promised to find out what they could about his daughter's situation, he had a feeling of real unease. He wasn't overly worried about the connection between Broken Ridge and local law enforcement. At least, not in the way others might have imagined.

It was Ty's mention of the barn that had done it. Jennifer Oates had committed suicide. She had hanged herself. She had tied a rope around a wooden support in the barn, and jumped from the top of the hayloft. Suicide

216

or not, suspicious or otherwise, it was enough to give Lock chills.

Ruth Price was in that same barn.

Chapter Forty

SHERIFF DWYER MASSAGED HIS TEMPLES with the tips of his fingers. He could feel a migraine forming at the front of his skull. He knew what had brought it on. It was the thought of the phone call he had to make.

Maybe she'd be out, or away from her desk. He could leave a brief message, then head out on patrol. With a little bit of luck, she might give up on reaching him. But he would have made the call, so he'd have done his part. Yeah, that might work.

He lifted the phone. The number was already programmed on his pre-set speed dials. He didn't have the name written next to it like the other numbers—his wife, who had as little to do with her sister as she could, their son who lived in Phoenix, the State Police, the local Fire Department—but it was in there nonetheless.

He hit the pre-set button and waited. It started to ring.

Someone picked up. Gretchen. Her voice was unmistakable. She had a very particular voice that she used to answer the phone. It made his skin crawl. It was so fake and phony, just like she was.

"Hello," she sing-songed.

"Gretchen, it's me. I got something I thought you might want to know about. I had a visitor this morning."

****

The phone call took around four minutes. It seemed a lot longer. Gretchen tended to freak out about stuff like that. Even after all these years, people were still turning up and asking awkward questions.

He'd had to explain to Gretchen that was why he'd put the guy off the idea. He hadn't told her over the phone what he'd said about her. He told her that his visitor had thought Broken Ridge's fees were steep compared to some other places.

She had been pissed when he'd said that. But he'd patiently explained to her that she didn't want the child of a parent who was already prone to hiring private investigators at Broken Ridge. She'd agreed.

That had always been the policy: never take into the program a child who wasn't being sent by someone who was completely onboard with how they did things. It cost the school money, but only in the short term. In the long term it was smart business.

He told Gretchen he'd see her at the next family dinner, and not to worry. This PI would go back, report to his client that he should go with a different program at another school and that would be that. Crisis averted.

Gretchen hadn't sounded convinced. She was paranoid. Always had been. Her old man had been the same. Thankfully, his wife hadn't inherited the gene. Only Gretchen had.

Gretchen had hung up on him while he was in mid-sentence. He'd stared at the phone for a moment. "You're welcome."

CHAPTER FORTY-ONE

O
N THE DRIVE OVER TO speak with the parents of Jennifer Oates, Lock called Don Price. He answered almost immediately. Whatever anyone thought of the man, including, and perhaps especially, Don's ex-wife, Lock had never doubted the man's love for his daughter.

"What do you have for me, Ryan? How's Ruth?"

Lock had been dreading this question. But there was no way to avoid it. What other question was her father going to ask?

The problem was that from early on, almost as soon as he had retained their services, Don Price had been pushing for a more forceful intervention. One that involved taking Ruth out of Broken Ridge without either his wife's or the school's permission.

221

Like Lock, Don Price's attorney had told him it was a crazy idea. His wife had custody. She had assigned just under half of that to Broken Ridge, as was the industry standard with these places. That meant any attempt to remove Ruth, without her mother's say-so, would be regarded as a serious matter by the authorities. In short, and somewhat ironically given how Ruth had been taken there, it would be seen as abduction. With all the legal ramifications that carried.

As soon as Broken Ridge knew that Ruth was missing, they would contact law enforcement. If Don Price was lucky they would be picked up before they crossed the state line and it became a federal case.

His best bet would be to get Ruth out of the United States. But even that wasn't without risk. There were extradition treaties and the US authorities had a very long, powerful reach. Which Don Price would have known, given his current work and status as a high-level employee with the State Department. Not only would he lose his job, and possibly his pension, he'd be a fugitive from justice. Until he was caught. And then he'd be in prison.

Of course, Lock knew that Don was aware of all of these things. But he was desperate, and desperate people often did foolish things. They also had a tendency, in Lock's experience, to be impulsive.

Lock had outlined a different strategy that didn't involve directly breaking the law so much as pushing at the edges. First, he had asked Don Price to let him and Ty establish whether Ruth was in harm's way. If she was, they would gather evidence, and present it directly to Don's wife. If she didn't respond by removing Ruth from Broken Ridge, they could then go to the relevant authorities, and to court to try for a legal remedy. If all that failed then, and only then, Lock would discuss the other, extra-legal, options open to them.

Reluctantly, Don Price had agreed. Like any concerned parent he didn't want to see his child go through any more torment than she absolutely had to. Lock got that. But first they had to establish that she was at risk. Maybe it was, as Ty had argued originally, not the worst thing in the world to be sent to be a place like this.

The reality, though, as Ty had quickly discovered, was less certain. There was discipline, and creating boundaries, neither of which was bad. And then there was manipulation and exerting psychological control to create short-term results with potentially damaging effects in the long term.

With all that in mind, Lock chose his next words with care. "Ruth doesn't appear to be in any immediate danger. She's in good shape physically. Overall, she seems to be holding up well, but we have some concerns."

Don Price began to interrupt, but Lock quickly cut him off: "In any case, Ty is on the inside now, and he's not going to allow anything to happen to her or any of the other kids in there. You have my word on that."

"What are your concerns?" Don Price asked.

Now Lock had to be even more careful with what he said. It was important that he chose the right words. At the moment, Donald Price was a loaded gun. The last thing Lock wanted to do was say the wrong thing, and flick off the safety.

Lock took a breath. "Our main concern is that the program at Broken Ridge may be detrimental to her well-being in the long term. If she stays there long enough."

"Come on, Ryan. Why don't you just come out and say what you have to say without all this dancing around? I've been in D.C. long enough to know when someone's trying to BS me."

"You told us Ruth is quite a sensitive kid, correct?"

"Yeah," said Don. "She has that whole teenager outer shell thing going, but she's sensitive to stuff, always has been. When she was growing up there were times I'd wish she was a little tougher, but that's not who she is."

"Okay. Well, from what we knew already, and Ty's now seen, this isn't a place best suited to kids who don't have a thick skin," said Lock.

"I knew that already. That's why I called you in the first place."

Lock could hear the frustration in Don's voice. It was tough to know whether it would be better to level with him, or whether that would be lighting the blue touch-paper. When he was placed in this kind of situation with a client, he usually asked himself how he would want someone to handle the situation if their roles were reversed. In this case it wasn't a hard question to answer. He'd want honesty. He'd want the truth. Even if it was hard to handle.

"Okay. She's not playing by their rules and they're punishing her for it."

The frustration that had been in Don Price's voice switched to something else. Panic. "What do you mean, punished? If one of those assholes has laid a finger on her, I swear, I'll—"

"Hold on. No one's touched her. That's not what I'm saying."

"Then how has she been punished?"

Lock told him about the barn, dialing down some of the details that Ty had given him. He emphasized to Don that she was with another girl, so she wasn't alone. They'd be able to look out for each other.

Don Price listened in silence. He was so quiet that, for a moment, Lock thought the call might have dropped.

"Like I said, she's not in any immediate danger, but it's not good either."

At the other end of the line, he heard Don exhale. "I think I should be there."

That was what Lock had worried about. The last thing they needed right now was Donald Price marching to the rescue. It would be a disaster. He would be arrested, Ruth would be sent back, and they would no longer have a clue about what was going on.

"Don, you know you can't just turn up there like the cavalry. That's not how it would work. We have to stick with our strategy. Gather evidence. Present it to Sandra, and if that doesn't work, present it to a judge."

"You think my ex didn't know what that place was like before she sent Ruth there?"

In any argument there were three sides. One side, the other side, and then the truth. For a divorced couple at loggerheads over how to raise a teenager that went double, maybe even treble.

"What it was really like? No, I'm not sure she did." Lock wasn't lying. He knew that Don was convinced his wife had punished Ruth to piss him off. Lock didn't doubt that there might have been something in that. But he also knew that the troubled-teen industry was extremely persuasive, with some very slick marketing. The kind of marketing that came with a multi-billion-dollar income stream.

"She's punishing me by punishing Ruth," Don said.

Lock didn't buy that. Of course people used kids during or after a divorce or separation. That was undeniable, not to mention commonplace. But very few mothers would place their daughter in harm's way to make a point, or for revenge.

"Listen to me," Lock said. "Our best chance here is to gather the evidence, then present it to Ruth's mother."

"I still think I should come down there."

"And I can't stop you. But I can advise strongly against it. You hired us to do a job. Let us do it. If our approach doesn't work, we can talk about doing things differently. But you have to let us try this first."

There was another silence. This time Lock took it as a sign that he might have gotten through. "Agreed?" he prompted.

"Okay," Don Price said finally.

"Good. If there are any new developments, I'll let you know immediately."

"Ryan?"

"Yeah?"

"Tell me I'm doing the right thing here."

CHAPTER FORTY-TWO

ARY HADN'T EATEN. HER PORTION of the food Rachel had brought them lay on the floor, untouched. Ruth knew this wasn't like her. Even when she was down, or depressed, Ruth hadn't seen her leave a meal. She was usually a comfort-eater. Ruth didn't blame her for that. There were so few actual pleasures here that food became really important to a lot of people.

She stood by the small window, staring into the far distance as she wondered what to do with the leftovers. She herself was full, and she couldn't just leave it in case it attracted more vermin. Someone would be here with lunch soon, too.

Ruth bagged it all up as best she could. Maybe she could hang the bag somewhere. She didn't like the idea of giving it back. Not when they were stuck in here by themselves, and relying on other people for food.

"You're definitely not hungry?" Ruth asked her.

Mary didn't reply. She kept staring straight ahead. That wasn't like her either. To shut Ruth out. To not eat.

"Mary?"

Still nothing.

Ruth walked over to where she was standing. "View kind of sucks."

No reaction to that either. Mary didn't look at her. It was as if nothing was registering anymore.

She decided to try something else. "I need you to be here for me too," she told Mary.

That got a reaction. Slowly, Mary turned her head to look at her. "This would be easier for you if I wasn't here. It would be easier for everyone."

CHAPTER FORTY-THREE

L OCK HAD BEEN SURPRISED TO find Jennifer
Oates's family living so near to Broken Ridge. It
was a little over an hour's drive away. In this part
of the country, with its vast spaces, and meager
population, that qualified as close by.

He used the time alone to work through a range of
scenarios and how he would manage them. If it came
down to it, and Ty thought that Ruth Price was in
immediate danger, they could remove her from Broken
Ridge. Perhaps they could even use what they already
knew about the place as leverage. Leverage that would
ensure law enforcement wasn't involved.

Ruth would have to be returned to her mother. Lock
would insist upon that. He would even help Don's ex-wife

to find an alternative program for her daughter. One that checked out.

****

At the house, Lock parked up next to a black Minivan, and got out. Two dogs greeted his arrival, running alongside the car, tails wagging, excited at the arrival of a visitor.

Jennifer's mother, Patricia Oates, was standing on the porch, waiting for him. The dogs hurtled around his ankles in circles, wrestling with each other, as he picked his way through the canine mayhem.

Patricia called them to her. They raced up the steps and onto the porch. Lock followed at a more sedate pace.

"Sorry about them. We don't get many visitors."

"No problem. I'm a dog guy," said Lock. "Thank you for taking the time to see me. I appreciate it."

Patricia Oates nodded. "Please, take a seat."

Lock sank into a chair as Patricia sat down opposite him, the two dogs arranging themselves at her feet, tails still wagging.

"Sorry," she said again. "Can I get you anything? Coffee? Some water? Juice?"

"No, thank you. I don't want to take up too much of your time."

"You wanted to ask me about Jenny?"

"Yes," said Lock. "Is your husband joining us?"

"No, he's out. Visiting with a friend."

231

He quickly gave her the same story that he'd sold the sheriff. This time he felt bad about the deception.

"I would say your client should keep looking," Patricia told him. "I wouldn't recommend that place to my worst enemy. Not after what happened."

This was the part of the conversation that Lock had been dreading. He knew how hard it must be for the woman to revisit the events surrounding her daughter's death. It wasn't something he would ask anyone to do lightly. Lock had his own ghosts. He understood how painful losing someone close to you was. It was an agony like no other. "I know this is difficult for you," he said, "but if you wouldn't mind, I'd like to ask you about the events surrounding your daughter's death."

Her look sharpened. "Why?"

"Because since I started looking into Broken Ridge on behalf of my client, I've become concerned that anyone is sending their child there."

That wasn't a lie. He was. Once you peeled past the glossy brochure and slick website, there was a lot to be concerned about. It wasn't just Broken Ridge either. There were plenty of institutions like it, some public, but most of them private.

Patricia sat back in her chair. "That's good to know. For the longest time we were told we were being paranoid. That we just wanted to find someone to blame."

"I've read the official accounts," he told her, "but I'd like to hear what you believe happened with your daughter."

She got up from the chair. "In that case, you'd better come inside. I'm going to need something a little stronger than coffee."

Lock followed her into the house. He sat in the living room and petted the two dogs as Patricia made him coffee and got herself a glass of wine. He didn't condone middle-of-the-day drinking, but he could hardly blame her for needing the prop.

He studied the silver-framed family photographs scattered around the room. Jennifer featured in most of them, either with her mom, her dad or her older sister, or all of them together as a family group. As a collection, there was an eerie quality to them. Jennifer remained in freeze frame at the age she had died, while in later photographs, everyone else had aged, put on weight, and gathered wrinkles. Fashions changed. Time moved on. Only she remained the same.

Patricia emerged from the kitchen with a mug of coffee and a glass of white wine. She handed the mug to Lock.

"Thank you."

The dogs rearranged themselves at her feet as she sat in a club chair next to the empty fireplace. "Jenny's father is suffering from Alzheimer's. Half the time he still thinks she's alive." She sighed. "I don't know whether it's a blessing or a curse."

"I'm sorry to hear that."

"He took what happened really hard. He blamed himself. He was the one who thought sending her there would be good for her."

Lock could imagine how the guilt of that decision would weigh on someone. Not that her father would have imagined any of what followed.

"I tried to tell him he couldn't have known," Patricia said. "But what was the point? He'd already convinced himself that it was his fault."

"And now?"

"He still thinks she's there."

"At Broken Ridge?"

She nodded.

Lock sipped his coffee. He had questions, but he was having trouble getting to them. Coming here, sitting in this room with a woman who had lost her daughter and had partly lost her husband, seemed intrusive. "Your other daughter?" he said finally.

"She lives in Phoenix with her husband. She doesn't like to talk about it."

"She was older?"

"By three years. They were close, but very different."

"Different how?"

"Well, Lacey was very well behaved. Good grades. Never acted out. Never argued with us. Never gave us any cause for worry. Just very level-headed."

"And Jennifer?"

234

Patricia took a gulp of wine. She cleared her throat before she spoke. "Excuse me." She had another sip of wine. "Jennifer was wild. Even when she was little. You know how toddlers can have tantrums? Well, she was like that right through. Don't get me wrong, she could be a sweetheart. But she acted out. And when she hit fourteen, fifteen, it went to a whole other level. Drinking. Parties. Boyfriends. That was why we decided we had to do something. We just couldn't cope anymore."

It was a familiar story to Lock. Some kids were just wild. It wasn't necessarily their parents' fault. That was simply how they were. For most it was a phase. But if you were a parent or guardian coping with it, there was no way of knowing that. Not when you were in the middle of the storm.

"It put a strain on our marriage," continued Patricia, "and it was starting to affect Lacey. Then, about three months before we sent Jennifer to Broken Ridge, three of her friends were killed. They'd been drinking and took someone's car without permission. It really freaked us out. It could have been Jenny in that car. That was when we felt like if we didn't do something we'd not be doing our job. We didn't have the know-how, so we tried to find people who did."

"I don't think anyone would blame you for making the decision you did," said Lock.

"Ironic, huh?" said Patricia. "We sent Jenny away to stop something bad happening to her."

235

"Tell me about your experience of Broken Ridge," Lock asked.

Patricia shrugged. The dogs at her feet stirred a little before settling themselves again. "They said all the right things. All the things that people in our position wanted to hear."

"Which were?"

"That we'd made the right decision by contacting them. That they'd dealt with far worse situations. That they could turn Jenny around. That they could get her back on track. Everything we wanted, they promised. So, we remortgaged our home and drove her there ourselves." Patricia put down her glass of wine on a side table. "She cried the whole way. Told us she'd behave. It was the hardest thing I ever did, leaving her there." She stopped to correct herself. "Second hardest."

Lock guessed that burying her daughter took the number-one spot. Not that he needed to ask or that she needed to say it out loud.

"That was part of the reason we moved out here. So we could be closer to her after she died. Does that sound crazy?"

He shook his head. "No. It sounds human."

She was close to tears now. Much more wine and Lock wasn't sure how much he'd be able to get out of her before she broke down entirely. "Can I ask you what you think happened to your daughter?"

She looked up at him. The tears began to dissolve, evaporating in anger. "I think they killed her."

"You mean drove her to kill herself?" Lock said.

"No. I think she was murdered, and they tried to make it look like suicide."

CHAPTER FORTY-FOUR

GRETCHEN PUSHED OPEN THE DOOR, and walked into the room. Her hands were already slick with sweat. But she couldn't be at rest until she had done this. She had to know.

It was too much of a coincidence. Or was it? All she knew was that she couldn't risk having a spy in their midst. Not right now.

She had made a promise to her father before he died that she would continue his good work. That she wouldn't allow anything, or anyone, to disrupt what he had started. He had warned her then of dark forces who would try to do just that. He had been right. They would.

Gently, so it didn't make a noise, she closed the door behind her. She took a deep breath. How would she explain being there if someone walked in? She'd think of something. She could tell them she wanted to make sure everything was as it should be. That their newest member of staff had everything he needed. Yes, that would work.

She crossed quickly to the other side of the room. She bent down, and opened the bag. All the while she listened for footfalls beyond the door.

It was quiet. Everyone was either in class or finishing lunch. That was where he would be. As long as she was quick no one would suspect a thing. And what was wrong with what she was doing anyway? It was in the best interests of everyone to make sure they weren't harboring a troublemaker.

Her hand slid inside the bag, pushing away the clothes that lay neatly folded on top. She touched something hard. Plastic. A box of some kind.

Her breath caught in her throat as she lifted it out and laid it on the floor. It was locked. But she knew what was inside. She wasn't stupid.

She placed it back in the bag. She placed the clothes on top. She opened one of the side pockets, and peered inside.

More evidence.

Her instinct had been right.

The question now was how best to handle this. Confront him with what she'd found? Call the sheriff? Terminate his employment?

None of those seemed satisfactory. Someone coming here to spy on them deserved to be punished. To be made an example of so that perhaps in future anyone else would think twice.

She had dealt with troublemakers before. Pushing them out often caused more problems. They went to the press. They agitated. They told lies and made up stories.

No, she would bide her time. She would watch the watcher.

She started at the sound of someone outside in the corridor. Quickly, she closed the side pocket, and stood up.

Whoever was outside walked past. The box she'd found troubled her. It meant that whoever this was meant business. She knew what she had to do. She would take it with her. See if they challenged her when they noticed it was gone.

She went back to the bag. Her hand reached inside, feeling for the carry handle.

CHAPTER FORTY-FIVE

TY FIGURED HE HAD ABOUT twenty minutes of free time between finishing lunch and being back in the dorm classroom to supervise the boys' study. Enough time to go check out the barn.

He got up from the table where he'd been sitting with the boys from his dorm. Chris saw him, and stood up too. "Hey, how you finding it so far?" he asked Ty.

"Good," said Ty, trying to close the conversation down. He dumped his tray on one of the metal racks, and headed for the door. Chris followed him. It was like having a shadow.

"You got a minute or two? I wanted to ask you a couple of things about being in the Marine Corps."

"I'm kind of busy now, Chris. Catch you after dinner?"

"Sure, sure. It's no biggie."

Ty strode past him and out of the dining hall. He headed down the corridor, pushed open the door and emerged into the bright sunshine. He hung a left, skirting around the outside of the building, and started toward the barn.

He was taking a risk. If he was seen, it would appear suspicious. Especially as he had already run down to the road to make a call earlier in the day.

If anyone asked him about it, he would blame his natural curiosity. He was pretty sure that Chris would buy that. Chris would probably buy any line that Ty fed him. As long as he was back in time to take care of his duties, he didn't see why there should be a problem.

About two hundred yards from the dining hall he heard someone calling after him. "Hey! Wait up!"

He turned to see Rachel. She was carrying a couple of canvas shopping bags and heading toward him. He stopped to allow her to catch up. "Where you headed?" she asked him.

He noticed that she was wearing makeup. A smear of lipstick and some eyeliner. He was fairly certain the girls were prohibited from having makeup in their possession, never mind putting it on. "Just stretching my legs," he said. "You?"

She held up the bags. "Taking Ruth and Mary some lunch. Want to come with me?"

The perfect alibi. Ty smiled. "Sure, I can do that."

They began walking. "You want me to carry those?" he asked her.

"Thanks." Rachel beamed. "You're probably a lot stronger than me."

There was a vibe off her that made him uncomfortable. It was the way she looked at him. He wouldn't have minded if she'd been ten years older. But she wasn't. She was still a kid, whether she realized it or not.

Ty took the bags, and kept moving. She struggled to keep pace with him. That was the idea. It was more difficult to bat your eyelids at someone if you had to run to keep pace with them.

"So, Mr. Cross? You married?"

Oh, boy, thought Ty. This kid is something else. "Nope."

"Girlfriend?"

Ty stopped and turned toward her. "You think you should be asking me personal questions like this?"

"Just being polite," said Rachel, the picture of innocence.

"Uh-huh."

"I dated a black guy back in high school," she said.

Now Ty was really uncomfortable. "Excuse me?"

Her face flushed crimson. "Just saying. I'm not prejudiced."

"I didn't think you were."

"He was older too," she added.

243

Ty put the bags on the ground. "Cut it out. For one thing, I'm old enough to be your father. For another, I work here, and you're a student. Which makes this an entirely inappropriate conversation."

"Maybe you should tell Chris that."

"Tell him what?"

"About me being a student and it being inappropriate."

For a second Ty wasn't sure how to respond. Had she just told him she was sleeping with Chris?

"Although the way he's been looking at you since you arrived," she went on, twirling a strand of hair around her finger, "maybe I have competition. Although I can definitely see the attraction."

Ty let go of one of the bags. His hand shot out and grabbed her wrist. "Cut this shit out right now. You hear me?"

"You're hurting me," she said.

He wasn't holding her wrist that tightly. It would be uncomfortable, but no more than that. "Do you understand what I'm saying to you?"

"Yes," she said.

He kept hold.

"I understand."

He let go of her wrist, and picked up the bag again. "I'll drop these off. Why don't you get back to class, or whatever it is you have next?"

She dug into her pocket. "You'll need this." She handed him a key attached to a small brass fob.

244

She was staring at the ground. Ty felt bad for her. He didn't know what had happened to this kid to make her act out like she just had, but something had. Something that wasn't good. "Go on," he said. "I'm not going to say anything about this."

She looked up. She was close to tears. She gave a little nod, all her bravado stripped away. "Thanks."

She started to walk away. "Hey!" Ty called her back. "It's going to be okay," he told her.

He wasn't sure, because the sun was behind her, but he thought she gave him a smile that looked like the first honest expression that had passed across her face in a long time.

CHAPTER FORTY-SIX

TY COULDN'T BELIEVE THAT ANYONE, least of all a school for teenagers with problems, would think it a good idea to place two teenage girls in a barn with no supervision, then lock the door. What if there was a fire or some other kind of emergency? It went beyond irresponsible. It was downright dangerous. Not to mention what had happened before in this barn, with a girl hanging herself.

He pulled off the padlock, and yanked the barn door open. He called out to the two girls inside. "Hey!"

When there was no immediate response, he walked in.

After the blinding sunshine, it took his eyes a few moments to adjust to the gloom. The place was a mess. He wouldn't have locked a dog in there, never mind a couple of kids.

He glanced over as someone moved to his right-hand side. It was Mary. She walked out of the darkness like a ghost. Her skin was pale, her face drained of color, and her expression was blank. Ruth appeared from behind her. She at least looked normal.

Ty held up the bags. "I brought you lunch."

Mary didn't even look at them. She walked past him, over to the dirty mattresses that were dumped in a corner, and lay down.

Ruth came up to him, and took the bags. "Thank you. We have some stuff that maybe you could take away. Mary wasn't hungry, and I don't want to leave stale food in here."

"Sure," said Ty. "Pack it up, and I'll take it with me."

Ruth went to the other side of the barn, and began unpacking what he'd brought.

"I'm the new member of staff," Ty said.

Neither girl said anything to that. Ty read it as fear. He could appear intimidating at the best of times. They didn't know him. And, on top of all that, they had good reason to be fearful of the staff here. After all, they'd just been locked in a barn for nothing. Ty had learned over the years that if you wanted to establish trust with another person, or an animal for that matter, you did it by actions, not words. Anyone who told another person to trust them tended to come off like a used-car salesman. He walked over to where Ruth was, and began to help her. Mary

247

stayed where she was, mute and withdrawn. After a few minutes, he asked Ruth: "Is she okay?"

Ruth shook her head. "This is the worst I've seen her."

"I'm going to try to speak to someone. See if I can't persuade them to let you guys out of here."

Ruth's expression was one of genuine shock.

Ty didn't blame her. All she had experienced from adults since she'd been taken from her home was harsh treatment and betrayal. She probably sensed some kind of a trap. "I can't promise anything," he continued, "but I'll do my best."

Ruth started as the barn door creaked loudly on unoiled hinges. Chris walked in. "There you are. Rachel told me you were down here."

This time it was Ty's decision to remain silent. Inside he was churning with rage. How could anyone think this was a good idea? This was the way you might treat an enemy, not a couple of kids who hadn't actually, as far as Ty could see, done anything wrong.

Chris headed over to them. He glanced at Mary. "What's her problem?" he said.

All Ty wanted to do right now was send the two girls out, and have them lock him in the barn with Chris for five minutes. See how much of a tough guy he'd be when faced with a grown adult. That was what he wanted to do. But he knew he couldn't. He had to keep playing the role he'd been assigned.

****

The barn door padlocked shut, Ty walked with Chris back up toward the dorm buildings. He wasn't sure how long he could keep this up. When Lock had asked him to go in under cover, he'd anticipated none of this. He'd known the regime at Broken Ridge would be harsh. He hadn't seen anything wrong with that. What he hadn't anticipated was the sadism he'd encountered.

"The barn always gets them," said Chris, with a smile. "They might go in there all defiant but they come out like little lambs."

Or dead, thought Ty.

CHAPTER FORTY-SEVEN

ON THE DRIVE BACK, LOCK turned over in his mind what he'd been told. Did he believe Jennifer's mother? Had her daughter been murdered—presumably, by someone at Broken Ridge? Or had she killed herself? Apart from inside a courtroom, was there even that much of a difference, given the circumstances of what had happened? In juvenile detention centers, in jails, in prisons, there were strict protocols for anyone who was suspected of having a mental-health problem. Even the hint of someone being a suicide risk and they were closely monitored, not locked away in an outbuilding with no supervision.

The outcome had been the same. Jennifer was gone, leaving behind a shattered family.

But if she had been murdered, it had been covered up. And a murder wasn't an easy event to cover up. It involved a lot of people either helping or, at the very least, turning a blind eye. Either way, with Ruth Price inside Broken Ridge, it was bad news.

The real question now for Lock was what to do about it. From what he'd been told less than an hour ago, Broken Ridge was less a place of safety than one of danger. Having counseled Don Price to hold tight, and let them gather intelligence, now Lock wasn't so sure. If it was his daughter, he'd want her out. But that still wouldn't get around the legal issues. It would still be just a stopgap.

Everything hinged on Don's ex-wife. If they could win her over, she could withdraw Ruth with no comeback. She would probably lose most of the money she had already spent – Broken Ridge's policy was to take most of their fees upfront – but her daughter would be safe.

The problem, as Lock saw it, was that she was hardly likely to listen seriously either to her former husband or, for that matter, to someone he'd hired. Lock needed someone to speak with her. Someone who could present the information they had gathered but appear as a broadly neutral third party.

He had someone in mind. He slowed his car, and pulled off the road so that he could make the call.

They answered almost immediately. Lock introduced himself. The person at the other end of the line asked how

251

they could help him. Lock explained that it was more a matter of how he could help them.

"I have a story for you."

CHAPTER FORTY-EIGHT

TY KNEW THAT SOMEONE HAD been in his room as soon as he walked in. They hadn't taken much trouble to conceal the fact. Or, if they had, they were incredibly sloppy. Or he'd interrupted them, and they'd gotten out without him seeing them, which seemed unlikely. It wasn't exactly ransacked, but his bag had been moved, and the zip was still open.

Kneeling down, he unzipped it the rest of the way and dug his hand in, past the clothes lying on top, feeling for the secure carrying case for his SIG Sauer.

Nothing. He peeled away the clothes, laying them on the floor.

Still no sign of it.

Finally, he stood back up, grabbed the bag, turned it over and tipped out the contents.

253

No sign of the case. His gun was gone.

Although he already knew someone had come in and taken it, he did a sweep of the room, then headed out.

Aidan Lewis was walking down the corridor. Ty stopped him. "Hey, Aidan, have you seen anyone going into my room?"

Aidan looked terrified by the very question. Ty knew that staff quarters were strictly off limits to the kids. Not that that would stop your average teenager.

"No, sir," said Aidan.

"Where is everyone?"

"In class. Working."

"Come with me," Ty told him.

Aidan followed him down the corridor and into the classroom. The rest of the boys were sitting, heads down, in silence, dutifully going through their workbooks.

Ty clapped his hands together. "Okay, stop what you're doing and listen up."

They all turned to stare at him. They looked as scared as Aidan had.

"Okay, someone was in my room, and took something from my bag," said Ty. He was looking for some kind of reaction from one of them. A snigger. A flushed face. Some kind of a tell. "If it's returned to me right now, I won't take any further action, and the whole thing will be forgotten."

Now he really did feel like some lame-ass old schoolteacher. But he wasn't sure what else he could do.

All he wanted was the gun back. No one would be able to open the case to get at it, but that wasn't the point. "Anyone know anything about this?"

Blank expressions. No one snuck a look at anyone else. Nothing.

"Like I said, if you tell me now that'll be an end to it. This doesn't have to be a big deal."

It must have sounded strange to a group of kids who were punished if they walked two steps rather than three behind the person in front of them. This was a place where the most minor infraction was made into a big deal. So maybe they didn't believe him.

"Okay, everybody up," Ty said.

The boys all stood. Now they really were scared. One of the younger boys was literally trembling, hands down by his sides, fingers drumming against his legs. That was too bad. Ty needed to find that gun case, and fast.

"Follow me."

They went out of the classroom, down the corridor, and into the dorm room. "Okay, I want everyone to stand by the bed of the person who's to their immediate right and look under their bed, then check their locker."

They shuffled into position and began to search. Ty stood in the doorway and watched.

"We're looking for a hard black plastic carry-case about this tall and this wide," he said, showing them the broad dimensions with his hands.

Gretchen's voice came from behind him. "Is everything okay here, Mr. Cross?"

CHAPTER FORTY-NINE

As Lock turned into the motel parking lot, he noticed a Sheriff's Department cruiser parked outside the office. Sheriff Dwyer was walking out. He waved at Lock, flagging him down. Lock pulled alongside the cruiser and got out.

"Didn't think you'd still be here," said the sheriff, with a smile.

Lock returned it. "Just taking my time with everything. I'm very thorough."

The sheriff tugged at the brim of his hat. "Good to know. Well, you have a safe journey home."

"Thanks," said Lock, getting back into the Explorer as the sheriff got behind the wheel of his own vehicle.

Lock watched him reverse out of the bay, pull a U-turn in the parking lot, and head back onto the road. The manager was by the window of his office, watching the sheriff leave. When he saw Lock looking at him, he ducked out of sight.

****

Parking in back, Lock headed to his room. He opened the door and stepped inside. A quick check confirmed his suspicion that someone had been there since he had left. Not that there was anything incriminating for them to find. Lock had made sure to take his gun, and laptop computer, with him.

Nothing was missing. Nothing was damaged. But the message was clear. Both from this and what the sheriff had said. They would prefer it if Lock packed up and got out of town.

Sadly for them, they were going to be disappointed. He thought about talking to the manager, but there would be no point. If he had let the sheriff into Lock's room, which was the most likely scenario, he wasn't going to admit it. If Lock challenged him directly, he'd only get himself kicked out. It was best left alone.

Lock headed back out. As he drove past the manager's office, he gave him a friendly wave. The manager nervously returned the favor, the look on his face all but confirming Lock's suspicions.

The sheriff turning up to search his room told Lock that someone was concerned. Which meant they had something to hide. Or something to lose. Very probably both.

So, he was not going to leave anytime soon: he was going to poke the hornet's nest a few more times, see what reaction he got.

CHAPTER FIFTY

TO RUTH'S RELIEF, MARY SEEMED to have rallied. Whatever catatonic state she'd plunged into had lifted as quickly as it had descended. Where there had been dark, brooding storm clouds, there seemed now to be blue skies. Not only was Mary talking, she had helped Ruth sweep the barn with an old broom they had found at the back of the hayloft. They'd also found a pack of playing cards at the bottom of the bag the new member of staff had brought to them. That was an inspired gift. Now that they had gotten past the shock of being locked in there, Ruth had realized that the great enemy they faced was boredom.

They spent the afternoon playing endless games of Crazy Eights and Hearts. The time passed much quicker. Mary's mood seemed to improve with every game.

For once, they were free to talk without fear of anyone reporting what they said to Gretchen or another member of staff. Mary wanted to talk about the injustice of it all. Ruth tried to steer the conversation toward what they would do when they left. Whenever that was.

"You're not scared about leaving?" Mary asked her.

Ruth studied the cards she was holding. "Scared? What do you mean?"

"I get scared that I won't be able to cope."

"You will. You're a lot stronger than you think," Ruth said, trying to reassure her. Although she wouldn't admit it, she knew what Mary was getting at. Here, everything was decided for you. From the time you got up until the time you went to bed, every waking moment was scheduled. You didn't have to make any decisions.

The outside world was different. It was full of decisions. Punishment wasn't just being locked in this old barn. It was the removal of all that structure.

But they had coped. It had been rocky, but they had come through.

Mary shook her head at the suggestion. "No, you're strong, Ruth. I'm not. I'm really not."

"You are! Look how you were when we were put in here, and look at you now."

The sadness flickered across Mary's face again. She started to tear up. Ruth's heart sank. She put her arms around her friend and hugged her tight. "This will all be over soon. I promise you."

261

Mary pulled away. She tried to smile. "I know."

They both turned toward the barn door as the padlock rattled. A second later a wedge of late-afternoon sunshine splashed across the floor. Rachel walked in, laden with another bag.

Ruth and Mary got to their feet. Rachel came over, put the bag down on the ground and gave them both a hug. "How are you doing?" she asked.

"Okay. Thanks for the cards," Ruth said.

"No problem. I can't stay too long. Everyone's going nuts up there. Apparently someone went into that new guy's room, and stole something. Gretchen's out for blood."

"At least we can't get the blame for that," said Mary.

Rachel looked at her. "You're feeling better."

Mary brightened again, the mini meltdown of a few moments ago forgotten again. "Yeah."

"Okay. Well, look, I'll come back in the morning. There's enough to get you through until then."

Ruth handed Rachel the bag they'd been brought at lunchtime. "Hey, what got stolen? Does anyone know?" she asked.

"No idea. But they're losing their minds over it. I know this place isn't great, but right now it's better than being up there."

Rachel headed back out. The door closed. The padlock clicked back into place.

"I'm going to take a nap," said Ruth. "Then we can have something to eat, and play more cards."

"Great."

Ruth walked over to the mattress in the corner and lay down. She'd found sleeping hard while Mary was still so on edge. She hadn't trusted her not to do something stupid.

A few minutes after closing her eyes, she had dozed off.

****

Mary waited until she was sure Ruth was asleep. Quietly she opened the bag that Rachel had brought them, and began to search through it.

She found what she was looking for at the very bottom. She pulled it out, handle first.

She ran the pad of her thumb along the blade. It wasn't very sharp. She pressed down harder until she pierced the skin. She squeezed her thumb against the side of her index finger until blood blossomed in a thin line. She closed her eyes. Her thumb pulsed with pain. She smiled to herself. It wasn't a good feeling, but somehow it was comforting. She wiped the smear of blood away, and looked around for somewhere she could hide the knife.

CHAPTER FIFTY-ONE

I T WAS A SMALL ENOUGH town so it hadn't taken Lock too much time to find out where the little old lady who had scolded Ty lived. He parked one street over, and walked to the house. He climbed three wooden stairs to the porch, and knocked on the front door.

He heard the lady inside before he saw her. She was muttering about having been woken from a nap. It wasn't a great start.

The front door opened and she peered at him through the screen. "I'm not buying anything."

"That's good because I'm not selling anything. I wanted to ask you a few questions about Broken Ridge."

The door slammed shut. He tapped on the frame again. "Ma'am."

"Go away or I'll call the police."

He was fairly sure she was still standing behind the door. He was also fairly certain that she wasn't about to call the police just yet.

Lock put a hand up to the side of the door, and leaned forward so that she would be able to hear him through the door without him having to shout. "Ma'am, my friend's daughter is at Broken Ridge, and he's very concerned for her safety. She was placed there by his ex-wife, and if we're going to get her out of that place, I need any information I can get."

There was no answer from behind the door.

"If you can't, or won't help me, I'll leave and I won't bother you again," he continued. "But I know you have some strong opinions about the place." He gave it a few seconds, turned and started back down the steps. His foot had barely fallen onto the last when he heard the door open again.

"You'd better come on in," she said, holding open the screen door.

Lock walked back up the steps and inside. He followed her into a small but neat-as-a-pin kitchen.

"Would you like something to drink?"

"Water would be great."

She opened the refrigerator and brought out a jug, took two glasses from a cabinet and poured them each a glass. They sat down at the small Formica-topped kitchen table. A grey and white cat scooted out from under it, rubbing

265

itself against Lock's legs before it disappeared through a cat flap.

"So how did you know to ask me about Broken Ridge?" the lady, whom he'd learned was called Miriam Toms, asked him.

"I've been asking around," Lock told her.

She rolled her eyes. "About the school? Bet that's made you real popular."

"Not especially," said Lock. "But I've always thought that popularity was kind of overrated."

Miriam Toms laughed. "You and me both."

Most people he'd asked about Broken Ridge had either gone quiet or feigned ignorance. The vibe he'd gotten was that it wasn't a subject that local people felt comfortable discussing, which was almost always a reliable indication of problems. A well-run school that brought money into an area was usually a source of civic pride rather than secrecy.

"Do you mind if I ask how you came to be so concerned about Broken Ridge?"

She laughed again, this time with an edge. "You don't know?"

Lock shook his head.

"I worked there. As a counselor."

It all made sense now to Lock. But it also concerned him slightly. If she was a disgruntled former employee she might have an axe to grind. Her objectivity could be called into question. "How long were you there for?"

"Three years, which, believe me, was more than long enough. I only stayed as long as I did because I liked the kids. And I thought that if I was there then perhaps I could be a moderating influence on that crazy bitch Gretchen Applewhite. Pardon my language."

The apology wasn't needed, but she didn't seem to him the kind of woman who wouldn't used such a word without there being some pretty strong emotion behind it. He wanted to ask her about Jennifer, whether she'd been there for that incident or, if not, whether she'd heard anything. But that could wait. He didn't want to spook her.

Instead, he asked, "What did you see that concerned you?"

She got up from the kitchen table and headed toward the living room. "We need a drink. If you don't then I definitely do."

****

Miriam Toms spent an hour giving him a run-down of what she had experienced at Broken Ridge. Most of it Lock had heard before, if not in relation to Broken Ridge then to one of the other thousand or so private schools of its type.

What surprised him was that so much bad practice could be concentrated in one place. If these schools could be dysfunctional then Broken Ridge would be the poster child. From punishments that would be ruled illegal in a county, state or federal prison to all kinds of abuse by staff members that should have seen them in court, to straight-up psychological manipulation and brain-washing that might not have been illegal but was certainly unethical, Miriam Toms related it all. With the kind of detail that made her highly credible.

Most alarming of all, it was clear from what she described that all of this was allowed to go on because of the school's leadership. There was also a dark undercurrent to it. A line that could be drawn from Gretchen Applewhite's domineering father, who had established the school in the first place, to her and, in turn, to the staff who implemented her philosophy and policies.

"Did you know Gretchen's father?" Lock asked Miriam.

"Not really. Only by reputation."

"Which was?"

"Well, no one round here spent any time with him unless they had to, or there was money to be made."

"Not a pleasant guy?"

"He was pretty aloof, and he had a temper. And he thought, because he ran the school people paid so much money to send their kids to, he was above everyone else."

"And Gretchen?"

"She looked at her father the way most people look at God. I think that was a big part of the problem. Especially after he passed."

"You mean, she's trying to prove a point to herself?"

"That's exactly what I mean. A lot of the stuff that Albert did would be considered cruel but there was some kind of method behind it. Gretchen does stuff because she wants to show just how tough she can be. That's when it gets dangerous there. Anyone even hints at challenging her authority, and she gets rid of them."

"And that's what you did?"

Miriam moved her glass around the tabletop in small circles. For a moment she seemed lost in her past. "Yes, I did. But way too late. I made the mistake of thinking that if I stayed around I could somehow put the brakes on the worst stuff."

"The worst stuff being?" Lock prompted.

"You'd think it would be physical violence. Like once I saw Gretchen totally lose it and drag a girl away from a fire pit session by her hair. But as bad as that sounds, it wasn't the worst thing she did. Not by a long way. The psychological stuff, the bullying, setting the others on one kid like a pack of wolves, that was what really did the damage. And Gretchen was good at that. She could manipulate people better than any politician, and what made it worse was that she seemed to get a kick out of it."

"She's a sadist?"

"I'm not even sure that's an adequate word for what she is. But, yes, she gets a lot of pleasure from seeing other people in pain."

'Was Jennifer Oates one of those people?" Lock asked.

Miriam's expression darkened. "One of them, yes."

269

CHAPTER FIFTY-TWO

T Y WATCHED AS THE FLAMES from the fires danced in Gretchen's eyes as she marched back and forth between the groups of students huddled around the pits

"If the person who stole from Mr. Cross does not come forward, every single one of you will be punished."

By Ty's estimate, her rant had been going on for a full ten minutes. If nothing else, he had to admire her lung capacity. She had barely stopped to draw breath.

Part of him regretted informing her of the theft. But he hadn't had much choice in the matter. Even though his sidearm was in a very secure carry-case – one that would likely take a locksmith to break into – it was still a gun that was in the possession of someone here. Likely a minor. Likely a minor whose behavior was unpredictable. And there was a good chance that it was a minor who wasn't used to handling a gun in a safe manner.

Gretchen stopped next to a group of girls. She tapped them on the shoulder one by one. That was their signal to stand up. She asked them all whether they had taken, or had knowledge of who had taken, Ty's property. One by one, they denied any involvement or knowledge. They sat back down. Even staff members weren't exempt. They, too, had to stand and deny knowledge.

As every person spoke, Gretchen stood in front of them, and stared into their eyes. Because she was shorter than most of the staff, and many of the students, especially the boys, it came off as comical and threatening in equal measure.

When she had asked everyone present, Gretchen walked back across to Ty. She stood behind him. It gave him the creeps. "This man came here to help us, to help each and every one of you, and this is how we have chosen to repay him. Shame on you. Shame on all of you."

Her voice was cracking with emotion. But it seemed forced. Put on. Like a performance by a bad actor.

"Not only do we have a thief among us. We have a liar," she continued. "And a coward. Whoever did this has until tomorrow morning to come forward. If no one comes forward, you will all be punished."

None of the kids said anything. Ty noticed that a couple of the boys in his group were shaking. He guessed that whatever the planned punishment was it wouldn't be fun.

The problem was that none of this actually solved the problem. Ty's gun was still out there somewhere. They couldn't assume that one of the kids wouldn't be able to get it out of the case.

Gretchen had started to walk away from the fire-pit area. Ty got up, and ran to catch her up. "Ms Applewhite?"

She turned. "Yes?"

"Listen, I know that how you deal with this is your call, but would you mind if I made a suggestion?"

Her expression told him that she wasn't looking for any suggestions, but she nodded. "Go on."

"Well, if one of the kids did take it, it has to be here somewhere. If we find it in one of the dorms, that at least narrows down who our thief might be."

It was so obvious that he felt kind of stupid suggesting it. But then again, no one else had. Gretchen seemed more fixated on the punishment she could mete out than in solving the problem.

She folded her arms. Not a good sign. She didn't like her authority being challenged. Not by anyone. She seemed to take it personally. Again, not a good personality trait for someone in her position. The great leaders Ty had worked with over the years had the ability to remove their ego from decisions, or at least keep it in check.

"Very well, then. Have the dorms searched. But they're all going to be punished tomorrow. Whether it's found now or not."

Ty didn't follow that logic, but he wasn't going to argue. All that mattered to him was finding his gun before something really bad happened.

He walked back to the fire pit, and gathered up Chris and the other staff members. The students stayed where they were.

Ty laid out his plan. Each dorm would search their neighboring dorm. That would mean there was less chance of someone deliberately overlooking the gun case if they had taken it, or knew who had.

Chris seemed pretty excited. "That's some Marine-grade thinking right there."

Ty did his best not to roll his eyes. It was the basic application of common sense.

"We could also offer them a little incentive," one of the younger female staff members suggested. "Tell them that whoever finds it will be spared being punished."

A similar thought had already crossed Ty's mind when Gretchen was speaking. If she'd said that whoever 'fessed up would be expelled there would probably have been a line all the way down to the main road.

"Gretchen will never go for that," said Chris.

"Okay, let's stick with the plan we have," said Ty.

273

The staff members broke off to gather the kids from their dorm and begin the search. Ty walked back to his group of boys.

****

An hour later, Ty led his group back out to the fire pits. They hadn't found the gun case. Neither had anyone else. Its location was still a mystery.

The search had turned up a bunch of contraband items, everything from a couple of girlie magazines in one of the boys' dorms to candy. As illicit items went, it struck Ty as a fairly pitiful collection, but Chris appeared pretty stoked.

"Y'see?" he said to Ty. "You can't trust these kids."

Ty was more concerned that the gun case hadn't turned up. It meant that whoever had taken it had gone to considerable lengths to hide it. As far as what they had found went, Ty doubted that some Snickers bars posed much of a threat. The girlie magazines that Chris was tossing onto one of the fires almost made Ty nostalgic for the days before the internet, when the merest peek at a naked woman had been a thrill.

"What about the other buildings?" Ty asked Chris.

"What about them?"

"Well, maybe we should take a look."

"But the students don't have access."

"They could have snuck in."

Chris grimaced. "I don't know. Gretchen really doesn't like anyone going near the ranch house. Not even staff."

"Can't hurt to ask her," said Ty.

CHAPTER FIFTY-THREE

GRETCHEN'S HAND CLOSED AROUND THE SIG Sauer. It was a nice weapon. Well maintained. Not cheap. Neither was the carry-case. It had taken her longer than she'd thought to get it open. In the end she'd had to use a drill with a diamond-tipped bit.

The phone on her desk rang. She put the gun back into its case and shoved it under her desk. She glanced at the phone's display. It was a Washington D.C. number. No doubt some neurotic parent wanted an update on how the kid they had messed up was doing.

Gretchen lifted the phone. "Broken Ridge Academy. Gretchen Applewhite speaking."

"Hi, my name is Susan Kranston. I'm calling from the *Washington Post*," said the woman at the other end of the line.

Gretchen held the phone away from her ear and stared at it.

"Hello? . . . Hello? . . . Are you there?"

CHAPTER FIFTY-FOUR

T Y KNOCKED AT THE RANCH-house door. When no one came, he turned the handle and pushed the door open. "Ms Applewhite?"

No one answered. Off in the distance, he could hear someone talking. It sounded like Gretchen, but he couldn't be certain.

He walked down the corridor, checking rooms as he went. The place was dark and musty. The furniture was old. Ty guessed it was probably the stuff Gretchen's parents had had when they'd first bought the place. He stepped into a living room. There were two couches and a piano. The piano was covered with framed pictures of Gretchen's father. There were several of Gretchen and her sister with him, and one of a woman Ty guessed was her mother.

278

Something else stood out about the photographs. No one was smiling.

Ty walked back out, and continued on down the corridor. Near the back of the house, he reached a closed door. He could hear Gretchen behind it. Her voice was high-pitched and agitated. She was practically screaming: "I'm warning you, missy. I have lawyers!"

Ty hesitated. This didn't seem like a good time, especially as he had just walked in. Then again, what the hell was he scared of? What was she going to do? Give him detention?

He knocked at the door.

On the other side, Gretchen fell silent for a moment.

"I have to go," he heard her say. "I suggest that in future you talk to our attorney."

The door opened. Gretchen stood there. She looked beyond angry, lips thinned, nostrils flared. Her hands were at her sides, bunched into fists.

"Sorry for intruding like this, but I didn't think you could hear me."

"What do you want?" she spat.

"I thought you should know that we've finished searching all the dorms, but we didn't find it."

"I'm not surprised," said Gretchen.

"And why is that?" Ty asked her.

"You're new here. You don't know what these young people are capable of. The deceit. The lies. The manipulation."

279

Gretchen was correct. He didn't think they were that bad. Not from what he'd seen. They seemed like a fairly regular group of kids, with all the good and bad that entailed.

"Anyway, I thought maybe we could search the other buildings."

A fresh tic of irritation flitted across Gretchen's face. "That's what you thought, is it?"

What was this woman's problem? Ty took a breath. "Yes, ma'am. If whoever took my gun case is as cunning as you say, they could have snuck off to hide it. Don't you think?"

"You know, if you'd just told me you had a firearm, I could have stored it for you. I have a gun safe. It's very secure, and hidden from prying eyes."

Ty made a mental note. Not that having a gun safe was anything out of the ordinary. In isolated parts of the country like this, gun ownership was common, often for good reason.

Gretchen bit down on her lower lip. "Anyway, why don't you go check the outbuildings first? The barn. I'll check here."

"If you want to get some sleep, I can check this place for you."

"This is my home, Mr. Cross. I don't want a stranger going through all my things."

Ty guessed that was fair. "I'll go look outside."

"You do that."

Ty walked back down the corridor. Man, the sooner he could finish up and get out of this place the better.

CHAPTER FIFTY-FIVE

L OCK'S HAND FELL TO HIS gun as he parked the Ford Explorer in back of the motel. About twenty feet away, a figure was crouched behind a dumpster. He had spotted them as he was backing into the space. Parking with the front of the vehicle pointing out was just one of many habits that had become engrained from years of working in close-protection security. Situational awareness was another.

Lock got out of the vehicle, making sure to leave the headlights on. He did his best to appear casual. If the person behind the dumpster intended to cause him harm, it was better they believed they had the element of surprise. For now, at least.

He slammed the door, and let out a loud sigh. Just a guy returning to his motel room after a long, frustrating day.

The dumpster was behind him, tucked into a corner of the parking lot. Unless the person was peeking round the side they'd be relying on what they heard to establish Lock's position.

Rather than walking away, in the opposite direction from the dumpster and toward his room, Lock lowered himself as quietly as he could to the ground, and crawled under the Explorer. He scooted round so that he was partially on his side, and facing the dumpster. Now all he had to do was wait.

He drew his SIG from its holster, and punched it out in front of him with his right hand, ready to pick off anyone who showed hostile intent. He had seen one person behind the dumpster. That didn't mean there weren't others.

With his left hand he pressed the button on the key fob that locked his vehicle's doors and activated the alarm and immobilizer. The car chirped. Lock counted slowly down from ten.

At eight, someone peeked quickly around the side of the dumpster. Lock watched as they peeked out again, taking longer this time.

They were looking for him. But not seeing him.

The Explorer's interior lights dimmed. The headlights stayed on.

The person, a man, walked out from behind the dumpster. He was, by Lock's estimate, white, a little over six feet, and in his mid to late forties.

He started toward Lock's vehicle. Lock noticed that he was carrying. As he walked his jacket slid back to reveal a holster.

The man moved another few feet and Lock lost sight of all but his legs. He kept coming toward the vehicle. Lock stilled his breathing, and waited.

Ten feet from the vehicle, just when Lock figured he'd be able to reach out, grab the guy's ankle and take him to the ground that way, the man changed direction. He turned at a forty-five-degree angle, headed for the side of the motel building, and the route Lock would likely have taken to get to his room.

Now he really had to hope that this was a lone operator. If he broke cover with someone else in the parking lot, it wouldn't be good.

He could wait. See if the guy returned after realizing Lock wasn't in his room. Take him out then. But there was no guarantee he would circle back this way.

Lock listened for any other movement. Met by silence, he belly-crawled out on the other side of the vehicle. He got to his feet and, crouching, jogged toward the rear wall. Hugging it, weapon still drawn, he made it to the corner. He listened. Again, nothing save the distant rumble of traffic along the road that ran along the front of the motel.

Punching the SIG out in front of him, he spun out from the corner, and came face to face with the barrel of a gun pointed straight at him. Lock had already begun to squeeze the trigger when he realized whom he was facing.

Lock eased up on the trigger, and lowered his SIG. The man facing him did the same. Both simultaneously exhaled.

"You never heard of calling someone first?" Lock asked Donald Price.

Don looked sheepish. "Sorry. I didn't want anyone to see me waiting for you. Then you'd disappeared and I thought someone might have gotten to you."

Lock didn't know whether to laugh or cry. Things were bad enough without being taken out in a motel parking lot by his own client. "Who? I think you're the only person here apart from me."

Don shook his head. "There was someone else when I arrived. Big guy with a beard. He had a gun too."

CHAPTER FIFTY-SIX

TY WAS TWO HUNDRED YARDS from the barn when he heard the first screams coming from inside. High-pitched. Hysterical.

He sprinted for the barn, covering the ground with long strides. The screaming kept up. Louder. Shriller. Screams that spoke of fear and a rising panic.

It took his mind a moment to process what he was hearing. It wasn't one person screaming but two. Ruth and Mary.

Strangely, the realization sparked a sense of relief. In order to scream, you had to be able to breathe. That meant, whatever was going on inside the barn, both girls were still alive.

Ty kept up his sprint. Arms and legs pistoning, he stumbled only once, reminded, for a second, of just how treacherous the ground beneath his feet could be.

A second later, his heart sank as he remembered that he hadn't picked up a key before he'd come down here. He cursed his own stupidity, but kept running. Before he turned back, if he did, he wanted to figure out what was going on in the barn.

Maybe it was something trivial. A rat. A big one. That could easily send two teenage girls who weren't in the best mental shape into a fit of hysterics.

But something about the sounds they were making told him it wasn't that. It was something altogether more serious.

He made it to the barn and called out to the two girls inside, "Ruth? Mary? You okay in there?"

The screaming fell away. Good news.

"Who's that?"

It sounded like Ruth, but he couldn't be sure.

"It's Mr. Cross. Listen, I don't have a key, but I'm going to get in anyway," he said, jogging to the front of the barn and looking for something he could use to pry open the door.

He wouldn't be able to break the lock, but the barn was old, the wood weather-beaten and worn. It wouldn't take all that much for a man with his strength to splinter it.

A full moon hanging high overhead made the search a little easier. But he couldn't find anything. No spades, or strips of metal. Nothing he could use. He would have to rely on brute strength.

"Step back from the door, okay?"

"Okay. But hurry," Ruth called out.

"Why? What's the problem?"

"It's Mary. She cut herself. It's bad, and I can't get it to stop bleeding."

Ty picked his spot and kicked out hard at the door. There was the satisfying sound of wood splintering as he made contact, but the door held. He took a couple of breaths and went again. Then a third time, a fourth and a fifth.

The sixth kick was the charm. The wood began to crack. A gap opened up that he could get his fingers inside. He wrenched at the door, levering it open even wider.

It still wasn't enough, though. He just couldn't get enough purchase. Splinters dug deep into his fingers and the palms of his hands.

He stepped back and let out one more almighty kick. The door gave way. He shoulder-charged it, forcing his way through and inside.

He was met by the sight of blood. A small kitchen knife, the kind you might use to peel an apple, lay discarded in the middle of the floor. Mary lay on her side on a dirty mattress. Her T-shirt was spattered with blood. So was the top of her jeans. Several fresh wounds ran across her left wrist.

Ruth was kneeling beside her. Her clothes were also soaked in Mary's blood. She flinched as Ty approached.

Right now Ty needed two pieces of information. Where she'd cut herself and how long ago. He knelt down next to the two girls. "Hey, listen, it's going to be okay. You're not in trouble. Not at all. I'm here to help you so you don't need to be scared of me. Ruth? You understand me?"

"Yes."

"Mary?"

Mary pushed herself up into a sitting position and backed tighter into the corner. She was making a high-pitched keening noise. The look in her eyes was primal, like that of a cornered wild animal.

"Mary?" he asked again.

She responded by pulling her knees up into her chest, making herself even smaller. She was beyond scared. Ty turned back to Ruth. "Ruth, I'm going to need your help. What happened here? Did she cut herself or did someone else do it?"

He was fairly certain that it was the former rather than the latter. But this place was nutty enough that he couldn't rule out any possibility.

"She did it herself," Ruth told him.

"Okay. Now, where did she cut herself, and when did she do it?"

"It's her arm." Ruth started to hyperventilate.

289

Ty did his best to keep his tone soothing. "Okay, that's good to know. When did it happen?"

"I don't know. I was having a nap. The noise woke me up."

"How long ago was that?"

"Just now. Maybe a minute or two."

That wasn't the worst answer. If she'd been bleeding like this for a couple of hours she would have been in real trouble. "Okay, Ruth, we need to slow the bleeding. I think Mary trusts you, so I'm going to need you to help me with this."

"Okay," said Ruth.

She still seemed freaked out, but at least she was listening to what he was saying and responding. The hysterics had stopped.

"So what we're going to do is. I'm going to make some fabric strips and you're going to use the ones I give you to press down where Mary's cut."

He crossed to the middle of the barn, picked up the bloodied knife and slashed some strips from the bottom of his shirt. He walked back with a few and showed Ruth what he wanted her to do with them. "Keep as much pressure on as you can, okay? The blood will start to soak through. That's fine. You keep the cloth where it is, and add another strip on top. Don't remove the strips to see if the bleeding has stopped. Just keep the pressure on."

He watched as Ruth took the cloth strips from him and took Mary's arm. She was a fast learner, doing precisely what he'd asked her to do.

"That's good. You're a natural. Now, you keep doing that, and I'm going to go get some help."

Both girls looked panicked. "No!" Mary screamed. "No! They'll punish me."

Ty took a breath. There was no way he was leaving here without these two girls. He was going to accompany them to hospital, whether Gretchen or anyone else agreed or not. And they weren't coming back.

"No one is going punish you. You have my word on that. But I need to get you, Mary, to hospital, and, Ruth, I want you to get checked over too. So I'm going to need to make a call, and the only phone I can use is up at the ranch."

"Okay," said Ruth.

"Sit tight and keep the pressure on her wrist. I'll be as fast as I can."

Ty got up, pushed his way through the broken barn door, and out into the night. All he could think about was getting to the ranch house, making the call, then grabbing whatever vehicle was to hand, loading Mary and Ruth into it, and getting them the hell out of there.

He was so wrapped up in what he had to do, he didn't even register the person waiting for him to emerge. By the time he saw them, and turned, they had already pulled the trigger.

291

CHAPTER FIFTY-SEVEN

GRETCHEN WAS SITTING ON THE porch of the ranch house when she heard the shots ring out. They sounded like they were coming from the barn. She started down the steps, stopped and turned back. If someone out there was shooting a gun, what the hell could she do about it? Especially unarmed and in her robe and slippers.

She pushed through the front door of the ranch house and made a beeline for her office. Inside, she walked quickly to the corner and opened a wooden cabinet to reveal a safe. She knelt down and began to spin the lock. The numbers came easily. Six digits. Her father's birthday.

As the safe clicked open, she thought she heard another gun shot, but she couldn't be sure. She looked inside.

It was gone.

The gun she had confiscated was gone.

Immediately, she knew who had taken it, and why.

Without closing the safe, she turned and ran as fast as she could out of the room. One of her slippers came off as she made it to the front porch. She didn't stop to get it. There was no time.

She cursed her big mouth. Why had she told Chris that Cross was a spy? Why hadn't she just kept what she knew to herself?

This was a disaster. There would be no coming back from this. Not after what had happened to others.

Everything was ruined. Everything she had worked for. That her father had worked for. Blown away.

CHAPTER FIFTY-EIGHT

THE BULLET CLIPPED THE VERY top of Ty's shoulder. Its glancing force spun him round. He let out a grunt, momentarily caught off guard, and dove for the ground as the gun fired again. The second shot was wide and low. It buried into the ground behind him.

Ty got back to his feet. Another muzzle flash burst through the darkness to his left. This time, he didn't wait around. He took off running, moving in an irregular zigzag to make himself a harder target. The more distance he could place between himself and the shooter, the better his chances. He threw up his right hand across his chest, and reached up to his left shoulder. His fingertips grew warm and sticky with blood.

Headlights snapped on behind him, lighting him up. He threw himself to the ground as another shot rang out. A vehicle engine roared into life. Tires spun against the baked ground. The vehicle, a pick-up truck, reversed at speed, and stopped. It stayed put, the rumble of the engine a low, threatening growl.

Ty lay there for a moment. He reached up with his other hand to where he'd been hit. The blood was oozing rather than pulsing. That was the good news. It meant the bullet had hit the top of his shoulder without puncturing an artery. Finally, he struggled back to his feet. He pushed himself forward, powered by sheer adrenalin, and the certain knowledge that if he didn't keep moving he was likely to wind up a dead man.

It was maybe five hundred yards from where he was now to the dormitories. A hundred yards further to the ranch house and the only line of communication to the outside world.

And the two girls were sitting in the barn. With no idea of who the shooter was, or their motive, he had to think about Ruth and Mary's safety as well as his own. Mary was already bleeding, and she had that sprained ankle. Ty already knew that Ruth wouldn't leave her. She was way too loyal to leave her friend to her fate. They would be sitting ducks.

Ty twisted his head round to look at where the first round had caught his shoulder. It was still bleeding, but it seemed to have slowed. The pain was bad, but manageable. He'd experienced worse.

Glancing back toward the pick-up truck from the hollow in the ground he'd found, he couldn't make out the driver. The glare from the headlights was too strong.

He heard the truck door open and slam shut again. The engine was still running. He saw a figure walk away from the pick-up. He stopped.

The figure stood parallel to the truck, about ten yards to the side of the driver's door. The narrowness of the hips, and the broadness of the shoulders told Ty it was a man. But his closeness to the glare of the lights made it difficult to see any more details. Apart from one. His right hand dangled casually by his side. In it was a gun. Ty couldn't be sure, but something told him it was his SIG.

Even with the throbbing pain in his shoulder, he couldn't help but smile at the irony of having been shot with his own weapon. If he didn't die from being shot again, he might just expire from sheer embarrassment.

Suddenly, the man standing next to the pick-up spun round. He was looking back at the barn. Someone was coming out, pushing their way through the shattered door.

Ty did some fast calculations. It was maybe a hundred yards from where he was to the shooter. There was no way he could make a frontal assault without getting caught by another round. Even allowing for the fact that the shooter was a pretty crappy shot, he'd be able to get off at least four more rounds. Each would be from a shorter distance than the previous one. He was almost bound to get lucky with one.

At the same time, Ty couldn't risk the shooter heading for Ruth. She, after all, was Ty's principal. In bodyguarding terms that meant the person whose life he had been charged with protecting. If that included catching a bullet for her, well, it was part of the job description. But maybe he could have his cake and eat it too.

He swept his hands across the ground in front of him. He found a small rock, dug it out of the dirt, scrambled to his feet, and launched it toward the pick-up truck. It fell short, but it had the desired effect.

The shooter spun back round. Ty took off running. Circling forward in a big sweep, outflanking the shooter on his right-hand side, pulling his attention away from the barn, and Ruth.

The shooter's hand came out, and he fired another shot. A puff of dust burst from the ground about two feet in front of Ty.

A better shot from that distance. Bad news for Ty. Maybe the guy was finding his range. Or perhaps his off-target shots had been down to nerves rather than ability. As Ty knew from personal experience, there was a world of difference between hitting a paper target on the range and taking out a real live flesh-and-blood human being.

The ground fell away as Ty kept running. The slope would offer him some protection. He kept moving in a broad sweep. Now he was closing in on the passenger side of the pick-up.

Looking up, he couldn't see the shooter. He had disappeared.

Maybe he had got back into the truck. Or he was hunkered down behind it, waiting for Ty to get into range and fire a shot when he couldn't miss.

Ty hit the ground again. Just because he couldn't see the shooter didn't mean the shooter couldn't see him. Standing in place would have made the guy's job a lot easier than Ty planned on making it.

He could make it out the side of the truck about thirty yards in front of him. He scanned the side window of the cab. It looked empty.

Then he saw the shooter's legs. He was standing on the driver's side. He seemed to be waiting.

Ty stayed put. He looked around for Ruth. She was nowhere to be seen. Maybe she had slipped back inside the barn. Or made a run for one of the dormitories.

The shooter was on the move again. He edged toward the back of the truck.

Ty crawled forward on his hands and knees in the opposite direction. If he could get behind the shooter he'd have some kind of a chance.

The shooter stopped. He switched direction once again. He marched back to the front of the truck. He kept coming. The gun was at his side, but he was heading straight for Ty, who was stuck in no man's land. He didn't have enough distance to make the next shot tough, and he wasn't close enough to rush the gunman. With no cover and no options, it was only a matter of time.

But he had one thing going for him. He could now see who was about to kill him.

Slowly, Ty got to his feet. He held up his arms in surrender. The shooter kept coming toward him, the gun at by his side.

There was no more than twenty feet between them. Ty stood alone, unarmed, and bleeding.

Chris Fontaine kept coming toward him. "Why'd you do it?" he said.

"Why'd I do what?" Ty asked.

Chris stopped and shook his head. "Come on, man. You know. Don't play dumb. Why'd you lie to me?"

Chapter Fifty-Nine

LOCK SLID INTO A CORNER booth at the diner. He made sure he was facing the door. If the bearded man with the gun had been waiting for him, he didn't want to take any chances. Donald Price sat opposite. He glanced at the menu and tossed it back on the tabletop as a waiter headed over.

"Coffee," Don told him.

"Make that two," said Lock.

Apart from theirs, only one other table was occupied. According to the sign on the door, the place was due to close for the evening in another hour.

"So?" said Lock.

Don Price knew what he was being asked. There was only one question to which Lock would want to know the answer. What the hell was he doing there when he'd been told repeatedly to stay away?

"I can't do this," said Don. "I know you've told me I shouldn't interfere, but this is my daughter we're talking about. If something happened to her, I'd never be able to forgive myself."

Lock waited. He wanted to make sure that Don had said everything he had to say before he made any comment. Then he said, "Ty's with her. She's fine."

"Is she? You said yourself that there could be long-term psychological damage. I've read up on some of these places. They use some of the same methods we use to break down detainees at black sites. You think I should just stand by and let them do that to Ruth?"

It was clear that Don wasn't about to be talked round. He hadn't come all that way for a chat. The plan had to change. "Tell me what you'd like to do," Lock said to him.

Don shot him a look that gave Lock chills. "What I'd *like* to do?"

"Okay," said Lock, "Let me rephrase that. What do you want to do?"

Don laid his hands, palm down, on the table. "I want to get Ruth the hell out of there. That's what I want to do. Did you know that a girl around my daughter's age killed herself there?"

Lock glanced out of the window as a Sheriff Department's patrol car pulled into the parking lot and parked up next to his Explorer. For once he found its

301

presence more reassuring than threatening. "Okay," he said. "I'll help you as far as I can."

Don Price glared at him. "What the hell does that mean? As far as you can? I contacted you because everyone told me that you get results. If I'd wanted a Boy Scout working for me, there are plenty of people out there who'd come a lot cheaper than you."

The waiter arrived with their coffee. He set down the two cups and swiftly retreated back to the counter. Right now Don Price was giving off waves of rage.

"Am I allowed to make a suggestion?"

"Go for it," said Don.

"Before we take the nuclear option with all that that entails, let me speak to Sandra. See if I can't persuade her to withdraw Ruth from Broken Ridge."

"There's no way she'll agree to that. Especially not if she knows that I'm the one behind it."

"So, we don't tell her. I can tell her I've been asked to look into the place by a concerned parent and I'm contacting others to see what they've heard. If that doesn't work, I have a reporter at the *Washington Post* doing some digging too. Maybe she could be persuaded to contact your ex."

"And how long would that all take? Listen to me, this has gone on long enough as it is. Every day Ruth's in that place is another day too many."

Lock leaned over the table toward Don. The cruiser was still parked next to his Explorer, but the patrol cop hadn't got out. "You see that cop out there?" Lock said. "You take Ruth out without your wife's permission and he's going to arrest you. You'll go to jail, and Ruth will go right back to Broken Ridge. Why don't you ask me how I know that's how it'll go down?"

"Why don't you just tell me?"

Lock explained about the family connection to the local sheriff, and to the money that Broken Ridge kicked across to the election campaigns.

Don took a sip of coffee. He swiped at his eyes. Lock couldn't be sure, but he thought the other man was crying.

"She's my daughter. I can't just leave her to rot away."

"I'm not asking you to," said Lock. He dug out his cell phone. "Let me call Sandra. If I don't get anywhere, we can talk about the other options."

Don looked at him, his eyes wet. "Okay."

"You're doing the right thing. Believe me, another night or two isn't about to make a difference."

CHAPTER SIXTY

I T WAS NOW OR NEVER. Ruth had never been surer of anything in her life. She didn't know what the argument between Chris and the new guy was about, but it didn't look like it would end well, and when it did there was no way of knowing what Chris would do next.

If she and Mary stayed where they were, they would be sitting ducks. Witnesses to a cold-blooded murder. And there was no way either Chris or Gretchen would allow any witnesses. Broken Ridge would be over.

In the gloom of the barn, Ruth knelt next to Mary. "How's your arm?"

Mary's voice barely rose above a whisper. "I think it's stopped bleeding."

"Okay, that's good, because we need to get out of here."

"I can't," said Mary. "My ankle still hurts. I'd only slow you down."

Ruth reached down and hauled her to her feet. "I'm not leaving you."

Mary didn't move. Ruth reached over and pushed away a strand of hair that had fallen over her friend's eyes. "Listen to me. If we don't get out of here, we're dead. You understand?"

Something flickered across Mary's face. It looked like fear. As far as Ruth could see, that was good. Mary hurting herself and talking about suicide was one thing. Actually confronting death was something else. It confirmed to Ruth what she'd suspected all along. Mary's self-harming was a cry for help, not a death wish.

"You don't want to die, do you?" Ruth pressed.

"No."

"Good. And neither do I."

She led Mary gently by the hand across to the splintered door. She could hear the two men talking not too far away, their words drowned in the rumble of the pick-up truck's engine.

"Okay, once we get out, stay close to me, and don't pay any attention to anything else."

Mary nodded, her eyes fixed on the floor. "Where are we going?"

"We'll get down to the road. Then we'll see if we can hitch a ride."

Even to Ruth's own ears it didn't sound like much of a plan. But it was the only one she had.

Keeping Mary's hand in hers, she edged toward the barn door. She squeezed through the narrow gap, pulling Mary with her. Staying close to the barn, they slipped down the side.

Ruth stopped at the corner. She glanced back toward the pick-up truck. Her heart leaped into her throat as she saw Chris standing over the man who had been the only one to help them. He was on his knees, head bowed toward the ground. Chris had the muzzle of the gun pressed into the top of the man's head, his finger poised on the trigger.

CHAPTER SIXTY-ONE

VEN IF IT MEANT WAKING up his ex-wife at an unnatural hour, and perhaps because that was exactly what it would do, Don Price wanted Lock to make the call immediately. Reluctantly, he agreed. They finished their coffee, paid the check, and headed outside. The patrol car was gone. Perhaps its presence had been a simple coincidence, not a fresh reminder that Lock had worn out his welcome in the town.

Lock leaned against the driver's door of the Explorer, and tapped a button on his cell-phone screen. It took a moment for the call to connect. It rang three times and went to voicemail.

He held up the cell phone so that Don could hear the message. "Voicemail," he said. He pulled the phone back, and was about to leave his name and number when Sandra picked up. She sounded groggy. "Hello?"

Lock introduced himself, using his real name this time. He apologized for the lateness of the call and launched into his pitch. He fudged his interest in Broken Ridge without directly lying. He told her he'd been hired by the parent of a student at Broken Ridge (true), who was concerned about the welfare of their child (true). He was canvassing other parents to see if they'd experienced any reason for concern.

Sandra listened patiently to everything he told her. "Well, I'll certainly look into it," she told him, "but everything seems fine so far. I get a letter from my daughter once a week. I'm sure if she was having problems she'd tell me."

Lock probed a little more. He was getting nowhere.

Next to him, Don Price was getting more and more agitated. "Did you tell her about the kid who died? The girl?"

Lock hit the mute button so that she wouldn't pick up the voice of her ex-husband in the background. "I swear, you interrupt me one more time, and I'm going to end this call right now."

"Okay, okay, but can you at least get her to call the school and ask to speak to Ruth?"

"Hello? Are you still there?" Sandra asked.

He tapped off the mute function. "Yes, sorry, I'm here."

"You really think I should be worried?" She sounded anxious.

Lock took a breath. "I don't wish to alarm you but, yes, I think there is cause for concern about how safe the students at Broken Ridge are. You know that as a private company it's not subject to the usual oversights and checks that a state high school or state or federal facility would be?"

She hesitated. Clearly she hadn't been aware of that, but she likely wasn't going to admit to her ignorance.

"There have also been a couple of students die while at Broken Ridge."

"Die?" Now she sounded panicked.

Lock shot Don a thumbs-up. "Yes." He ran through the story of Jennifer Oates and her parents' suspicions that it hadn't been suicide. "But even if she did take her own life that still leaves a lot of questions over how they handled looking after someone who was vulnerable."

"Mr. Lock, can I ask you a question?"

"Of course."

At the other end of the line, Sandra paused. "How much is my husband paying you to try to undermine me like this?"

The question took Lock aback. She hadn't given a hint that she knew he was working for Don through their entire conversation. He wasn't about to deny it. It would get him nowhere. It would only antagonize her further. But it did make him wonder how she knew. That could be a question for another day. "It doesn't matter what I'm being paid, Mrs. Price."

"It's Ms Andrews, these days," she corrected him.

"I was skeptical too. But what I told you about Jennifer, and the other concerns I have, those are all genuine. I give you my word. I don't think it's a safe place for your daughter."

"Good night, Mr. Lock," she said. "And please don't contact me again. Oh, and you can tell Don that Ruth's not going anywhere. And that tomorrow morning I'll be contacting his boss at the State Department and filing a complaint."

Lock stared at the call-ended screen for a moment. He started to speak. Don cut him off. "I heard her," he said.

"How'd she know I was working for you?" Lock asked him.

"The hell if I know."

CHAPTER SIXTY-TWO

GRETCHEN SAT AT HER DESK, her head in her hands. She was coming apart. She was on the very edge of the precipice. So was Broken Ridge. Everything her father had worked so hard for was at risk. And it was all her fault for allowing things to spin out of control, like she had.

The phone next to her rang. She started at the sound.

She stared at it. Scared to pick it up. Fearful of who was at the other end of the line.

This was ridiculous, she told herself. She had to gather herself. To get a grip.

She snatched it up. She cleared her throat. She tried to find her singsong telephone voice. The one that told the world everything was fine. "Good evening, you've reached Broken Ridge, Gretchen Applewhite speaking."

"I'm sorry to call you this late, Ms Applewhite. This is Sandra Andrews, Ruth Price's mother."

Gretchen didn't say anything.

"Hello? Are you there?"

"Yes, I'm here. How may I help you?"

"You're probably going to think I'm being silly. I just got a call from my ex-husband. He works at the State Department and, anyway, he's worried about our daughter."

Somewhere in the back of Gretchen's mind a loud siren began to blare. *The State Department?*

"I feel ridiculous even calling you, but I wonder if perhaps I could speak to Ruth."

Gretchen tried to think of something. Usually she dealt with situations like this with ease. She would patiently explain to a parent that calls had to be prearranged. That unscheduled calls disrupted the routine and upset the student. There were a hundred and one ways to deal with a call like this. Especially one that was made so late.

All Gretchen needed to do was to explain that all the students were in bed. Asleep. This time, though, she couldn't find the words. She couldn't find any words. She put the phone down on her desk and stared at it. She could hear Ruth's mother ask if she was there.

The State Department. That meant the federal government. Suddenly the new staff member and the man in town who'd been asking questions took on an even more sinister resonance. The forces conspiring against them were darker, stronger, more malevolent than even she could have imagined.

Hurriedly, she snatched up the phone, and cut off the call. There was only one thing she could do now. Only one way of saving Broken Ridge. Or, at least, buying some time.

She would have to move fast.

CHAPTER SIXTY-THREE

IS HEAD BOWED, THE MUZZLE of his own gun pressing painfully into the top of his skull, Ty kept his eyes closed and chose what might just be his final words with extreme care. If Chris did pull the trigger, at least it would be a bodyguard's end.

Out of the corner of his eye, Ty had already watched Ruth Price and her friend, Mary, slip out of the barn and into the desert night. The longer he talked, the more distance they'd have from Broken Ridge. And, as a not inconsiderable bonus, the longer he talked, the longer he lived.

There was one other factor at play. Perhaps the most crucial one of all. The longer Chris Fontaine delayed pulling the trigger, the less chance there was that he actually would.

"Can I ask you something, Chris?"

"Go ahead."

"How'd you figure out I was under cover?"

"I didn't. Gretchen did."

Ty took the risk of moving his head so that he was looking up at Chris. It was a strange feeling to be staring up the barrel of your own gun. "And how did she find out?"

Chris smirked. "You must have thought I was a real hick, getting taken in by all your Marine Corps bull crap."

Now Ty had an insight into why Chris was so upset. He felt Ty had made him look stupid. He'd humiliated him. At least, that was how he saw it. It didn't strike Ty as a good enough reason to murder someone. But then again Ty's ego wasn't so fragile that he had to get his rocks off sleeping with underage girls and bossing around a group of spotty teenagers.

"That part wasn't a lie, Chris. I was in the Marines. Served the tours I told you about. The only thing I lied about was my real name and why I was here. And I couldn't exactly have told Gretchen the truth about either of those things."

"You're a liar."

"I can prove it."

"Oh, yeah? How are you going to do that? You really think I'm going to let you up? How dumb do you think I am?"

With a bit of luck, you'll be just dumb enough, thought Ty.

"You don't need to let me go. You don't even have to let me stand up, if you don't want to. But I can still prove it."

"How?"

Ty closed his eyes and said a silent prayer of thanks. That was all he needed to hear. Human curiosity had come to his rescue, the overwhelming need to know. Assuming that Chris's hands weren't so sweaty that his finger slipped on the trigger, biomechanics should take care of the rest.

"I have a United States Marine Corps tattoo on my right arm," said Ty. "I got it after I finished my first tour of Iraq."

"Bullshit."

"Look for yourself if you don't believe me. It's a pretty easy thing to check."

Chris seemed torn between wariness and curiosity. Ty slowly lifted his hand, ready to roll back the sleeve of his shirt. As he moved, his hand rose in a slow arc toward the barrel of the gun.

"No!" Chris shouted.

Ty's arm froze.

"I'll do it," said Chris. "Put your hand down."

Ty complied with the request. He lowered his arm so that his hand was back by his side. He'd guessed that when he'd moved first, Chris would want to take back control of the situation.

In a standoff it was always preferable to let the other person think that what was happening was their idea.

Ty glanced up at him. As he tilted his head so that he could see Chris, a fresh channel of sweat trickled its way down past his left eyebrow and into his eye. "You really going to kill me?" Ty asked.

"You think I don't have it in me?" Chris responded.

With the gun in his right hand, Chris reached over to pull up Ty's sleeve.

"I don't know. Do you?" said Ty.

Chris stared down at him, his fingers grasping the fabric as he began to roll the sleeve up. "Maybe it's not my first time. You ever think of that?"

The way he'd said that was chilling. It didn't come off like a boast. Or a threat. More as a calmly stated matter of record. There was a look on his face that Ty hadn't seen before. It was as if a mask had melted away to reveal a completely different person underneath. Ty, who didn't scare easily, found it chilling.

"Know what?" said Ty, focusing all his attention on Chris's right hand. The hand that was holding the gun that was still pointed at his head.

"What?" Chris said, with a sneer, as he stared Ty down.

Ty could tell that Chris was getting off on this. At having another man, a man he had been afraid of, now at his mercy.

"I believe you," said Ty. "I sincerely do." He felt Chris's fingers against his biceps as the man's fingers eased

317

back the sleeve of his shirt. Chris was still staring him down. Any second now, he would glance over to see if Ty had also been telling the truth about the tattoo. When he did, Ty would have one chance to save himself from getting his brains blown out.

"So who was it, Chris? Who'd you kill?"

Chris answered with a smirk.

"Was it that kid Jennifer?" Ty said.

The smirk dissolved. Maybe Ty had hit a nerve.

"She get tired of you like Rachel had? I mean, I know you like 'em young."

Ty saw Chris's hand tighten around the SIG. He glanced over at Ty's arm.

With his toes dug into the ground, Ty pushed off hard, using his gluteal muscles and thighs to propel himself forward. The barrel of the gun slipped over the top of his head as his shoulders slammed into Chris's hips. Pain surged all the way down his spine from his injured shoulder. The gun went off, the noise deafening. Chris lost his balance and fell backwards. Ty went with him, launching an elbow at his face as they rolled.

Ty's elbow went wide. It slammed painfully into the ground. The impact sent a fresh bolt of searing pain through his body.

Chris still had hold of the gun. Trapped under the weight of Ty's body, he tried to wriggle back to get the distance to draw down.

Ty followed him. Pushing off with his feet, he managed to stay on top. He drew a fist back and slammed it hard into the side of Chris's face.

Chris kept pushing back, trying to get out from under Ty and back onto his feet. His hand twisted round, his finger on the trigger. He started to squeeze off another shot. Ty rolled off him. Chris fired. Ty felt the round part the air next to him.

Chris started to get back to his feet. Ty was lying on his side, facing his opponent. If Chris managed to get up with Ty still on the ground, it would all be over.

Fighting through the pain in his shoulder, Ty shot out a hand, and grabbed Chris's right foot. He pulled back as hard as he could. Chris swayed for a second, desperately fighting to keep his balance.

He tried to kick his foot free, but Ty kept a firm hold it. He twisted and wrenched it as hard as he could. He hung on, twisting it hard to one side. Chris yelled in pain, and, finally, lost his balance, firing the gun again as he fell.

A puff of dust pinged up from the ground, only inches behind Ty, as Chris toppled over backwards.

With no time to waste, Ty scrambled toward him. He launched himself for Chris's right arm. Pinning it under his knees, making sure he couldn't fire another round in his direction, Ty drew back a fist and punched Chris hard in the chest. The blow caught him flush in the solar plexus.

Chris gasped, all the air rushing from his lungs. He struggled for breath.

This was Ty's chance. He moved for the gun. Chris tightened his grip on it. Ty grabbed his wrist, and bent it back at the joint. His fingers opened. Ty reached over with his other free hand and lifted the gun clear of his grip.

He let go of Chris's wrist, and switched the gun to his right hand. It was Ty's index finger that slipped over the trigger. He pointed the gun at Chris Fontaine's head.

He would have enjoyed nothing more than pulling the trigger, and blowing the man's head off. But there were too many questions still unanswered.

Ty's finger drew back from the trigger. He kept his grip around the gun tight, drew his hand, and smashed the butt of the SIG hard into Chris's mouth, taking out two of his front teeth with one mighty blow.

Chris screamed in pain. His hand flew up to shield his face from another blow. Ty got to his feet. He stood over Chris for a moment, still tempted to pull the trigger and finish him off. Instead, he reached down, grabbed Chris by the hair and yanked him onto his feet, spun him round, and jabbed the barrel hard into the bottom of his spine.

"Move. Before I change my mind about killing you," Ty barked.

CHAPTER SIXTY-FOUR

BOTH HANDS CLAMPED FIRMLY OVER her ears, Mary stood at the side of the road with Ruth. The sound of gunfire from earlier seemed to have tipped her completely over the edge. Ruth had had to half drag, half cajole her friend all the way there. She couldn't leave her behind, especially not now, but it would have been a lot easier to get away on her own.

At least now they had reached the main road, they could wait. Next to her, Mary sank into a crouching position, and began to sway back and forth. So far they hadn't seen a single vehicle. Not that they'd been there very long. Maybe only a few minutes at most. But Ruth knew that if they saw one, and the driver picked out Mary in their headlights, they'd keep driving.

Ruth came up behind Mary, grasped her uninjured arm and peeled her hand away from her ear. Mary's head whipped round. "No one's going to stop if you're sitting here like this."

Mary started to make a high-pitched keening noise. It was as much as Ruth could do not to slap her. "Listen, I'm scared too," she said. "But we both have to be strong if we're going to get out of here. And when we do, I'm going to get you help, okay? Real help, from people who know what they're doing."

The keening noise stopped. Her words appeared to be getting through. She pulled Mary to her feet. "How's your arm?" she asked.

Mary swallowed hard, trying to compose herself. "I think it's stopped bleeding."

"Okay," said Ruth. "That's good. Now, you think you can walk some more?"

"It really hurts."

"I know. But there might not be anyone out here for a while, so we need to keep moving. The further we can walk, the safer we'll be."

Mary seemed to comprehend that basic logic. Ruth lifted Mary's good arm and draped it around her shoulder. "Here, you can lean on me."

"Okay."

Slowly, Ruth led her along the side of the road. Mary was slumped against her so heavily that it was difficult to keep her balance.

Looking up, Ruth saw two pinpricks of light off in the distance. She blinked, trying to make sure that her imagination wasn't playing a trick on her.

The lights grew brighter. They were headed straight for them. A car maybe. Or a truck.

Ruth stopped walking. Mary slumped against her even more heavily, almost pulling her off her feet and down into the culvert that ran parallel to that stretch of the road.

The height of the lights from the road suggested it was a car rather than a truck or a bus. It was moving fast. Every second the headlights grew bigger and more vivid.

Ruth could barely stay still. Escape was close. So close she could almost taste it.

Soon Broken Ridge would be nothing more than a memory. There was no way that anyone, not even the local cops, would take one look at Mary and drive them back there. She would have to be taken to a hospital to be checked out. Questions would be asked. Phone calls would be made. Even if her dad hadn't acknowledged her letters she was sure he wouldn't ignore her when he found out where she'd been sent, and how she'd been treated.

"Okay," Ruth told Mary. "We can't risk this driver not seeing us out here."

With Mary still hanging onto her, Ruth began to edge out into the road. Mary started to panic. She let go of Ruth, and began to hobble back to the side. "What if it's Gretchen or someone? Out here to take us back?"

323

"We're going to have to risk it," said Ruth, as she moved to the very center of the road, held her arms above her head and began to wave frantically as the vehicle's headlights carved a path toward her.

It was less than a quarter-mile away now. She waved her arms and screamed, "Stop! Stop!"

She heard the grinding metallic sound of brakes being applied. The vehicle slowed. She could see now that it was a Minivan. Gretchen didn't own one. Neither did any of the other staff.

The van slowed and came to a stop. She couldn't make out the driver through the glare. But she heard the driver's door open. Looking down she saw heavy work boots hitting the black top.

A man moved toward her. He looked like someone who had fresh walked out of the Appalachian Mountains. He was wearing boot-cut denim jeans, and a plaid shirt. His head was shaved to the scalp and he had a bushy brown beard that had grown all the way down to his belly, and he wore small, round-wired eyeglasses.

As he drew closer, he towered over Ruth. She could feel herself shrinking back. He smiled, but he still looked intimidating. "What are you doing out here in the cold?"

Ruth stood her ground. So, he looked scary. But what did that tell her? Nothing. Hell, Gretchen looked like a sweet old grandma until you got to know her. Appearances were deceptive, especially when it came to adults.

And, what choice did they have? It could be another hour or more before someone else drove down this road. "We need a ride into town. My friend's hurt."

The man folded his arms. "Your friend?"

Ruth looked around. Mary was nowhere to be seen. She seemed to have vanished into the night. "She was here a second ago," said Ruth, frantically scanning both sides of the road for a sign of Mary.

"Well, she ain't here now, is she?"

There was still no sign of her. "Mary?" Ruth called out. "Where'd you go?"

The bearded man was looking at her like she had a screw loose. "You shouldn't be out here on your own."

Ruth didn't know what to say. If she admitted it, and he realized where she'd come from, he might just put her in the van and drive her back there. Mary's injuries had been their—her—ticket out of there. She had to find her.

"My friend, she's hurt. Bleeding. I have to get her to hospital."

The man's face seemed to soften. "Hurt? How? What happened?"

Again, Ruth wasn't sure what to say. Mary cutting herself felt private somehow. To tell a stranger that she had harmed herself seemed like a betrayal of confidence. "I have to find her," Ruth told him, turning away.

"She was here a minute ago?"

Ruth walked back to the very edge of the road. She looked down into the culvert to see if Mary had climbed

325

into it. Maybe she had freaked out when the van had stopped, panicked and decided to hide.

"Listen, I can't stay here all night with you looking for this friend of yours. Get in the van and I'll take you home."

Ruth couldn't see Mary. She walked back behind the van, along the side of the road, checking the culvert. There was still no sign of her.

The driver had gone back toward the van. He opened the driver's door.

"Can you wait for a minute? She can't have gone far."

"Sorry," said the driver. "You want me to give you a ride into town, then hop in. If you don't, that's fine, too, because I ain't waiting around for your friend."

Frantic, Ruth called out Mary's name again. There was no response.

The man was offering her a ride. If she passed up this opportunity she might not get another. She could raise the alarm when she got to town. Get people out here to look for Mary.

"Okay," Ruth told the driver. "I'm coming."

She walked round to the other side of the van, opened the passenger door, and climbed in. The driver got in next to her. He closed his door, started the engine and put the van into gear.

Ruth pressed her face against the window, hoping to glimpse her friend as the van moved off. She was free of

Broken Ridge, but she couldn't shake a nagging sensation that somehow she wasn't free just yet.

She looked at the driver. His eyes were fixed on the road ahead, his features set. He reached a hand across and pushed a button that locked both doors.

"I can't believe I finally found you," he told her.

CHAPTER SIXTY-FIVE

L OCK SAT IN THE EXPLORER with Donald Price. The diner's parking lot was empty now, the place closed until morning. For the past ten minutes they had been going round in circles. Don wanted to go get his daughter, or at least speak to her. Lock attempted to persuade him it was a bad idea.

"We tried it your way," said Don, not for the first time since Sandra had hung up on Lock. "Now let's try it mine."

"Don, it's after midnight. Those kids are tucked up in bed by now. If we roll up there, they'll call the cops, and we'll be arrested. And then where will you be?"

"At least I'll know my daughter's safe."

328

The argument was starting to wear on Lock. Why was it always the gigs that seemed like the easiest money that turned into the biggest nightmares?

He took a breath, and repeated pretty much what he'd been saying for the past ten minutes. "And then what? She's still going to be there and you'll have weakened your hand. There's no point playing your best card until you have to."

"Point taken. So why don't I play it? Get in there, get Ruth and take her out."

Lock sighed. "Perhaps because you don't actually have custody."

"Your partner Tyrone said that what she's going through could cause her long-term problems. Come on, Ryan, what kind of father would I be if I just stood idly by and let that happen?"

He had a point. Lock knew he did. A lot of men walked away from their kids after a divorce. Not always because they wanted to, but because they felt it was for the best. The system was weighted against men in a divorce, especially when it came to children. Lock got why mothers were favored in court. But he also knew that divorce could sour people to the point where they forgot that what mattered above all else was the children caught in the middle. This situation was pretty much a textbook case. Only the stakes were a lot higher.

Don Price was not going to back down. His mind was set. The best thing Lock could do for a client under these circumstances was try to find a way to accommodate what they wanted without it coming back to bite either of them in the ass.

In this case, they might not be able to march straight in and demand to see Don's daughter. But Ty had told him security was low grade. The main barrier to escape was the remote location and vastness of the landscape around Broken Ridge. If you were trying to break out, that was a problem. But if you were trying to break in, it offered an advantage.

Plus, Ruth was in some kind of a barn that was well away from the main dorms. That would also make things easier, and mean there was less chance of anyone else seeing them. Lock was worried about Ty, too. Not something that happened often. Ty was more than capable of taking care of himself. But his silence, even allowing for the communication problems they faced, had started to nag at him.

Lock started the engine.

"Where we going?" asked Don.

"We're going to check on Ruth. But we're doing it my way, and after you've seen her, assuming she's safe and well, we're going to leave. I need your word on that," Lock said, taking one hand from the steering-wheel and reaching out so Don could shake on it.

Don hesitated.

"It's either this, or you're on your own. I pull out and take Ty with me. Then there's no one to keep an eye out for your daughter. Those are your choices so take it or leave it."

They shook hands.

"I have your word?" said Lock.

"Yes," said Don. "You have my word. But if they've hurt her . . ."

He didn't need to finish the sentence. Lock knew how it would have ended. Knowing what he did about Don's background, he was aware that he wasn't a man to make idle threats.

Saying a prayer that Ruth would be fine, Lock pulled out of the diner's parking lot and onto the main road. It was a straight shot from there to Broken Ridge.

"Take us about twenty minutes. A little less if I put my foot down," Lock informed his passenger.

"Then put your foot down," said Don, his jacket riding up to reveal the gun on his hip. It was a Glock 19, standard State Department issue for a man with Don's type of responsibilities. Not that Lock had ever seen anyone rolling through the State Department offices in D.C. with one.

"You're not thinking of using that, are you?" he asked, with a brief nod to the gun.

"Of course not."

Lock knew that was a lie. Don might not have been planning on drawing his weapon, but you didn't carry a gun unless it was at least a possibility. But Lock was hardly going to take it from him. "Do me a favor, would you?"

"What's that? asked Don.

"When we get there, leave the gun in the vehicle."

"I told you, I'm not planning on using it. And, anyway, you're packing."

"Yeah, but this is work for me. I'm not emotionally involved."

"Okay, okay. Whatever. If it makes you happy, I'll leave it in the car. Now can you step on the gas?"

Lock jammed his foot on the pedal. The Explorer lurched forward along the empty desert road. Lock wanted to get there so that Don could see his daughter. Then they could go back to the motel and decide upon their next move.

"So?" said Lock. "This guy with the rifle you thought was hanging around back at the motel before I got there. Tell me what he looked like again."

"I dunno. Tall, heavy-set, bushy beard. Like some kind of mountain man. Why? You have an idea who it might be?"

"Yeah, but it doesn't make any sense why he'd be looking for me."

CHAPTER SIXTY-SIX

RUTH PRICE SAT IN THE passenger seat and did her best to stay calm. Every few seconds the man would glance at her and smile. Even if he hadn't locked the doors there was no way she could get out while the van was moving. The worst part was that she had no idea who he was or what he wanted with her. At Broken Ridge she at least had the comfort of knowing what she was dealing with.

The bearded man began to whistle, a soft, reedy sound. It sounded familiar but Ruth couldn't place it.

"So," she said, doing her best to sound matter-of-fact, "where are we headed?"

The man smiled again, his eyes twinkling. "Already told you, I'm taking you home."

"Home?"

"Yeah," he said. "Where else would we be going at this time of night? Your mom will be excited to see you. You know, I knew it was you, as soon as I saw you standing out on that road."

He reached over and patted Ruth's knee. She shrank into the corner of the seat, leaning in against the door.

"It's going to be a surprise. You know her birthday's coming up soon."

Ruth stared at him. Her mother's birthday wasn't for three more months. "She sent you to get me?" she asked, careful to stay out of knee-patting reach.

"Not exactly, no. Like I said, I wanted it to be a surprise. But it's time you came home. We've missed you."

We? What did he mean "we"? He was talking like he knew her.

"It's not easy for me to say this but we should have never sent you to that place."

Finally, Ruth had had enough. If he was going to do something to her, he would do it.

"Why do you keep saying "we" like you know me?"

He looked over at her. The smile fell away. He didn't look angry so much as sad. "It's the beard, isn't it?"

"What is? What's the beard?"

"It's why you don't recognize me."

She rifled her brain. Had she seen this man somewhere before? No, she was sure she hadn't. So why did he seem so sure that he knew her? Was he some kind of weird stalker who picked up kids trying to run away from Broken Ridge?

"It's me, Jenny," he said. "It's your father."

"My father? You're not my father. My father's Donald Price."

The man scowled. "That's not funny. Not funny at all. Did your mom put you up to this?" He reached over and made a grab for her arm.

She pulled away. "I don't know what you're talking about. You're not my father, and my name's not Jenny. It's Ruth."

"She did, didn't she? This was her idea. She's always coming out with stuff like that, trying to confuse me. Telling me I have someone's name wrong. But you listen to me, it's not funny."

The van slowed. He pulled in off the road. Out of instinct, Ruth reached for the door handle. "Let me out of here, okay?" she screamed.

"See?" he shouted back at her. "This is why we had to send you away in the first place. This kind of attitude. Now, you stop this right this minute. You hear me?"

He leaned across toward her. She lifted her leg and kicked out as hard as she could. Her foot caught him in the chest.

He raised his hand to strike her. She flinched. At the last second, he stopped himself. "I'm taking you home," he said. "And no one's going to stop me. You hear me?"

CHAPTER SIXTY-SEVEN

TY PUSHED CHRIS ON AHEAD of him. As far as he could tell, the bleeding from his shoulder had all but stopped. When his captive slowed, he jabbed the barrel of the SIG into the base of Chris's spine. At one point, Chris half turned around. "Could you quit that?" he whined at Ty.

"Listen, asshole, count yourself lucky I haven't returned the favor and put a bullet in you yet."

Chris turned back round and kept walking. He didn't say anything else until they had reached the ranch house. That was where the only working link to the outside world was. Before he did anything else, including searching for Ruth, he planned on calling up the cavalry in the form of his business partner.

He prodded Chris up the stairs, onto the front porch, and toward the front door. The ranch house lay in darkness. Somehow, Ty doubted that Gretchen had retired to bed, not with everything that was going on.

Chris stopped at the front door. Ty made sure he was close in behind him. It wouldn't have surprised him if they found Gretchen on the other side, cradling a shotgun over her lap while she sat in her rocking chair. Having already caught one bullet this evening, Ty didn't plan on catching another. That honor could go to the man in front of him.

"Go ahead," prompted Ty, with another dig to Chris's spine.

Maybe Chris had the same concerns, because he didn't seem eager to walk in and face his boss.

"Open the door."

Chris reached out and turned the handle. It hadn't been locked. He pushed through and into the gloom. Ty stayed a few paces behind him and scanned the hallway. There was no one to be seen.

The place was quiet. Only the ticking of an old clock in the corner of the living room disturbed the peace.

Chris called out to Gretchen.

No answer.

With Ty at his back, the two men moved through the ranch house. They found no one. If Gretchen had skipped out, they would have seen her on the road that led out of the ranch. She had to be somewhere.

Not knowing where she was heightened Ty's growing sense of unease. There was no way back from what had just happened. Gretchen and the local cops might have been able to explain away the last few deaths as misadventure or suicide. This would be different. They must know that Ty and Lock would make sure the place was closed down and that people went to prison.

That alone would raise the stakes for everyone here. The place generated huge sums of money. But it was also all that Gretchen had going for her. Take away Broken Ridge, and she was just a bat-shit crazy woman with a bad attitude. This place was her life. Ty didn't see her giving up on it without a fight.

Standing in the middle of the ranch house, the thought set him on edge. There was one thing more dangerous than someone backed into a corner. Someone who also felt like they had nothing left to lose.

They kept moving. Ty keeping Chris in front of him, a human shield, as they rounded every corner.

In the office, Ty made straight for the phone. He picked it up from its cradle, held it in one hand and quickly punched in Lock's cell phone number.

It was only when he put the phone to his ear that he realized it was dead. He walked over to where it was plugged into the wall socket. The cable had been ripped out, the wall socket smashed, the wires inside pulled out.

Ty turned to Chris. "Where does she keep the cell-phone blocker?"

Chris hesitated.

Ty pointed the gun straight at him. "Let me explain a couple of things to you really quick. You've already shot me, so I'm not all that fussed about keeping you alive. And if you don't help me out here then I truly don't have any reason to keep you around."

It's over there," said Chris, pointing to a cabinet behind the desk.

"You know how to disable it?"

"Gretchen doesn't let anyone near it apart from her."

Ty marched over to the cabinet. It was padlocked. No great surprise.

He raised the SIG, leveling the barrel at the lock.

"What the hell are you doing?" Chris shouted.

Ty shrugged. "What? You're worried that I'm going to damage it?"

He blasted two quick rounds into the cabinet. He dug out his cell phone. He was low on battery, but he had a signal.

Hallelujah.

He tapped on the screen, pulled out Lock's number and hit the call icon. The connection was fussy. Static crackled. But after a few seconds Lock answered.

"Ty? Where are you?"

"Up here in the ranch house."

"Okay, good, we're almost there. Be about five minutes."

"We?" asked Ty.

"I got Donald Price with me."

Terrific, thought Ty. That was all they needed.

When Don Price arrived to find his daughter missing, and all this chaos, he'd go ballistic. Their biggest problem would be preventing him from burning the place to the ground.

A thought struck Ty. Something that Gretchen had mentioned earlier. "Where does she keep the guns? She told me she had a gun safe."

"I don't know," said Chris. "She gave me yours after she told me you'd been sent in to spy on us. I don't know anything about a gun safe."

"Bullshit."

"Why would I lie?"

"Okay then, start looking."

Together they began to search the office. Ty found it, concealed behind a regular-looking wooden cabinet door. He pulled it open. The safe wasn't locked. He threw its door wide.

It was empty.

CHAPTER SIXTY-EIGHT

S O WHAT DO YOU PLAN on doing with me?" Chris asked Ty, as they headed back out of the ranch house and toward the dormitories.

"That depends."

"On what?"

"Whether you give me any more trouble or not. If you do, I'm going to shoot you."

"And if I don't?"

Ty took a second to think about what he should say. "Tell you what, you help me find Gretchen, make sure the kids are safe, and explain to the authorities how badly this place needs to be shut down, I'll try to help you out."

"How are you going to do that? I shot you."

"I can say the gun went off accidentally. Happens all the time."

"You'd do that for me?" said Chris, sounding so grateful it bordered on pathetic.

"If you do what I ask, then sure," said Ty.

In truth, he had no intention of helping Chris Fontaine once this was resolved. None at all. He wouldn't hurt him, but the guy deserved to stand before a judge and jury.

"I can't believe you'd do that for me after what I did."

"Neither can I," said Ty.

****

Thirty seconds later, they reached the first dormitory. Chris pulled the door open, and walked in, Ty close behind him. For once the arrows marked on the walls performed a useful function. If Ty stayed two arrows behind, he would have enough time to deal with Chris turning and attempting to disarm him.

Inside, the quiet was eerie. They came to a classroom. Ty gestured for Chris to walk past, then stopped at the door and pushed it open with the toe of his boot. It took him a second or two to process what he was looking at.

Papers and workbooks were crumpled up, torn and scattered across the floor. The partitions that had separated each student from their neighbor had been ripped down. One had been thrown through a window. It sat, held in place by jagged shards of glass, half inside and half out.

Chris followed Ty and stood behind him, taking in the chaos. Ty pulled out his cell phone, and tapped on its light. He swept the beam across the walls, picking out fragments of graffiti. It took him just a few seconds to grasp the message that the person or persons who had written it had wanted to convey. Chris must have got it, too, because before Ty could stop him, he had turned on his heel and made a mad rush back toward the door and down the corridor.

Ty started after him, then stopped. Running made his shoulder scream with pain. But that wasn't why he had decided not to go after Chris. If he'd been in Chris's shoes, Ty would have run too. And he wouldn't have stopped until he was a long way from Broken Ridge.

Ty pulled up Lock's number again. He hit the call icon.

"Almost there, Ty. You okay?"

"Yeah. But keep your eyes wide open. I think we got some really bad shit about to go down."

At the other end of the line, he heard Lock shout something he couldn't make out. The call dropped.

Outside, someone let out a high-pitched scream. It was followed by the whipcrack of a single gunshot, then more shouting. Punching his gun out ahead of him, Ty charged into the corridor.

It was empty. He moved as quickly as he could to the first dorm room. He kicked the door open, and rushed in, gun high. He took in the room with a single sweep from left to right.

343

No one.

He backed out. Went to the next room. Repeated. No one there either.

The gun safe had been empty, and now so was the dormitory.

CHAPTER SIXTY-NINE

Seventy-eight seconds earlier

A S LOCK MADE THE TURN onto the approach road to Broken Ridge, Ty's name flashed on his cell.

"Almost there, Ty. You okay?"

"Yeah. But keep your eyes wide open, I think we got some really bad shit about to go down."

Before he could respond there was a rush of movement from the side of the road. Someone ran directly in front of the front of the Explorer.

Yanking down hard on the steering-wheel, Lock stood on the brake pedal. The wheels spun, struggling to maintain grip on the dirt. The Explorer shuddered and shook. Next to him, Don was thrown hard against the door.

The person who'd run in front of them disappeared from view. Lock struggled with the wheel, and eased up on the brakes, trying to stop the Explorer toppling over as it hurtled off the dirt road.

The vehicle spun. Lock felt it tilt. He struggled to keep hold of the wheel as the tires on the passenger side lost contact with the ground.

The vehicle rolled. There was a whooshing sound as front and side airbags deployed, throwing Lock back into his seat. The Explorer rolled again. Everything that wasn't secured flew about the cabin.

Lock's mind flashed inexorably to a lonely Topanga Canyon road on a rain-lashed night that had changed him for ever. An acid-splash of bile rose at the back of his throat.

Finally, the Explorer settled in the dust. Lock's hand fell immediately to his side. He flipped open the pouch holding his Gerber knife, and pulled it out. Reaching up, he slashed through the seatbelt. He jabbed the point of the blade into the front air bag, and slashed that too. He repeated the same action with the side air bag.

He took a moment to get his bearings. Aligning his position with land and sky, he realized the Explorer had done a full roll, landing back on its wheels. A stroke of luck, making getting out a lot easier than if it had finished on its side.

He looked across at Don Price. His eyes were closed. Lock reached over, and touched his neck, feeling for a pulse. Don stirred, pushing out his hand to swat him away. "Get the hell off me."

"You okay?"

"Terrific. Now what the hell was that?"

Lock reached for his door and opened it. "Why don't we go see?" He jumped out, legs wobbly from the aftermath of the crash. He looked around, unable to make out anyone in the darkness. Drawing his gun, he walked to the front of the Explorer. He checked the front for a person-sized dent. It was intact. So was the windshield. Good news for whoever had run in front of them.

He heard someone move close by. He spun round, pointing his SIG in their direction as, behind him, Don clambered out of the passenger side, his gun also in his hand.

If the bad trouble Ty had warned him about had just forced him off the road, then Lock was about to give them the good news. He narrowed his eyes, adjusting to the gloom. The pad of his index finger settled on the trigger.

He moved it back as a teenage girl stepped down from the road toward them. She had a ghostly white complexion and red hair. A blood-soaked strip of cloth was wrapped tight around one of her arms.

Lock exhaled. He had come within a split second of ending her life twice within the space of a minute. Fear gave way to anger. "What the hell are you doing jumping out like that? I could have killed you."

The girl looked at him evenly. "So why didn't you?"

CHAPTER SEVENTY

THE GUN FELT GOOD IN Jacob's hand. Finally, he had the power. He was the one in control. People would do what he said now.

He looked at the other kids. They were scared. Scared of him. Like he had been scared of them once upon a time. Even the level sixes were frightened. Maybe especially the sixes. All those perfect little rule followers who had looked down on him. Who had treated him worse than dirt.

It was all so different now. The level ones were in charge, and the sixes were at the bottom of the heap. Not all of the level ones had followed him. Most hadn't. That was okay. He didn't need much help. In the end only two had come in with him. Both boys who, like him, had been there for over a year without making it past level one. Boys

349

the staff had picked on, and other kids had bullied because they were different somehow, or wouldn't do as they were told.

One, Adam, was a scrawny fourteen-year-old with ears that stuck out and made him a target. Not that anyone was laughing at his ears now. Nor were they calling Jacob's other friend, Corey, who was fifteen and stuttered, any names. Not when he was holding a gun to the back of Little Miss Perfect Rachel's head as the other kids followed Jacob's instructions to light the fire pits.

Tonight they were going to have some fun around the fire pits that no one would ever forget. And Jacob was going to have his say, without anyone telling him he was wrong. So was Adam, and so was Corey, and so were any of the other kids who'd been bullied and picked on.

There would be one rule for the fire pit. You could say what you wanted. You could tell the truth. The real truth. Not the truth you thought Gretchen Applewhite and the other staff wanted to hear.

But before that, Jacob was going to start things out with a special piece of entertainment. Something that would set the mood.

Gretchen always had to be the center of attention. And Jacob was going to make sure she was. One final time.

After all, none of this would have been happening without her. Not just because she had made him who he was but because, once she was done torturing him, she had made the mistake of believing he was incapable of revenge.

350

After the electro-shock therapy sessions, all three of them, he had shuffled and drooled around Broken Ridge for real. He hadn't been able to lift his feet or control what his mouth did. But, as time passed, his body and his nervous system had recovered. Only he had decided to stay the same, at least as far as everyone was concerned.

That was when he noticed something interesting beginning to happen. Because of how he behaved, the staff ignored him. It was as if they thought he was deaf. They didn't guard what they said when he was around. It was as if he was invisible. Gretchen even put him to work cleaning up in the ranch house. That was when he had discovered the safe. Only thing he had to do after that was gather a few recruits to his cause (which wasn't difficult) and bide his time.

Jacob had known that, sooner or later, something would give. The place would begin its descent into chaos. When it did, he would be ready. Ready to pay back Gretchen and all the others for what they had done to him. The level ones would be powerful, and the level sixes would be ground into the dust. Jacob was going to take Gretchen's stupid system and turn it upside down.

After all, Jacob reasoned, what could she do to him now that she hadn't already done?

****

351

Ty hunkered down at the corner of the dormitory building closest to the fire pits. The scene in front of him verged on surreal. Three of the students, armed with handguns and a rifle, were holding the rest at gunpoint. They barked orders to a handful of the younger students who were busy lighting the fires, while the rest had been forced into their usual positions around the pits.

Of all the sights Ty had anticipated confronting when he'd heard the gunshots, this wasn't one. From the look of shock on the faces of the small group of staff members who were huddled together in the middle of the fire pits, he wasn't the only one who'd been taken by surprise.

As he looked out from the corner of the building, there was another shock. Not only had Chris gone to ground, Gretchen was nowhere to be seen either.

Ty quickly shifted back into work mode. He was facing a hostage shooting with three gunmen holding at least a hundred captives. So far they didn't appear to have killed or injured anyone. That could change in the blink of an eye.

The three holding the weapons didn't appear to have any level of training. But that could work for or against the people being held. Gunmen with training were a more difficult threat to deal with. But those with no training or experience were apt to panic and take someone out without meaning to. In any case, calling them gunmen seemed to be a stretch. They were runty teenage boys who hadn't started shaving yet.

There was one positive, though. The situation seemed to be relatively stable. In a mass hostage situation, the two critical points were, by definition, at the beginning and the end of the event. As far as Ty could tell they hadn't started out by shooting anyone, which made it less likely that they would do so now. Less likely, but not certain.

Although he was outgunned three to one, the three shooters would be no match for him. Plus, they were out in the open. Hostages would be able to scatter. But—and there was no getting away from this—if he did something now, it was certain that there would be casualties. He'd likely have to shoot at least one of the boys holding weapons. That wasn't a decision to take lightly. Not if it could be avoided.

He decided upon a tactical retreat. He'd stay close enough to take action if the situation changed, and try to make contact again with Lock, and law enforcement.

He backed up slowly, melting around the side of the dorm building. Out of sight of the three shooters. Ty squatted, his back against the dorm wall. His shoulder throbbed and he tried to lift his left arm. No go. He could barely get it away from his side. Too bad. Getting it seen to would have to wait.

He laid his SIG on the ground for a moment and took out his cell phone, ready to try Lock again. He didn't know what had caused his partner to terminate their last call, but it hadn't sounded good.

353

He was about make the call when someone shouted from around the corner. Ty didn't catch what they'd said. A low buzz of chatter rose from dead silence.

Pocketing his phone, Ty picked up his gun again and duck-walked back down the side of the building. When he reached the corner, he took a quick peek around.

The surreal scene clicked up another notch. The fire pits had all been lit, bathing the hostages in dancing orange light. One of the teenage shooters was pushing someone toward the center pit at gunpoint. Gretchen.

The shooter stopped, and picked up a red two-gallon can. The can would be full of an accelerant, either gasoline or something similar. He turned back to the kid who was directing everything: Jacob. Jacob gave him a thumbs-up.

The kid raised the gas can above Gretchen's head, and began to pour, dousing her with it. Gasoline. Ty could smell it from where he was. Gretchen began to whimper and moan, her cries muffled by the thick silver tape wrapped tight around her mouth. Her hands were cinched tightly behind her back with a length of rope.

Jacob watched her distress with a smile. The tormented now the tormentor.

Gretchen half turned, and took a step, making a run for it. The kid with the gas can was caught flat-footed. She had three steps on him. She picked up her pace. One of the kids sitting down swiveled around, put out their leg and tripped her as she ran past.

Gretchen stumbled, and fell forward. She face-planted into the ground, no arms ready to break her fall. The shooter caught up with her. He tipped the final contents of the gas can over her, starting at her slippers and working all the way up to her head.

Face down in the dirt, Gretchen wriggled and writhed. One of the staff members, an older woman, got up from where she was sitting. "Enough! Stop this right now."

Jacob turned, raised his gun and shot the woman in the chest. She fell back. He dropped another round, that one into her head. "No talking!" he shouted. "Those are the rules."

Ty's blood chilled. Glancing back to Gretchen, he caught a look at the student who had tripped her, foiling her escape. It was one of the girls from Ruth's dorm.

CHAPTER SEVENTY-ONE

DON PRICE GRABBED THE GIRL by the shoulders and shook her. "Where's my daughter? I need to find her."

Lock pulled him away from her. "Take it easy."

Don spun round, spittle flecking the corners of his mouth. "Don't tell me to take it easy. I need to find Ruth."

Something seemed to register with the girl, who had been inches from being killed by Lock's vehicle. He took a step toward her. "Ruth Price. Do you know her?"

"Ruth's my friend. Why? Who are you?"

Don shouldered his way past Lock. This time he kept his hands to himself. "I'm Ruth's father. I came here to get her. Now, can you tell me where she is?"

The girl stared at him. It was as if she was experiencing everything from behind some kind of screen. "I don't know. We were in the barn together."

Don turned back toward Lock. "You hear that? She's in the barn. Let's go."

"No, we got out. A man helped us."

"Okay, so where is she now?" Lock asked, trying to coax some kind of sense out of her.

"I don't know."

Don looked like he was about to explode again. Lock placed himself between Ruth's father and the girl. This was going to take a little time. The girl wasn't lying, or being difficult, he was sure of that. She was in shock. "What's your name?" he asked.

"Mary. I'm Mary. Ruth's my friend."

"Okay, Mary," said Lock. "I'm going to get someone to take a look at your arm for you, and make sure you're somewhere safe. How does that sound?"

She was staring at him. He still wasn't sure he was getting through to her, but it was a start.

"Okay," she said.

"Now, Mary, you were with Ruth. Where did she go?"

"We went down to the road," she said. "There was a Minivan. Ruth got into it. It drove off. I don't know where."

"That's good. You're doing really well. Now, can you tell me anything else about this van? Did you see who else was in it?"

357

"It was a man."

"And what did this man look like? Can you describe him to me?"

The blank look drifted across Mary's face again.

"Was he white? Black? Old? Young?"

"White. Kind of old. He had like this big, bushy beard."

Behind them, Don Price cursed.

"And the Minivan?" Lock pressed, his mind turning over, pieces falling into place. "What can you tell me about that? What color was it?"

"Black. It was black."

"And you're sure that Ruth got into it, and it drove off with her inside?"

Mary nodded.

"Which way did it go?" Lock asked.

She pointed across to the east, away from town. "That way."

"Okay," said Lock. "You did really good."

"Take her with you," he shouted to Don, tossing him the keys for the Explorer. "Drop her at the first emergency room. Then you can go on and get your daughter."

"You know where she is?"

"I have a good idea where she's headed."

"Where?"

Lock gave him brief directions and an address he could plug into the Explorer's GPS system. "The man with the beard. I don't think he's going to hurt her so when you find Ruth take it easy on him, okay? Oh, and as soon you

358

can, call the local sheriff, state troopers, and the feds. We're going to need bodies up here, and fast."

"What are you talking about—the man with the beard? Who is he? Why won't he hurt Ruth?" Don asked.

A fresh crack of gunfire broke the silence. It was coming from the school. Whatever was going on, and whoever was firing, it wasn't good. Lock turned and took off running.

CHAPTER SEVENTY-TWO

TY SQUATTED, HIS BACK AGAINST the dorm building, his cell phone pressed to his ear. "Ryan?" he whispered.

"I'm almost there. What's the gunfire?"

"Some of the kids have turned the tables. There are three of them, and they're armed. We got two staff members dead, and one about to barbecue. I have three rounds left."

"Okay. I have extra clips and I'm almost there. Cops should be on their way, too."

The news didn't fill Ty with confidence. It was likely that local law enforcement would be first to the scene. They could easily blunder in and turn a crisis into a catastrophe. The three kids with weapons were well dispersed among the others.

"When you hit the ranch house, circle east. That'll bring you down to where I'm at, by the last dorm building."

"Copy. Sit tight."

****

Jacob counted off the hands raised in the air. Apart from the remaining staff members, only a handful of students had kept their hands down. Part of him admired their guts. Not that guts would stop him killing them when the time came.

He crouched next to Gretchen, and whispered, "Bad news, Ms Applewhite. A majority want to see you on the fire."

She whimpered, her neck twisting round, her eyes rolling white with terror. Jacob smiled. After all this time, she had a window into his world. She felt as he had. Knowing that something bad was about to done to you and there was no way to stop it.

"Jake!"

Jacob looked at Adam. He had his gun up. He was pointing it at the corner of the dorm building.

****

Ty stood, arms by his sides, palms open, facing the fire pits, one step out from the corner.

"What? The FNG doesn't get an invitation to the party of the year?" he said to Jacob. "That's kind of rude, don't you think?"

Jacob didn't seem fazed, but the other two shooters were nervy. That could go either way. Bad, if they developed an itchy trigger finger. Good, if they'd been thrown off balance by his gatecrashing their event.

"The FNG?" Jacob asked.

Ty rolled his eyes. Kids these days. "It stands for 'the fucking new guy'. Pardon my language."

Jacob raised his gun. There was forty feet between him and Ty. A tough shot with a handgun for a kid who didn't look like he'd spent any time on a gun range.

Jacob waved the weapon at him. "Come sit down."

Ty shifted his weight, ready to move. His eyes flicked between the two shooters who had guns on him. "No can do."

Lips peeled back from his teeth, Jacob snarled at him, "I told you to sit down."

"Okay," said Ty. "But I need to tell you something first. I came here to make sure Ruth Price was safe. I was hired by her father."

Ty's eyes kept darting between the shooters. It was all well and good giving a speech. It wouldn't look so hot if he caught another bullet before he finished it.

So far, Jacob didn't seem all that impressed by what Ty was telling him. "And?"

"What's happened here is wrong. What Gretchen's done is wrong. People going along with it are wrong too. But so is this."

The two other shooters were looking at Jacob. Trying to see his reaction. Looking to take their cue from what he did or said. Which told Ty that if Jacob called it a day, so would they. They were followers.

"You toss her on that fire, and you're no better than she is," Ty continued. "You're worse."

"How do you make that out?"

"You know what you're doing's messed up. You didn't come in here like this. You do this, and she's won. She's turned you into something you're not."

Jacob glanced down at the ground. He lowered his weapon. No one said anything. Ty took a breath. It seemed like he'd gotten through.

Jacob raised his head. "Shoot him," he said to Adam, raising his gun.

Ty pivoted back, as Adam fired. The corner of the building fragmented, a chunk of wood and plaster puffing out, as he dove for cover.

He heard someone rushing toward his position. Ty drew his SIG, and tucked in tight, refusing to offer his back to whoever was barreling toward him. His back against the wall, Ty waited.

A second later, Adam rounded the corner. He came in tight, rather than giving himself some distance between the open ground and the wall. Ty spun, angling downwards, and caught him flush in the face with the elbow of his right hand.

The kid's legs wobbled. He fell. Ty followed him to the ground. He threw two fast jabs, the SIG still in his hand, the gun catching Adam in the face, breaking his nose, and crushing a cheekbone.

The gun fell from Adam's hand. Ty reached down, grabbed it and threw it behind them, safely out of reach. He reached down, and pulled Adam back to his feet, dazed and bleeding.

"Ty!"

Lock's voice from behind him. A blur of movement. Ty looked left. Jacob was standing there, gun raised. He was within ten feet, his finger on the trigger, the gun pointed straight at Ty.

A shot from behind Ty. Muzzle flash and a deafening bang. Jacob stumbled back, Lock's bullet catching him in the middle of his chest, an inch below his rib cage.

Another shot from Lock's gun. This one an inch above the first. Jacob's expression was one of shock, like he couldn't believe what had just happened to him. He sat down with a bump, then fell onto his back.

Ty rushed to the corner. The third shooter was standing there, dumbfounded. Ty punched out his SIG, aiming at him. "Put it down!" he screamed.

The kid's hand went limp. The rifle he'd been holding dropped. Ty watched Rachel break from where she was sitting, and grab the stock. Two of the older boys rushed the shooter, taking him to the ground.

Ty turned back to where Lock was crouched over Jacob. He had taken the boy's gun and now ejected the clip with a tap of his palm.

Lock's chin dropped to his chest. He swallowed hard. He reached out a hand to brush a stray strand of hair away from the boy's eye. His hand passed over Jacob's face twice more, closing his eyes, giving him a little dignity in death.

Adam was lying on his side. Ty walked back to retrieve his weapon. Then he went to Lock, who was still crouching over Jacob. Lock was crying without making any noise. His chest rose and fell.

Ty put a hand down to his friend's shoulder. "It was him or me, Ryan."

"Doesn't make it right," said Lock.

CHAPTER SEVENTY-THREE

D ON PRICE SPED UP THE driveway toward the black Minivan. He exited the Explorer at speed, running toward the front door. The porch light was on. He stopped in his tracks as he saw three people sitting on the porch. One was a middle-aged woman. The other a slightly older man with a long bushy beard. The third person was his daughter, Ruth.

When he saw her, he stopped dead in his tracks. She looked at him, but didn't move. Don couldn't see a gun, and Ruth didn't seem distressed. She was clearly exhausted, and tearful, but fine.

The woman got up and started down the steps toward him. Don met her halfway. "It's okay," said the woman. "She's fine."

Don wasn't sure where to start. "Who are you? What the hell is going on?

The woman smiled. "You'll have to lower your voice. My husband is easily upset."

"No kidding," said Don. "Now, do you mind telling me why you have my daughter?"

"Don't you want to talk to her first? I know it's been a while since you've seen each other."

Caught off-guard, Don managed a mumbled "Sure."

He walked past the woman and up the stairs. The man with the beard got up. His eyes darted to Don, then to Ruth and back again.

"Jenny? Who is this?" he asked Ruth.

Ruth reached out and patted the man's hand. "It's okay. Don't worry."

She got up and walked toward Don. Her eyes were filled with tears. So were Don's. She took a step toward him. He wrapped his arms around her, hugging her tight. Wanting never to let go.

They stayed like that. Both crying and holding onto each other.

The woman walked up the steps and onto the porch. She gently coaxed the bearded man up from where he was sitting. "Come on, bed time."

"But who's that man with Jenny?" he asked.

"If you come with me, I'll tell you."

367

Hesitantly, the man got up and followed her inside. She kept her hand resting gently on his elbow as she guided him through the front door.

Eventually Don let go of Ruth. He took a step back. "You're okay?"

"I'm tougher than I look."

CHAPTER SEVENTY-FOUR

Three days later

R YAN LOCK KNOCKED AT THE hospital-room door and waited for a reply.

From the other side, Ty shouted, "Come on in."

He pushed the door open and walked in. Ty was reclining in bed, his feet jutting out over the edge. His bedside locker was covered with cards and flowers. Head propped up by three pillows, he was watching TV. Pinched between his fingers was what looked suspiciously like a joint.

"Oh, it's you." He sounded deflated.

"Sorry, who were you hoping for?"

"That cute little brunette nurse promised me a sponge bath."

Unlike Lock, who had an aversion to hospitals, Ty had seemed to embrace the entire experience. Especially when it came to interactions with the female medical staff. And, from what Lock had seen, the feeling appeared to be mutual. On every other visit, he had walked in to find Ty surrounded by a coterie of admiring medical professionals.

"You know smoking isn't allowed in here, Tyrone."

Ty looked from the hand-rolled cigarette to Lock. "I ain't smoking. This here's medicinal."

"Medicinal?"

"You heard me. Pain management. Hey, you couldn't order me up a pizza from that Italian place down the street, could you?"

Lock laughed. Perhaps the first time he'd laughed since the shootings at Broken Ridge. "I take it you're feeling better, then."

Ty swiveled his neck, and glanced at his bandaged shoulder. "This ain't shit. Done worse to myself shaving."

Ty was playing it off, but Lock knew different. Even if the bullet had only clipped his shoulder, it had still done some damage. Thankfully it had missed the subclavian artery, and the collarbone, but it had still blown out a small chunk of his trapezius muscle, which meant he'd need physiotherapy.

Much of what had allowed Ty to deal with being shot, particularly in the hours immediately after it had happened, was his psychological toughness. Lock had seen people survive and fight after being shot if they could deal with the shock. He'd also seen people die because they'd not been able to cope with the psychological impact.

It had helped that Ty had been focused on salvaging what he could from the mess he'd found at Broken Ridge. He had been handed a mission. With no time to dwell on himself he'd powered through it because that was who he was, and what he'd been trained to do. Not that Lock was about to tell him any of that.

"You feel well enough to have some visitors?" Lock asked his friend.

"Sure. Send 'em on in."

"You might want to get rid of that joint before I get rid of it for you," said Lock.

"Oh, yeah," said Ty, taking one final hit, then stubbing it out in a small ashtray and stowing it underneath his bed.

Lock opened the door. "Come on in."

He held the door open for Ruth and her friend, Mary. They had both insisted on seeing Ty before they went home.

The girls walked in, both a little nervous. Ruth sniffed the air. "What's that smell?"

"It's medicine," said Lock, leaving Ty to explain that one.

Lock edged back out of the door and into the corridor. Mary's parents, with Don Price and his ex-wife Sandra were there. Lock counted as some kind of progress Don being able to occupy the same physical space as his ex-wife without either of them screaming at each other.

If their daughter's narrow escape hadn't exactly brought reconciliation, it seemed to have returned a measure of sanity, not to mention perspective. Part of that was, no doubt, down to the amount of damage Sandra had to undo if she ever wanted to have any kind of relationship with her daughter.

Between them they had agreed to share custody of Ruth. Sandra was going to move to D.C., so that Ruth could be enrolled in a school there and be closer to her dad. A regular school that didn't rely upon psychological manipulation and electro-shock therapy to deal with its students when they stepped out of line.

Mary's parents came over to Lock. They thanked him again for what he and Ty had done. While someone outside the situation might have blamed them, Lock didn't. They had been desperate and looking for help. Gretchen had exploited that need, as she had with so many other parents, and she'd paid the ultimate price.

There was the sound of laughter from Ty's room. It spilled out into the corridor. After everything that had happened, it was good to hear something that reminded Lock of the good in people.

CHAPTER SEVENTY-FIVE

Six weeks later

THE UPS TRUCK ROLLED DOWN the quiet suburban street and came to a stop outside a picture-perfect two-story Cape Cod-style house. Inside, Brice Walker put the truck into Park, switched off the engine and glanced at his partner, Mike.

"You forget your glasses again?"

Mike reached into his shirt pocket and, with a flourish, pulled out a pair of black-framed reading glasses. "New pair!"

"Good. So who we got?"

Mike grabbed the clipboard and flicked past the cover page. "Gabriel Mansur. Fourteen. Going to Coral Bay in Florida. We have an eight o'clock flight out of LAX."

"Not LAX." Brice hated taking kids through LAX. The place was a zoo, and if the kid made a fuss it got even worse.

"Sorry, man."

"Okay, let's go through the check."

Mike flicked back to the front page. Brice reached behind him and grabbed the equipment bag.

"Okay," said Mike. "Let's see here," he said, squinting at the list. "Pepper spray? Two canisters."

Brice rummaged around in the bag, found the pepper spray, and handed one to Mike. Mike struck a line through *pepper spray*. His finger moved down the list.

"Handcuffs. Two pairs."

"Here. Let's just hope this one ain't a fighter."

ACKNOWLEDGEMENTS

Special mention and sincere thanks to Naomi Gargano, Mike Davies, Anthony Downes, Joe Dugan, Frances Mojica and all the readers who have bought, borrowed, stolen, read and reviewed the Ryan Lock series over the years. I appreciate each and every one of you.

Thanks also to friends and family on both sides of the Atlantic who have kept me going during the writing of what was, at times, an emotionally draining story.

Most of all, love and thanks to M and C.

THE RYAN LOCK SERIES

Lockdown

Deadlock

Lock & Load (Short)

Gridlock

The Devil's Bounty

The Innocent

Fire Point

Budapest/48 (Short)

The Edge of Alone

The Byron Tibor Series

Post

Blood Country

Made in United States
North Haven, CT
13 September 2022

24000860R00212